Series by Julie Johnstone

Scottish Medieval Romance Books:

Highlander Vows: Entangled Hearts Series
When a Laird Loves a Lady, Book 1
Wicked Highland Wishes, Book 2
Christmas in the Scot's Arms, Book 3
When a Highlander Loses His Heart, Book 4
How a Scot Surrenders to a Lady, Book 5
When a Warrior Woos a Lass, Book 6
When a Scot Gives His Heart, Book 7
When a Highlander Weds a Hellion, Book 8
How to Heal a Highland Heart, Book 9
The Heart of a Highlander, Book 10
Highlander Vows: Entangled Hearts Boxset, Books 1-4

Renegade Scots Series
Outlaw King, Book 1
Highland Defender, Book 2
Highland Avenger, Book 3

Regency Romance Books:

A Whisper of Scandal Series
Bargaining with a Rake, Book 1
Conspiring with a Rogue, Book 2
Dancing with a Devil, Book 3
After Forever, Book 4
The Dangerous Duke of Dinnisfree, Book 5

A Once Upon A Rogue Series
My Fair Duchess, Book 1
My Seductive Innocent, Book 2
My Enchanting Hoyden, Book 3
My Daring Duchess, Book 4

Lords of Deception Series
What a Rogue Wants, Book 1

Danby Regency Christmas Novellas
The Redemption of a Dissolute Earl, Book 1
Season For Surrender, Book 2
It's in the Duke's Kiss, Book 3

Regency Anthologies
A Summons from the Duke of Danby (Regency Christmas Summons, Book 2)
Thwarting the Duke (When the Duke Comes to Town, Book 2)

Regency Romance Box Sets
A Whisper of Scandal Trilogy (Books 1-3)
Dukes, Duchesses & Dashing Noblemen (A Once Upon a Rogue Regency Novels, Books 1-3)

Paranormal Books:

The Siren Saga
Echoes in the Silence, Book 1

The Heart of A Highlander

Highlander Vows: Entangled Hearts, Book 10

by
Julie Johnstone

The Heart of A Highlander
Copyright © 2019 by Julie Johnstone, DBA Darbyshire Publishing
Cover Design by The Midnight Muse
Editing by Double Vision Editorial

All rights reserved. No part of this book may be reproduced in any form by any electronic or mechanical means—except in the case of brief quotations embodied in critical articles or reviews—without written permission.

The characters and events portrayed in this book are fictitious. Any similarity to real persons, living or dead, is purely coincidental and not intended by the author.

> Want the inside scoop on what I'm writing?
> You can join my newsletter here:
> juliejohnstoneauthor.com/subscribe
>
> You'll get early glimpses into books
> and the chance at ARCS and prizes!

Dedication

For lovers of magic and legends and mystical highland ways!

And for my mother who always has my back. I love you!

And a special thanks to my good friend Madeline Martin who is not only an amazing writer and conference roomie but a rock star plotter! She helped me untie a knot I had tied myself in!

Author's Note

I have taken great pains to make sure the words I used in writing this story were as historically accurate as possible. However, given that I am writing to a modern audience, there are some instances when I chose to use a word that was not in existence in the fourteenth century, as they simply did not have a word at that time to correctly convey the meaning of the sentence.

If you're interested in when my books go on sale, or want to be one of the first to know about my new releases, please follow me on BookBub! You'll get quick book notifications every time there's a new pre-order, book on sale, or new release. You can follow me on BookBub here: www.bookbub.com/authors/julie-johnstone

All the best,
Julie

Playlist

I'll Be – Edwin McCain

Hanging by a Moment – Lifehouse

You are the Reason – Calum Scott

Say Something – A Great Big World and Christina Aguilera

Stay – Rhianna with guest lyrics by Mikky Ekko

I Won't Give Up – Jason Mraz

Ho Hey – The Lumineers

I Will Wait – Mumford & Sons

Over My Head – The Fray

Use Somebody – Kings of Leon

Love, Love, Love – Of Monsters and Men

Prologue

1340
Isle of Mull, Scotland

Every man had a weakness, and for Laird MacQuerrie, his had been his wife. His chest ached something fierce, as if he were the one who'd been stabbed through the heart two days ago and not his sweet Agnes. He could hardly believe she was gone, but the proof was his crying bairn, Ada, whom he cradled in his arms. Ada had never cried when Agnes had held her. He was doing it all wrong; he was certain of it. He loosened his grip and stared down at his daughter. So fragile. So innocent.

So red-faced and loud.

Her fresh wail echoed throughout the packed great hall as Father Dorian sprinkled the holy water on her forehead. His clanspeople stood still, their grim expressions mirroring his feelings. They'd loved Agnes, too. He ran a soothing finger over the soft, plump skin of Ada's wet cheek, and his chest squeezed with loss.

Agnes... Ye should be here, Wife.

Big, gray eyes looked up at him, eyes the exact color of the sky before the rain broke through.

Make certain Ada remembers me.

It had been Agnes's one plea before she had succumbed to the knife wound she'd sustained. He gritted his teeth. If only she hadn't come to the rescue when a murderous swine had attempted to relieve a fairy of her pouch, which purportedly held magical dust…

Of all the places in Scotland, why did his island have to be saddled with those two featherbrained fae, Hortense and Portense? They hadn't even had the ability to save themselves from the men who'd attacked Hortense. He clenched his jaw, shoving down his anger at the fae. Agnes would not have been pleased with him. She had adored them, and the fae were forbidden by their own law to harm a human, even one attempting to hurt them.

Oh, Agnes. Why did ye get involved?

"Laird." A tap on his shoulder accompanied the softly spoken word near his ear.

He frowned at the interruption of the Blessing, but it had to be pressing for them to have done so. Turning, he took in his first-in-command, Connely. "Aye?"

Connely swept a hand toward the great hall door. MacQuerrie sighed. Hortense and her sister, Portense, stood just inside the entrance to the great hall.

"Laird," Hortense called, dipping a curtsy beset with the awkwardness of a fairy not used to doing such things. "We've come to give Ada a gift."

His first instinct was to deny them entrance, but he knew deep down it was not their fault Agnes had died. She would have wanted him to allow them to bestow what they wished upon Ada. He nodded to Connely, who waved to the guards to let the fae pass.

They seemed to glide just above the rushes that covered the floor of the great hall. As they moved down the center of the path formed by the two long lines of MacQuerries, the clanspeople's heads swiveled to follow the fairies' progress. When they reached him, Hortense gave him a sad look that made the ache in his chest flare hot.

"I'm so sorry, Laird MacQuerrie," Hortense said. She opened her mouth to say more but looked uncertain.

"We wanted to bless Ada with gifts," Portense jumped in, filling the silence left by Hortense, "in our gratitude for Agnes's sacrifice to save my sister."

Hortense nodded enthusiastically. Portense snapped her fingers, and a pouch appeared. "'Twas my idea," the fairy said, to which Hortense gasped. "I told Hortense to be watchful down by the water, but she did nae listen and now..."

"I am watchful." Hortense scowled at her sister. "And us coming here was *my* idea. I feel horrid that Agnes gave her life for mine."

MacQuerrie's throat was too tight with raw emotion to speak.

"Ye should feel horrid," Portense said in a chastising voice as she opened her pouch and dipped her fingers inside. When she withdrew them, her fingertips shimmered silver. "Hold the bairn away from ye, if ye please."

Unsure, the MacQuerrie glanced to the priest, who shrugged helplessly, a shocked look upon his face. Agnes's voice filled his head again: *The fae are good and kind.* He sighed. His wife had never been one to give trust easily. Knowing this, he stretched out his arms so that Ada was not pressed against his chest anymore. She splayed her arms and scrunched up her face. Her tiny hands balled into fists as she cried.

Portense set her hand to Ada's forehead, and when the child immediately stopped crying, he relaxed. The fairy smiled knowingly at him, then fixed all her attention upon Ada as Portense held her fingers above his daughter. "I give to ye the gift of beauty," she announced in a loud, sure voice. When Hortense scoffed at her sister's pronouncement, Portense frowned. "Is there something wrong with my gift?"

He wanted to know the same thing. He was half-ready to snatch his daughter away from the fairies. Hortense elbowed her sister out of the way and now stood in front of him. The gesture triggered a memory of Agnes laughing at how humanlike the fae were in how they argued as human siblings did.

"Yer gift," Hortense said, her voice dripping with scorn, "is nae a real gift."

MacQuerrie instinctively started to pull Ada back to protect her, but Hortense stopped him with a hand to his arm. The power radiating from the warm touch of her fingertips upon his skin rendered him unable to move. She smiled reassuringly at him. "'Tis nae a harmful gift." She smirked at Portense. "Just a useless one. Beauty fades and will nae protect the bairn." Hortense held out her arms. "Give me the bairn to set things right."

Immediately, he could once again move, but he was reluctant to do as bid. Yet, despite his hesitation, he found himself handing Ada over without even realizing what he was doing until it was done. When she started to cry, her nursemaid, Esther, came to Hortense's side and cooed at Ada to quiet her, which immediately worked. Hortense dipped her fingers in her pouch, which appeared out of nowhere, just as her sister's pouch had. This fairy's fingers also shimmered silver when she took them back out.

"I bestow upon Ada the power to make a king," she said, shaking her fingers above Ada's forehead and heart. Silver specks fell through the air to land upon the bairn and then disappeared.

The words triggered an avalanche of whispers from the

clan. "King Maker," they muttered, one after another, sounding like a swarm of bees.

"Silence!" MacQuerrie boomed. Then to Hortense, he said, "What do ye mean ye will give my daughter the power to make a king?" Such a gift sounded as if it would attract great danger.

Hortense smiled at him. "Not *will give*, Laird. I have already done it." She placed her hand over Ada's heart. "Yer daughter now possesses the gift within her."

"Ye've done it now," Portense announced, slapping a palm to her forehead. "Ye've given a curse, nae a gift!"

"A curse?" MacQuerrie bellowed.

"Och!" Hortense scoffed, her silvery-blond brows dipping together. "I gave a great gift. Yer daughter will wield immense power."

Fear spiked his blood at the notion of such a thing.

"See there?" Portense exclaimed, pointing at him. "See how his eyes are wide and his nostrils flare? See how pale his face has become? He kens yer gift is an ill-conceived one."

"How?" Hortense demanded, her jaw setting. The fairy set her hands on her hips and glanced between him and her sister.

"Ye nae ever have the clarity to see yer own foolishness," Portense grumbled. "Men will hunt the lass and use her for her power," she said slowly as if her sister were a simpleminded child.

Hortense's face flushed. "Ye always wish to appear so wise, so superior."

Portense gasped. "What?"

"Here." Hortense yanked open her pouch and tilted it above Ada, who was now quiet, as if she were under a spell. "The sweet lass will nae wield the power until the day she weds."

An uproar of chatter came from the clan, and the sisters scuttled backward from him with Ada. He struggled to hear the rest of what the sisters said. Yet, from how they argued and the way Esther's mouth parted with shock, he did not think it could be good. The fairies faced each other now, and Esther stood behind them, gawking. Hortense's lips moved as she once again said something and tilted up her pouch. One lone silver speck fell.

He wanted to snatch his daughter away from Hortense, but he found he could not move once more. "Esther," he bellowed. "Take the bairn!"

"*Stillande!*" Hortense and Portense pronounced in unison, blinking at each other with surprise.

"Laird, I kinnae move," Esther cried out.

"Nor I!"

"I kinnae move, either!"

The calls came fast from MacQuerrie clanspeople behind him.

Father Dorian said, "Nor can I, Laird."

"Ladies," MacQuerrie said, looking at the fairies. "Release me."

"Just a moment," they answered, voices sweet and once more in unison.

"Dunnae fash yerself, Laird. I'll make this right," Portense said. And with that, she shoved her sister, who went flying forward, and then Portense quickly turned over her own pouch and dumped the contents on Ada.

The bairn let out her first laugh, and MacQuerrie could not help but stare at his daughter in amazement and pride. "She laughed!"

Portense did not spare him a glance. As Hortense charged toward her sister and Ada, Portense quickly rushed out words as she shook her fingers. "Yer gift will only activate if ye willingly choose yer husband." With that, she shot her sister a triumphant grin. "There. I've fixed yer mess."

"Oh, Sister!" Hortense wailed. "We are both fools, but ye remain the biggest. I had already set things right with the second part of my words."

Second part? MacQuerrie frowned. He had not heard the second part.

"Please tell me ye have some fae dust left," Hortense wailed, snatching his attention back to her.

Portense bit her lip and peered inside her pouch. When she looked up, worry danced over her delicate features. "Nay. Do ye?"

"Nay," Hortense said, worry as equally evident in her voice as it was on her sister's face. "That word, *willing*, do ye believe—"

"Nay," Portense interrupted. "It will nae be enough. But what ye added…" She bit her lip. "Ada could willingly choose a husband to save someone or something. Did ye nae think of that?"

Hortense burst into tears, and suddenly, MacQuerrie could move. He closed the distance to Portense and snatched Ada from her. As he pulled his daughter to his chest, he glanced between the sisters, who were fading. "Where are ye going?" he demanded.

"To the fae world," they said together. "We dunnae have any more dust. We must replenish it. If our father will let us…"

Ada grabbed his finger, and he glanced down. "How the devil long will that take?"

When he received no answer, he looked up to find the fae gone. Their so-called gifts to his daughter rang in his mind: beauty, and the power to make a king. She would most definitely be hunted when word got out, and he had no doubt it would. His clan had started to move, and the excited chatter was near deafening. The chant of *King Maker* filled the hall.

This would be impossible to contain.

One

1362
Isle of Mull, Scotland

Brothwell was the devil, or as close to it as a person could be and still be human. Ada MacQuerrie stared at her stepbrother, fully expecting horns to pop out of his pointy head at any minute.

"Ada." Brothwell's gaze narrowed on her, and he snapped his fingers in front of her face. "Are ye hearing what I am saying to ye?"

It would be impossible *not* to hear the man. He was standing so close she could see spittle fly from his mouth every time he enunciated. She longed to tell Brothwell just how misguided she thought he was, but she clenched her teeth on the desire, lest the words escape her. It would not serve her well to anger her stepbrother, being at his mercy as she currently was. Any way she tackled her current predicament, the path would lead her back to Brothwell's benevolence. His current goodwill would expire the moment he realized she did not intend to choose a husband from the supporters of the Steward whom he had presented to her. That left one option: running. So far, it had been impossible to get away given Brothwell had ordered the guards to be her shadows since her father's death four days prior.

"Are ye ignoring me?" Brothwell demanded. He grabbed her chin and brought his lips a hairsbreadth from hers.

Her stepsister, Marjorie, who had always been quick to side with her brother, surprisingly did not respond. Instead, she pressed her lips together and glanced down at her feet.

"What think ye, Marjorie? Is little Ada ignoring me?" he asked. Silence stretched for a moment, to which Brothwell blew out a loud, irritated breath.

Marjorie slowly looked up, and Ada could have sworn she saw tension in the woman's face. "Aye," Marjorie replied, her voice little more than a whisper. "She's ignoring ye."

Ada had not expected Marjorie to come to her defense. Still, it stung all the same when she didn't.

Brothwell squeezed Ada's chin. "Ye think yerself better than us. Ye always have."

"That's nae true," Ada denied. "I have always treated Marjorie as my true sister and ye as my true brother."

"Nay, sister dear, ye treated us as the bastards we are every time ye did nae listen to us, though Marjorie is five summers older than ye, and I'm twelve summers older."

"Ye told me to do things that ye kenned my father would nae approve of," she replied.

"Siblings would have stuck together," he snapped. "Like Marjorie and me. Is that nae right, Marjorie?"

Marjorie nodded and offered a tight smile.

"Even now, with yer father dead and me as yer new laird and keeper, ye are refusing to obey and choose a husband."

"Ye wish me to wed a man for the Steward, and ye ken my father supported King David. I—"

Brothwell grabbed her arm and hauled her from her

seat. "Yer father is dead. Ye will support whomever I tell ye to."

"Brothwell," Marjorie cut in, "might I be excused?"

"Nay!" he thundered. "Dunnae ye find it fun to watch Ada squirm?"

In the past, Marjorie would have nodded readily, but she had seemed a bit different lately, less inclined to torment Ada. She suspected it had something to do with the warrior Bram MacLean, who had been here for a while but was now gone. She did not know for certain, though. Still, even if Marjorie no longer supported her brother, she was no fool. She knew not to anger Brothwell.

Marjorie finally gave a nod to Brothwell's question, and he grinned, motioning to the guard standing in front of the closed great hall door. "Tell James to bring in Esther."

Ada's eyes widened. "Why do ye have Esther?" she demanded, looking toward the door. It was already opening. Her dear, sweet companion of many years appeared with a guard on either side of her. Esther was really the mother Ada had never had, as her stepmother had never taken to her.

"Esther is here to persuade ye to do my bidding with haste," Brothwell answered. "Choose a husband, *willingly*, within the next fortnight or ye will nae like what I do."

"Dunnae do it, Ada!" Esther bellowed.

Brothwell sliced his hand through the air toward the guard, and the man smacked Esther across the face. She cried out, as did Ada when she tried to run to her.

Her stepbrother tightened his grip. "Do ye wish to see her hurt, Ada?"

Ada's heart thundered, and her stomach knotted.

"Brothwell," Esther yelled, "yer father is nae the rightful king! He made ye a bastard! Why do ye even support him?"

Brothwell shoved Ada away and stormed toward Esther, raising his hand as if to strike her.

"Brothwell, nay!" Ada screamed, lunging toward him and grabbing his arm. What Esther said was true: the Steward had taken Marjorie and Brothwell's mother as his mistress long ago but had refused to make her his wife, even when she bore them. To say it aloud, to remind Brothwell, was dangerous. She feared Esther had pushed Brothwell too far.

"Brother, Esther is an old, babbling fool." Ada shot Esther a pleading look to cooperate and stay quiet. "I ken as ye do that yer father did what he had to for Scotland, which makes him a great man."

The lie made her stomach turn, and she prayed her disgust did not show on her face. The Steward was a horrid man, but in the long years since Brothwell's father had turned his mother away, Brothwell had concluded that his father had made a great sacrifice for Scotland by wedding a woman other than Brothwell's mother. The truth was, his wife had brought him more power than Brothwell and Marjorie's mother ever could have.

"I need to teach yer companion her place," Brothwell said, jerking out of Ada's hold and once again raising his hand to Esther. She flinched but held her ground.

"I'll do as ye say!" Ada blurted. "I'll choose a husband!"

"Ada!" Esther cried out, and Ada glared at her, willing her to silence.

"Cease talking, Esther," Ada commanded, knowing Esther's loose tongue would worsen matters. The woman was stubborn and outspoken. If only she cowered or stayed quiet in this moment, she would live another day. A day they could use to figure out how to escape.

Brothwell turned to her. "Ye finally relinquish yer misguided loyalties to King David?"

Ada nodded as her mind turned on how to get away from the guards. "My father is dead, and as ye have said, ye are my laird now."

Brothwell held his hand out to her. What did he want her to do? Take it? The thought repelled her, but she reached for it, willing to grovel briefly to keep Esther safe. He smirked at Ada when her fingers grazed his, and he pulled his hand away. "Nay, sister dear. Kiss my ring."

She gritted her teeth. The conniving liar! The thief! He had convinced her ill and confused father that he should give Brothwell the ring of the laird, thereby giving his support to the Steward.

Oh, Father! Her heart ached. *I ken ye did nae ken what ye were doing.*

"Ada," Brothwell said. The word was a reminder, and Ada forced herself to kiss the ring, though doing so made her want to retch.

"Ye are a clever lass, and ye have pleased me today. My father will recognize me when he becomes king. He has vowed to claim me as his son, which will bring this clan more land, more coin, and more power. And I will be generous to ye."

Brothwell was a fool. The Steward would never acknowledge him as his son, nor Marjorie as his daughter. He was using Brothwell, but Ada bit her tongue on saying words that would only fall on deaf ears.

Brothwell reached out and grabbed her by the neck, drawing her close once more. "Since ye have pleased me, I have a gift for ye."

Ada could only imagine, and it made her tremble.

"I've decided to have a tournament here in a fortnight. Yer stubbornness in nae choosing a husband from the men I already presented was actually a blessing."

Heaven above, what was about to happen? She saw Esther's uneasy look, and she prayed her longtime companion would hold her silence just a bit longer.

"I was nae thinking properly," Brothwell said.

"Nay?" she asked weakly.

"Nay!" He squeezed her neck, causing a shooting pain that made her wince, but his hold did not lessen. "Ye are the King Maker! I was simply putting men before ye that supported the Steward, but I thought too small. When men hear ye are to finally choose a husband, they will come from far and wide. Yer hand will command the greatest warriors, and they will join forces with me to aid me in putting my father on the throne."

Ada knew she should hold her silence, but she could not. "Whatever makes ye think any man that would willingly betray his king will nae betray ye? They will come in hope of becoming king themselves or of putting whomever they support on the throne."

To her surprise, Brothwell agreed. "Aye...some will."

Esther's eyes had narrowed into two gleaming slits of disgust, and Ada had to wonder if she looked the same way.

"Ye are verra astute, Ada," Brothwell went on. "But I already considered this. The men will believe that all they must do is fight in the tournament to win the chance to woo ye. But any man who dunnae pass a test of fealty to me and my father will nae advance in the tournament. All ye must do is choose a husband from the last two men standing, and I will allow him to woo ye. See how generous I am?"

The urge to slap him was so strong, Ada had to curl her hands into fists to control herself, but even allowing that was a grave error.

Brothwell's face flushed red, and she realized too late that he'd seen her action. He shoved her aside, reared his hand back, and hit Esther so hard, she fell to her knees, head hanging down.

"Ye monster!" Ada screeched. She surged toward Esther, but Brothwell stopped her with a viselike grip on her wrist.

"See what ye made me do?" he demanded.

She nodded without hesitation as blood dripped from Esther's lip onto the floor beside her.

"Will ye make me hurt her more?" he asked.

"Nay, nay," Ada whispered, tears and rage constricting her throat. "I'm sorry. I—" What could she say? She had to gain his trust. "I had hoped for love," she blurted, which was the God's truth.

"We have all hoped for love at one time, Ada," Brothwell said.

Surprised by his admission, she could do no more than gape. He glanced at his sister, who had obviously stiffened, and then Marjorie said, "We must all make sacrifices, Ada. This is yers. Do ye ken me?"

"I ken ye," Ada replied, though she had no intention of willingly picking a husband from the treacherous lot her stepbrother intended to present to her. She, Esther, and Maximilian—an orphan who was like a little brother to her—would simply have to escape. Somehow. Some way. Ada's hounds, Freya and Hella, whom Brothwell had shut out of the great hall earlier, began to howl at the door as if they could hear her thoughts.

The fire horn sounded to alert the clan as flames split the

darkness and licked the black sky. The heat from the fire Ada had started singed her face—her entire body, really. The flames crackled in her ears as shouting voices joined the roar of the fire, and the castle's inhabitants, normally asleep at this hour, poured into the courtyard.

The guards started yelling as the horses Ada had released thundered away from the stables. The ground beneath her feet vibrated as she stood, unmoving with the shock of what she'd just done.

Father, ye'd be proud.

The thought broke through her stupor, and she scrambled into action. Her clanspeople already rushed toward her, along with Brothwell's warriors. Chaos swallowed everyone up just as she'd planned so the tower guards would rush to help. Then she, Esther, and Maximilian could flee unnoticed through the gates. It would be daybreak before things settled and possibly longer before their absence was noted.

She turned to Esther, who had been with her since Brothwell's tantrum in the great hall, and nodded, indicating they should start the second part of their escape plan. All would be fine. She had to believe that.

"The horses!" someone shouted. "We must catch the horses!"

"I'll do it!" Ada yelled.

Siddoway, one of Brothwell's men, stopped in front of her. "Ye're certain?"

Ada nodded, the fire from the stable illuminating the man's uneasy face. "Aye. Dunnae fash about any horses that have escaped. I'll bring them back."

Siddoway nodded. "They should nae have gotten far."

Since she'd purposely opened the inner gate earlier, she knew well the horses had gotten farther than Siddoway believed, but she simply said, "Ye can rely upon me." The guard gave a nod and turned away, and Ada motioned to Esther, who'd stood quietly, to follow her.

When Ada looked to the guard towers, she exhaled, relieved to see Maximilian standing by the right tower. In the glow of the moonlight he looked very small, though at twelve summers, he was as tall as she was already. Freya and Hella were positioned by his side, a feat only Maximilian could accomplish as the one who fed the hounds. He was the only other person they listened to besides Ada.

She glanced around to ensure no one had taken note of Maximilian and the hounds. Thankfully, everyone was now consumed with the fire, including the guards who had left their towers. They'd be punished for that. Brothwell would be livid come morning, but she refused to feel guilty about the punishment the two guards, who'd helped to keep her prisoner in her own home, would receive.

With every step she and Esther took toward Maximilian, Freya, and Hella, she expected Brothwell to appear and call her back, but they reached the boy and two hounds and all hurried between the guard towers and into the darkness under the guise of securing any escaped horses.

"I cannot believe it's this easy," Ada murmured as they took the path to the cave that would lead to the woods. Beyond that would be freedom.

"I believe it," Esther said, her voice hushed. "Brothwell is so cocksure that it dunnae occur to him that ye would dare defy him. His ego is our salvation."

Ada nodded, glad the moon was bright ahead of them so they could see their way. She took a breath, and smoke filled her lungs, making her cough. "I wish I'd not had to set fire to the stables."

Maximilian took her hand and squeezed it. "'Twas the

only way, my lady," he replied as they made their way from the courtyard and the view of the guards.

She squeezed Maximilian's hand back, a gesture they'd long exchanged since years before when her father had brought the dirty, scared orphan home with him from where he'd found Maximilian in the woods. Ada had taken to him immediately, and he'd been as her little brother ever since.

"Esther, how far to Iona Nunnery?" Ada asked.

"A sennight on horseback, if I recall correctly. It's been many years since I've been there. Max—"

"I've got them," Maximilian interrupted Esther, then released Ada's hand. He quickly stopped two horses that had been about to gallop by them with soft words and a click of his tongue.

Ada and Esther laughed, and Freya and Hella barked. "'Tis a gift," Ada said, as she often had before. Maximilian was blessed with an oddly powerful ability to relate to animals of almost any sort. They seemed to know what he was asking and did what he said.

Ada mounted one horse, and Esther and Maximilian mounted the other. Freya and Hella stood between them. Ada bit her lip, worry for her dogs rising. "What if they kinnae find their way there?"

"Maximilian," Esther urged, "tell the wee beasties to follow the water west."

He dismounted and kneeled before Freya and Hella, putting a hand on each hound's back. "Go west, lasses," Maximilian ordered.

If Ada had not known better, she would have sworn her hounds had nodded in the moonlight. Once Maximilian had remounted beside Esther, they turned the horses toward the west, galloped down the path, past the cave, and started up the hill toward freedom. Ada hesitated, waving Maximilian and Esther toward the woods, and then she glanced over her shoulder at the home she feared she would never see again. She took a deep breath for courage, and as she turned around on her horse once more, Freya and Hella began to bark ferociously and charged ahead of her horse, who took a fright, reared up unexpectedly, and threw Ada off.

She fell to the ground with a hard thud and had to roll to her right to keep from being crushed as the horse pranced backward, neighing. Specks of bright light danced before her eyes, and she lay there for a moment, trying to take a proper breath. But when Esther's scream cut through the silence, Ada scrambled to her feet and started to race up the hill toward Esther. Before she even got halfway up, however, Brothwell and Marjorie appeared with four guards, two mounted beside Brothwell and two now on foot. Each of the dismounted guards held Esther and Maximilian in front of them, swords pointed at her friends. Freya and Hella came racing toward Ada.

"Ye disappoint me, sister dear," Brothwell called.

He could not have come looking for her. She would have seen him. Which meant he had to have been out of the keep for some reason… She wanted to burst into angry tears as she absorbed the scene before her and what it meant, but she did not have the luxury of allowing herself to show such emotion. Brothwell would deem it weak, and now that they'd been foiled by fate, her future would be set by her stepbrother. She felt ill, but Maximilian and Esther needed her, so she swallowed the lump of fear lodged in her throat, trying to think of a lie that could possibly spare Esther and Maximilian. "I—"

"I suggest ye think before ye speak, Ada," Marjorie said, her tone cutting as Ada would expect, but there was also an odd tension in her voice. "The boy already confessed ye were fleeing."

"I'm sorry, my lady, I had to protect Esther. Brothwell threatened to kill her," Maximilian burst out and was hit over the head for his efforts. He cried out, Esther bellowed, and Ada bit her tongue to stop herself from making things worse by speaking the harsh words she wanted to fling at Brothwell.

Ada's heart squeezed at Maximilian's bravery. "I ordered them to come with me," Ada said calmly. "Please, ye kinnae hold them accountable."

"But I do," Brothwell replied coldly. He dismounted and started toward her, and as he did, Freya and Hella began to growl low, then louder as he advanced on her. "Order the hounds to stand down," he bit out.

Ada opened her mouth to do so, but suddenly the dogs charged from her side and launched at him, Freya latching onto his arm and Hella to his leg. Brothwell howled in pain, and his mounted guards thundered toward them. Panicking, Ada closed the distance between Brothwell and her hounds, and flung herself in front of the dogs, who would surely be killed by the guards.

"Hella, Freya, release!" she cried, followed by, "Away!" They did as she commanded, just as the guards reached Ada and the first one dismounted, bow and arrow already lifting to shoot the hounds. Ada threw up her hands. "Brothwell, please. Please dunnae allow them to hurt my hounds. I swear," she said, turning toward him and falling to her knees in front of where he stood, cradling his arm. "I swear they just thought to protect me. I'll do as ye say. I'll—"

"Shoot them," Brothwell commanded.

"Nay!" Ada shouted.

"Those hounds were sent as gifts from the fae to Lady

Ada," Esther called out to Ada's shock. The lie was bold. Ada had found the hounds in the woods years ago, before Brothwell, Marjorie, and their mother had come to live with them. Ada had nearly tripped over Hella and Freya one day when she'd been walking. They had been no more than two small white balls of fur at the time. Ada held her breath, praying Brothwell would believe Esther's lie.

"From the fae?" Brothwell repeated, wariness in his voice now.

"Aye. Sent to watch over Lady Ada. If ye hurt the hounds, my lord, it could have an effect on her gift."

"A verra good point," Brothwell said, his tone congenial—too congenial for Brothwell. He motioned to Esther and Maximilian. "Take them to my special place and guard them." Maximilian and Esther both glared at the guards as they started dragging Ada's friends toward the waiting mounts.

"What are ye going to do with them?" Ada asked, her heart pounding with fear.

"That depends on ye, Ada," Brothwell said, his voice cold. "If ye attempt to escape again, I'll kill them." She didn't doubt his words, which contained no hint of compassion. "If ye dunnae do as I say, I'll kill them. If ye displease me in *any* way, I'll have them beaten. Do ye ken me?"

She nodded, unable to choke out words through her constricted throat. With Esther and Maximilian captured, her own fate was sealed. She would sacrifice herself and her dreams to keep them safe.

Two

William MacLean stared at the MacLean warriors, who had snuck up on him and now surrounded him with weapons raised. The desire of his own clansmen to hurt him, possibly kill him, glittered in their narrowed gazes. He moved his hand to the hilt of his sword, glad he'd not yet taken off his weapon and disrobed. The grime from the weeks-long journey he'd just completed to return to his home—or what once had been his home—clung to him, but better dirty than dead. He'd not traveled back to his old home, a place he'd foresworn, simply to be cut down before he saw King David, who had called him here and away from his latest mission the king had sent him on.

"It warms my heart that ye men were so anxious to see me that ye formed a welcoming party to greet me before I could even step foot in the castle to meet with *our* king who called me here," William said, glancing up toward the seagate stairs. Two shadowy figures were illuminated slightly by the full moon as they made their way up the stone steps toward Duart Castle. William let out a shrill whistle for them to stop, a signal that both Lannrick Kinntoch and Thomas Fraser should know from their time fighting alongside him for the king the last few months, but neither man paused. It was his own fault, he supposed. He had been their commander for some time now, since the king had sent them to him to aid in missions. He'd trained them to listen without questioning orders, and this night he'd ordered them to go straight to the great hall without stopping. That's what he got for being prideful, for not keeping them with him in case he encountered a problem like this.

He'd wanted to wash off first to present a good picture to his clansmen and clanswomen in hopes that they would be more welcoming of him now than when he'd left over two years prior, in the shadow of his father and brother Bram's treachery of King David. But by the grim-looking MacLean men circling him, however, he could see they still did not consider him one of them anymore, despite the fact that the MacLean had declared William's loyalty to clan, country, and king. They still suspected that he'd become a traitor to the king as his brother and father had. It appeared it didn't matter one whit that he'd spent the last two years of his life on mission after mission for King David, aiding the king in seizing the castles of real traitors.

"Ye're smart enough to ken we're nae here to welcome ye," said James MacLean, one of the older warriors who sat on the MacLean council.

"How did ye ken I was coming today?" William asked, ignoring any tug of emotion caused by the fact that James, whom he'd once thought of as family, still did not trust him.

"I saw the missive King David sent to ye, as well as yer response to the king and the MacLean."

"Then ye ken that King David trusts me and Alex—I mean, the MacLean—trusts me. I have fought in the king's name for two years. If our king and our laird dunnae believe me a traitor, then why do ye?"

The men around him shifted, and James spoke once more. "Yer father and yer brother were traitors. My son is dead because of them!"

William's neck heated in shame. Everything James was saying was true, and it made William feel as if he were a betrayer, but he wasn't. His father and brother had each betrayed the king at different times. His father's betrayal had cost many MacLean warriors their lives when they had fought warriors his father had led against the king for the Steward. And later, James's son had died protecting the king during an ambush after William's brother had alerted the Steward as to where the king was traveling. Still, William had argued the point enough to know that words would never change their minds. It seemed the actions he'd hoped would prove his loyalty, reestablish his good name, and earn the trust of his entire clan might not change what they now believed of him, either.

James pointed his sword at William. "I dunnae ken what sorcery ye used to convince the king and our laird that ye are nae a traitor, but we"—he motioned to the men with him—"dunnae believe yer lies."

William swept his gaze over the men before him. Each one had been personally affected by the actions of his father and brother. The hatred on their faces made him want to turn around and leave, but fleeing again would not gain their forgiveness, nor could he defy the king's order to appear before him. "I am nae a traitor," he repeated, his words stiff.

"Bah! Ye are making yerself more powerful!" James said, pointing two fingers at his eyes and then at William's. "I see what ye are doing. We all do." He waved a hand around at the men again. "Ye are probably trying to become king yerself or to aid the Steward's cause!"

"Aye!" chorused the men around him.

"Raise yer sword now, traitor!" James said. "'Tis time to

die!"

A tic began in William's right eye. He blinked a few times until it dissipated. "James, I dunnae wish to fight ye. Ye taught me to defend myself alongside my father, remember?"

"Oh aye, I remember. It makes the betrayal so much worse, *Wolf*."

William flinched. He hadn't minded the nickname he'd been given as one of the enforcers of the king's will, but coming from James, the nickname sounded twisted. James smirked, and William had a feeling his old friend had seen his reaction.

"Let us see if ye are as ferocious and deadly as they say."

"Again, I dunnae want to fight ye, James," he reiterated.

James shrugged. "Ye can die fighting or die standing there. Either way, ye will die this night."

William reacted instinctually to the slight movement of James's sword hand. The man moved to slice William down his breastbone, and William jerked his own sword up. Their blades clanked, cutting through the silence, and then the high-pitched sound of William's sword grating along the length of James's rang in William's ears, along with his now-rushing blood. With a swivel of his wrist, he relieved James of his weapon, which went flying upward. William reached out and caught James's blade with his left hand, then pointed both swords at the man.

"Ye can either stand aside," William said through clenched teeth, "or I can use ye to practice a little double-sworded trick the Dark Riders taught me while I trained with them."

Invoking the name of the ferocious warriors had the desired effect. James looked momentarily fearful that William might now possess some of the magical powers the

Dark Riders were thought to have. He used the momentary advantage to dodge past James, only to come face-to-face with four more angry warriors.

He knocked two men down in quick succession, but the other two came at him before he could get his sword or James's back up. A blade pressed hard against his windpipe from behind.

"Do ye have any last words?" James asked, panting in William's ear.

"Aye," William said, rage pumping through his blood. All he'd wanted in the years since his father and brother had betrayed their clan and king was to cast away the shame and convince people he was honorable. And he'd failed. "Dunnae ever come at a man from behind unless ye are certain of exactly what he's capable of."

With that, William jerked up his hand and grasped the blade at his throat, the sharp edge slicing into his skin, and held it just long enough to rear his head back into James's nose. Bone crunched, and James's howling rang in William's ears. The men in front of him lunged forward, and as they did, William raised the swords in his hands, not wanting to hurt the men but not wanting to die.

"Stand down!" thundered a voice from the darkness. Laird Alex MacLean appeared in the moonlight, holding a torch. Thomas and Lannrick were by his side.

Everyone stilled, and William glared at Thomas and Lannrick. "Did ye nae hear me whistle?"

"Oh aye," Lannrick said, amusement clear in his voice. "But ye did order us nae to stop to so much as to take a breath until we got to the great hall."

"That ye did," Thomas agreed, sounding equally amused. "And so we obeyed."

"What the devil is going on here, James?" the MacLean

demanded, striding toward them.

"He's a traitor," James growled. "He's nae welcome here."

William's neck heated with shame once more.

The MacLean jerked James toward him by the man's plaid. "As far as I ken, I'm still yer laird and David is still yer king. I say William is welcome, as does yer king. To defy me is to be banished from the clan, but to defy yer king is yer death. Do ye wish to continue down this path? I can send one of William's comrades to retrieve the king from the great hall where he is dining and let him ken ye tried to kill a member of his personal guard."

A long silence stretched through the darkness, and the disgrace William had long felt suddenly scalded him along with anger. No matter what he did, the sins of his father and brother would never be forgotten, and they would be considered his own sins forever. Why had he thought it could be different? His father had died fighting against the king, and his brother had fled to the king's enemy some time ago, so he might as well be dead. William had thought one day he would live here peacefully again, but this was no longer his home.

"Dunnae fash yerself, James," William said to the man's stubborn silence. If he'd been in James's place, mayhap he would have felt the same way. "I'm only here at the king's behest. This is nae my home any longer."

"That is likely the only thing we agree on, Wolf," James replied. "It seems, Laird, that the problem is solved."

The MacLean shoved James away. "Nae to my satisfaction. I am yer laird. Ye seem to have forgotten that when ye refused to obey my command, so I dunnae have need of ye on my council or as a clansman any longer."

"Alex," James said, his astonishment clear in his voice.

William was shocked, too. He could not believe that the MacLean would go to such a length for him. Or perhaps it was more to keep order in his clan. Yes, that seemed more likely.

The MacLean stared at James, his gaze hard and cold. "Collect yer things and leave my lands. If I see ye in the morning, I'll tell the king ye defied him, and I'd wager ye'll be missing yer head by midday."

"Ye'll see, Alex," James said, pointing a finger at William. "'Tis only a matter of time until he follows in his father's and brother's footsteps. And when he does, ye'll come searching for me, begging me to return to counsel ye."

"Dunnae hold yer breath," the MacLean said. "Now, away with ye before I take yer head off myself just to shut yer mouth."

"Come on, men," James ordered, and the warriors followed James away.

"Thank ye for yer trust," William said to the MacLean.

Alex turned to him, his searching eyes glinting in the moonlight. "I dunnae place the sins of yer brother and yer father upon yer head." He clapped William on the shoulder. "Give it more time. The others will come around."

"The only way these men would ever trust me again is if my brother and father were found innocent of betraying our clan and the king, and we both ken that my father died a traitor and my brother lives as one. These men think I have treason in my blood."

"It dunnae matter what they believe, William," Thomas said, speaking up. "Ye ken what is in yer heart, and so does God."

William nodded. Thomas would know better than anyone. He fought for King David now, but there was a time when he'd been loyal to the Steward, driven to it by a twisted past. "How do ye do it?" he asked Thomas. "How do ye ignore what people say about ye? How they look at ye with distrust?"

"I see it. I hear it. But I caused it. Ye, ye did nae cause yer woes, so ignore them or ye will go mad trying to change their minds. Some minds kinnae be changed."

"'Tis good advice," the MacLean said. "Now come. The king sent me to fetch ye when these two showed up at the great hall without ye. He's eager to talk to ye."

"Do ye ken what this is about?" William asked, falling into step beside Alex, who was already turning toward the castle. King David had been unusually vague in the summons he'd sent. Usually, he gave at least a hint at what mission was to come next, but the missive that had brought William here had been a simple command to present himself within a fortnight.

"Nay," the MacLean replied, glancing at him. "The king has always been a most secretive man. He claims it's how he has kept his throne. The only man I've ever kenned him to confide in is Iain MacLeod. But I've heard even the MacLeod say that though he's King David's closest friend, he's nae privy to all the king's endeavors."

"Well, if he summoned all three of us here," Lannrick said, "surely that means he's pleased with how we work together. Mayhap he's going to reward us."

"Twice I've seen the king reward a warrior he was pleased with," William said, cutting his gaze to Alex. "Both times the warrior in question ended up wed when he did nae want to be."

The MacLean chuckled. "It turned out verra well for me. Are ye saying the Savage Slayer—"

"Brodee," William interrupted, feeling a special allegiance to his closest friend. "He dunnae care to be called the Savage Slayer," he finished by way of explanation as they reached the top of the seagate stairs.

"Noted," the MacLean said, and they made their way into the inner courtyard of the MacLean stronghold. "Ye ken I did nae mean anything by it. I like Brodee. I thought he was rather proud of the moniker he'd earned as the king's right hand."

William shrugged. "I think it once served a purpose for him but no longer does since his wife tamed him."

"So," the MacLean said with a smirk, "Brodee has found he likes the wife the king thrust upon him well enough?"

William chuckled. "Ye could say he's rather fond of her."

The MacLean paused at the main castle door and faced William. "Then it seems to me, that if ye should find yerself rewarded by the king this day and taking a wife happens to be part of yer reward, ye can all be at ease kenning how pleased Brodee and I both are."

"I've heard many more stories where it did nae turn out so well," Lannrick muttered.

"Aye," Thomas agreed. "I'd rather nae be the recipient of such a gift."

Alex chuckled. "William, ye're being awfully quiet. Would ye mind much if the king gifted ye a wife?"

Yes, he would. He did not want a wife. Most women were not to be trusted. Like his mother. Hell, most men were not to be trusted or counted upon, either. Too many people whom he had thought he could rely upon had left or turned their backs on him.

"Aye, I'd mind," he said, choosing not to say more.

Alex assessed him for a long, silent moment, and William half expected his laird to ask why, but the man surprised him with a nod and a look that bespoke of understanding. "Come," the MacLean said. "Let us end yer suspense."

Three

King David greeted them in the solar and quickly sent Lannrick, Thomas, and the MacLean on their way. Once the door was shut behind them, the king's smile, which had been consistent since he'd greeted them, immediately disappeared.

William wasn't completely surprised. King David was known for his abrupt changes in mood. William watched the king's progress back to the table from the door, and then he waited as the king poured a goblet of wine, then another, and handed one to William. Now that *did* surprise him.

"Drink this," King David instructed, spearing William with a contemplative gaze.

William gladly consumed the wine, welcoming the warmth as it made a path down his throat and into his belly. His journey to Duart Castle had been long, and he was tired and sorely lacking in patience at the moment, which was something he most definitely needed for a conversation with the king.

King David leaned against the edge of the table and brought his wine goblet to his lips as he regarded William. A sudden, unexpected feeling that the king did not know where to begin or was loath to begin at all struck William. Both options were novelties for the king, he knew. David was a man of action. He simply charged ahead, often plowing over others in the process, but everything he did was always, truly in his heart, for the good of Scotland.

Finally, the king let out a long breath, set his goblet on the table, and asked, "What would ye do to vindicate yer father and brother? What would ye give?"

What the devil was the king about with these questions? "If they could be exonerated, which they kinnae, I'd give anything," William said.

"I thought ye might say that," David said, sighing, then drummed his fingers against the edge of the table. "I've watched ye as ye have worked tirelessly alongside Blackswell," the king said, mentioning William's closet friend, who was also the king's right hand. "And I've watched ye lead yer own group of men. I ken everything ye've done, every dangerous mission ye have volunteered for, ye have done so to remove the shadow of shame ye live under—"

"Sire, that's true," William cut in, "but I would have volunteered for the missions even if my father and brother had nae betrayed ye. Ye are the rightful king, and I consider it my duty and an honor to serve ye."

"I ken that, William. 'Tis why I called ye here today. I find myself in an unconscionable position of either breaking a sworn vow to someone or risking losing my throne." The king's gaze pierced through the distance between them. His expression looked almost guilty.

Uneasiness stirred in William's gut as David stood and shifted from foot to foot, almost anxiously, like someone with a secret. "If ye were king, which would ye chose: to break a vow or fight to hold yer throne?"

William did not even have to consider it. "The vow is to one, but on yer throne, ye serve the good of many. I'd break the vow if it meant keeping my throne."

King David nodded. "I have come to the same conclusion, but it dunnae make me feel better. What is the worth of a king who breaks his vows?"

The agony in David's voice over what he must do was exactly why William knew that David was a good king. He waved a hand toward a seat. "Sit with me, William. I need to tell ye something."

The uneasiness William was feeling began to grow, and he quickly took a seat as did the king. "Years ago," the king started, "when I was captured by the English and imprisoned, I developed a very small network of men to aid me on the outside while I was trapped by the English. There were four men in this circle, and I had kenned each of them since my boyhood. These men had, at one time or another, proven to me that I had their absolute, undying loyalty, and each of these men had at some point risked their life to save mine. I kenned, despite what hardships they might face by serving me, they would do so unquestionably."

William nodded. Was the king bringing him into this inner circle? Revealing things William could not even imagine? King David leaned forward so that his elbows rested on the table, and his gaze bore into William. "William, yer father was one of these men."

"What?" The word cracked in his throat, and shock rendered him unable to say more.

"Yer father was one of four men I trusted above all others. I had kenned him since we were verra young lads. Do ye ken the history?"

Instead of immediately answering, William ticked off the facts he knew in his mind. His father had not been a MacLean by birth; he'd been born into the MacThorn clan. His grandfather had been laird, and William's father had become laird when his grandfather was killed saving King David's father. Then years later, the MacThorn clan was destroyed during a battle with the English that William's father went to on the king's command. "My grandfather saved yer father's life, and my father aided ye in a battle against the English, a battle that destroyed our clan."

"Aye," the king confirmed. "When I was verra young."

William nodded. "My father took the MacLean name, as the MacThorn clan was too weak to rebuild. There were nae enough of them left."

"Aye," King David said, sighing. "Yer grandfather gave his life serving my father, and yer father gave his clan serving me. Yer grandfather and my father were friends, and that is how yer father and I came to apprentice together, and how I later came to call on his aid, first in battle, and then when I was captured by the English, I did nae hesitate to call upon yer father for aid. Times were just as treacherous then as they are now." The king held up his sword hand. "I counted only four men as those I kenned in my heart I could trust with my most secret missions. *Four men.*" The king lifted four fingers. "And then myself." He raised his thumb. "Together, we took back my throne and kept me upon it. Yer father was among those men."

"And then he betrayed ye," William said, heat stealing into his face.

"Nay," the king said. "He did nae betray me, William. Yer father died in service to me."

William stared wordlessly at the king as his heart began to pound heavily. "That kinnae be. He betrayed ye. He told the Steward where ye would strike in the Battle of Glenfurrie, and—"

"He did tell my nephew, 'tis true, but yer father told him because we planned it to be so."

"Ye planned it to be so?" William repeated, still struggling to form a proper sentence with the roar of confusion in his ears.

"Aye. Just listen for a moment," the king said in the most patient voice William had ever heard the normally impatient king use. "When King Edward captured me and imprisoned me in Odiham Castle those years ago, I suspected almost immediately that my nephew would make a move for my throne. That was when I reached out to the four men I told ye I trusted above all others."

"Who are the other three men?" William asked.

"Iain MacLeod," the king began, "Archibald Douglas, and Grant Macaulay."

William nodded. Archibald Douglas was cousin to the Earl of Douglas and the illegitimate son of Sir James Douglas, and William happened to know Archibald had served as a page of sorts to David before he was king. But William was not certain what connection Grant Macaulay, cousin to the MacLeod laird, had to the king. Had Grant trained with King David and the MacLeod when they were younger? William sifted through faded memories trying to recall what he knew of Grant Macaulay. He had a wicked scar down the length of his right cheek that he'd received while a prisoner at the Earl of March's castle.

"Each of these men has sacrificed a great deal for me— yer father obviously the most, since he gave his life. After I gathered with the men I'd called to me at my prison, we all agreed that my nephew was already doing things that appeared to point to him preparing to take my throne. So the men became my spies, using the connections they had to learn of any plots that might be afoot. Yer father was responsible for keeping me alive more times than I can count by discovering plots against me. Hell, yer father constantly being away on missions for me was what drove yer mother away. That always weighed heavy upon me."

William frowned. "I did nae ken that. He never said why she had left, simply that she had." His chest jerked. It didn't change that his mother had not cared enough to stay and that she had left him when he was but a lad of thirteen summers, but at least now he knew the real reason.

"He could nae tell ye," the king went on, oblivious to William's inner thoughts. "To do so would have revealed his work for me. But I ken yer mother was tired of being left alone with ye boys. Men like ye, men like yer father, give much for Scotland."

When the king gave him an expectant look, William nodded, feeling David would not continue until he got some sort of indication that William understood there would be more sacrifice than he'd already offered.

The king heaved a sigh and continued. "Yer father had a mission to ascertain whether the MacQuerrie laird had turned against me. Do ye ken the MacQuerries?"

"Only a legend about the laird's daughter," William replied. "But it is nae one worthy of repeating." The idea that a lass could make the king of Scotland was ridiculous.

The king's lips flattened into a hard line. "The legend is true, William. 'Tis why it was important to discover if MacQuerrie had turned against me. I verra much have a stake in who his daughter will wed, and she must wed a man loyal to me."

"Sire, I dunnae mean any disrespect, but the legend says the lass—"

"Ada," the king interrupted, his eyes narrowing to an intense look. "Her name is Ada, and the legend is true. Dunnae tell me ye dunnae believe in the fae?"

William rubbed the back of his neck. He knew the king, and most in Scotland, believed in the fae. He also knew the MacLeod laird and his entire clan credited the fae with the

MacLeod clan's prosperity and very survival. The MacLean had told him long ago that the MacLeods had a flag they swore had been given to one of the long-ago MacLeod lairds, and that the flag carried special powers the MacLeods could call upon in dire times. William didn't want to argue with the king, but he didn't want to lie to him, either. "I believe in things I can see," William replied slowly.

"Aye," the king said with a nod. "So do I. And I have met fae, been saved by fae, and heard fae predict the future for several people, and every word of it came true. I have even witnessed a fairy bestowing a gift upon a man. I tell ye, fae are real and so is their power. And knowing this as I do, the lass Ada, when she weds, will have the power to either keep me on the throne or snatch it from me. I spoke with her father long ago, and he pledged his undying loyalty to me and vowed he would wed his daughter to a man utterly loyal to me. But over the last five years, the laird's stepson has been more in control of the clan than the laird, and now the MacQuerrie is dead. Which means his stepson is now laird. I've heard increasingly disturbing reports that the stepson was loyal to my nephew, who is his father."

"I beg yer pardon?" William said, dumbfounded.

The king waved a dismissive hand. "My nephew has sired bastards all over Scotland, and the new MacQuerrie laird, Brothwell, is but one amongst them. But he is the most dangerous one. He is now laird of a strong clan, and he is the one who will decide who the lass Ada weds. But I've jumped too far ahead…"

William could do little more than nod. His thoughts were bumping into one another with all he had learned.

David continued. "Yer father came to me three years ago with his concern that the MacQuerrie's stepson, Brothwell, would eventually gain control over the

MacQuerrie clan and that Brothwell was nae loyal to me. Yer father proposed going there and spying on the stepson—an easy enough task for yer father because he and the MacQuerrie were friends. When yer father returned to me, he confirmed our suspicions, but it was worse than I'd imagined. The MacQuerrie was ill but hiding it from everyone; his mind was slipping. Yer father told me he would forget everyday things, and Brothwell was taking advantage of it. Yer father believed Brothwell, unbeknownst to the MacQuerrie, was recruiting other clans to the Steward's side. After much discussion with yer father and the other men in my inner circle, we decided the best thing to do was to plant yer father as a spy and as someone who might aid us in battles by giving the other side false information. But in order for anyone to trust him, it had to look like he and I had fallen out and that yer father was betraying me."

"Yer mistress," William said, the truth hitting him like a swift punch in the gut.

"Aye. We argued publicly over my mistress. Yer father did nae approve of her, and then he left and went to Brothwell. He fed him false information about where I would strike at the Battle of Glenfurrie, but Brothwell and my nephew are clever. They sent a troop of men to where yer father had told Brothwell I would be, *and* they sent a larger troop of men to where my troops really were. We were outmanned, and yer father was there, seemingly fighting for Brothwell, but I saw him and he nae ever raised a sword against a man of mine. 'Twas why he died."

William was at once enraged to know the truth, though glad to know it at the same time. His father had not been a traitor. A wave of relief slammed into him, followed by searing-hot shame that he'd believed his father capable of such a ruse. Why hadn't he questioned it? Why had he been so quick to condemn his father? He knew part of the reason. His throat grew tight with the memory of how easily he'd believed the worst of a man who had given him everything.

Jesus. William yanked a hand through his hair. The things he'd said to his father... Memories came at him, piercing his heart like arrows. The words he'd said...

Christ, those god-awful words...

William clenched his teeth as he recalled telling his father he was ashamed to be his son when his father had told him he was departing the clan to pledge loyalty to the Steward. His father had never hinted that he was working for the king. "Why didn't he tell me?" William groaned, unable to repress the question.

The king grasped him by the shoulder, and his sorrowful gaze held William's. "Everyone had to believe—most especially ye and yer brother."

Bram.

William's head began to pound to match the ferocious rhythm of his heart. "Is Bram working for ye, as well?" he asked, hope and fear tangling inside him. He'd turned his back on Bram just as quickly as he'd rebuffed his father, and if Bram had been innocent, too...

He clenched his fists, and nausea roiled within him. His father was dead. He'd turned his back on Bram completely when he thought him a traitor, too. There was no taking back how he had acted, but was there a chance to set things right with Bram?

"Aye," the king said, his brow furrowing. "Or he was," the king replied, frustration in his tone. "I am unsure at this time if Bram has nae turned against me truly for Brothwell's sister, which was the cover we originally created for him."

Regret and guilt washed over William, making him feel

as if he were going to drown under the deluge of emotion. He swallowed the hard lump in his throat. Even if he had wanted to question the king now, ask for answers, he could not. His throat had tightened in an effort to restrain the bellow of rage that wanted to escape him.

King David nodded as if he understood William's plight. "Once people thought that I believed yer father to be a traitor and we had publicly quarreled, it was easy for him to go to the MacQuerrie clan to seek refuge and then gain acceptance by Brothwell. Once he had that, yer father easily discovered that Brothwell was, indeed, recruiting men to aid in my nephew's plot to steal my throne. The MacQuerie laird was apparently already losing his grip on his memory even three years ago, so Brothwell was able to easily manipulate him. Yer father learned the names of some of the lairds who were vile traitors when Brothwell had spoken of their fealty to the Steward."

King David stood and began pacing the great hall. He jerked his hands through his hair, clearly agitated, and he finally paused in front of the table where William still sat. The king's fist came down hard upon the table, making the wine goblets rattle. The king's gaze, blazing with rage, met William's. "These are greedy men who always want more. More power. More land. More coin. They dunnae ever care for the commoners, though. They have joined forces with my nephew to drive me from the throne. He promises them the *more* they want. Do ye think he will give it to them, William?"

It was not a question, but a point the king was making. "Nay," William answered anyway. "Of course the Steward will nae. He wants all the power himself. All the land. All the coin."

"Aye." The king fell back into the chair he had vacated

only moments before. "But people filled with greed are blind to their own folly. They would put a man on the throne who will give them less say than I do. I kinnae allow that to happen. Nae because I wish to stay king." David suddenly laughed. It was a bitter sound. "Well, of course I do, but more importantly, I love Scotland with my heart and my soul, and my nephew would destroy our home as surely as I am standing before ye this day."

William inclined his head in agreement, and King David took a long breath before continuing. "Yer father uncovered four of the twelve lairds loyal to the Stewart. That is why what he was doing was kept secret from everyone except the other three men in the circle. Nae anyone else kenned that yer father was spying for me. Nae the MacLean and nae Bram. He only learned the truth when yer father was killed."

"Do ye believe Brothwell kenned my father was yer spy?" William asked, clenching his jaw against another wave of murderous rage. He would kill Brothwell.

"Nay. As I said, yer father appeared loyal to Brothwell in battle the day he was struck down by one of my men. I will live with the regret that I did nae foresee such an outcome."

William's throat constricted even more with the information that his father had ridden into battle appearing the traitor. "Why have ye nae sent someone to kill Brothwell since ye ken that he's treasonous?"

"I've thought about it," the king replied. "Believe me, I have. But the man's belief that he is invincible and his tie to my nephew make him too valuable to end his life just now. He makes mistakes because he's so cocksure, and his mistakes have aided me in my pursuit of learning which other lairds are plotting against me. As I said, yer father discovered four of them. After he was killed, I met with the MacLeod, Archibald, and Grant. I took their counsel and decided to approach yer brother and bring him into our circle, but only if he was more than willing and wished it."

The king swiped a hand over his face. "Bram was the natural choice, as it would nae seem suspicious at all to Brothwell if Bram appeared at the MacQuerrie stronghold claiming he wished to join forces with Brothwell since it seemed yer father died in service to the man, cut down by one of my warriors." The king let out a long, shuddering breath. "When we approached Bram and he learned the truth of yer father's fealty, he was verra eager to take up yer father's work." The king paused, his gaze sorrowful. "I'm sorry that I could nae tell ye before now, William. I'm sorry that ye have had to live believing yer father and brother were traitors. I've seen how it tortured ye, but I have also seen how ye have made yerself into a fine man and warrior, despite yer hardships."

"Where is Bram? Did he truly fall for Brothwell's sister Marjorie, or is that rumor also a lie?" William demanded, uncaring of any consequence he might face for speaking to the king so curtly.

"Bram was accepted immediately by Brothwell, as we had hoped, and Bram discovered five more lairds who were plotting against me. Yer brother was able to pass the names along to me. As to what has happened to him, I truly dunnae ken. Whether he has real affections for Marjorie or nae, I kinnae say, either. At first, it was a good way to get information—to pretend to care for her—and a good excuse to convince everyone here he had betrayed us. Yet, from the things he wrote in his correspondence to me, I do believe yer brother has developed feelings for her, and I suspect he slipped in his ruse because of it. I have nae heard from him in quite a while, which makes me think he has been discovered, or—" the king eyed William "—he has truly turned traitor for the heart of a woman."

William had thought his brother a traitor once; he would not do so again. "I dunnae believe it," William said.

The king offered a grim smile. "Neither do I. I have tried to find out what has happened to Bram. I've sent men to try to breach Brothwell's inner circle, but nae one has been successful. I was waiting and hoping Bram would contact me, but it's as if he's disappeared. The men I sent were able to ascertain that he was no longer at Brothwell's home. They say Brothwell sent him on a mission. And I recently received word that Brothwell is holding a tournament in a sennight to choose a husband for Ada MacQuerrie. I kinnae let that happen. I may nae ken Ada's loyalty, but I ken Brothwell's undoubtedly, and now that Ada's father is dead, there will be no stopping Brothwell in wedding Ada to a man loyal to the Steward."

It suddenly clicked in William's mind as to why the king had called William to him and why he was sharing all of this now. The king wanted to use him. And William would let him. He'd do just about anything to exonerate his father and brother, and if he could become close to Brothwell, he could discover what had truly happened to Bram, and whether he was alive or dead. And if Bram was not dead, William would find him. Then he would discover the remaining lairds who were in league with Brothwell, and he would clear his own family's name.

"Ye want me to snatch the lass?" he asked, preparing to argue for the rest of what he wanted, for the ability to find Bram and exonerate his family.

"Nae just take her," the king said, a vicious smile twisting his lips. "I want ye to wed her. 'Tis how her powers will be activated. And I trust ye to use her to serve me."

The king's announcement left William frozen. He could not seem to find the words to agree to the command.

The king leaned forward and gripped William by the neck. "I ken what I'm asking of ye."

"I dunnae wish for a wife," William said. Truth be told, he was surprised he'd even gotten those words out. He had not wanted a wife since the day his mother left and he'd seen what a woman could do to a man. She had cut him deeply, but it had nearly cleaved his father in two. "Kinnae ye ask someone else to do that part of it?"

The king shook his head. "I wish I could. I vowed to yer father I'd nae ever tell ye or yer brother about his work for me. He did nae wish for ye two to follow in his path after yer mother left him. As I said, he believed his long absences were part of why she fled."

And he'd likely be right, William thought, a spark of a memory coming to him: his father alone, crying softly and saying William's mother's name over and over.

Christ, no, he did not want to take a wife.

William's heart thudded, and King David's gaze turned desperate, pleading.

The king is afraid. He is fearful of the lass rumored to hold the power to make or keep a king.

"But ye are the only one who can do it," David said. "Brothwell will think ye have come to follow in yer brother's and father's footsteps, if he dunnae ken Bram is a spy. And if he does ken it—"

"I'll be handing myself to the enemy," William finished for the king.

"Aye," David replied, his voice as grave as his face. "Either way, I'd wager my life he will nae be able to resist letting ye compete, and that will give ye a chance to convince him that ye are there to join forces with him." The king squeezed William's neck. "I ken I ask a great deal. Once ye have the names, ye can flee to crush my enemies, and find yer brother. Once yer brother is proved still loyal, yer family name can be cleared. Do we have a pact?"

There was only one answer William could give. He had not wanted to take a wife, but he had to try to take this lass. But then what? "Will I continue to work in yer inner circle after this?"

"Aye," the king replied. "Of course."

"I did nae plan on taking a wife," William reiterated. "I dunnae have any interest in a wife and family, only in serving ye."

And gaining respect once more.

The king offered a triumphant smile. "As far as I'm concerned, ye need nae ever see her again after she aids ye. If ye desire, I'll set her up in a castle to be guarded always. But first, ye must win her hand. What say ye?"

William swallowed, his mouth too dry. The king was right. He could wed this lass, Ada, and use her to aid the king, but that did not mean he had to let her close or even live with her. He had a sudden recollection of offering Brodee advice on his wife: he'd told him simply to let her close. It had been easy counsel to give because it was not his life being altered. This, however... This was different. *He* was different.

"Aye," William said, sealing his fate.

Four

Ada stood on the platform to the left of the arena, where all the men who had come to fight in the tournament were gathered. Such intense hopelessness washed over her that her knees felt as if they would buckle. Beside her, Hella lumbered to her feet and bared her teeth in a snarl as Brothwell approached. At Ada's left thigh, Freya growled low and the ferocious sound increased with each step Brothwell took.

"Tell those damned hounds to stand down," he muttered, glaring at both dogs.

Ada clicked her tongue twice, and Hella immediately obeyed. But Freya continued to voice her displeasure. Ada set her hand to Freya's head, which was level with Ada's hip, and she ran her fingers over the gentle slope of the thick, white fur that covered Freya's neck.

"Freya, nay," Ada gently chided. After a moment, Freya quieted, but her ears went back and her teeth remained bared. Ada glanced at Brothwell's still-bandaged arm and leg, courtesy of Hella and Freya, and knew the only reason Brothwell had not had her hounds killed is because he believed Esther's lie that the faes had given the dogs to Ada. Fresh worry for Esther and Maximilian coursed through her. She had tried to discover where Brothwell was keeping them, but to no avail.

"Where are they?" Ada demanded, unable to hold her tongue.

"As I have told ye repeatedly," Brothwell said, moving directly in front of her, "once ye choose yer husband and are wed, I will release them from where they are being held captive. They're on this island."

"They are safe and fed?" she asked, as she did every day.

"Of course, Ada. I'm nae a monster."

She pressed her lips together in disagreement.

"I'm nae," Brothwell growled. "I simply do what I must to aid my father. Ye would do the same."

She felt an unwanted shaft of pity for Brothwell, one she'd felt before. In him, she could see and hear the desperation to be acknowledged and loved by the Steward, but it did not excuse that he was forcing her to wed a man of his choosing so Brothwell could manipulate her once her gift started working. She didn't understand the gift the fae had supposedly given her. She did not feel anything special within her. She only knew that she believed in her heart that King David should be king. Brothwell would make her betray her own heart, though, unless she could escape. But without any help, it was hopeless. Her throat grew tight with the need to cry, but she forced herself to swallow, then swallowed again, ridding herself of the weak need. She would not cry.

"Ah, there's Marjorie!" Brothwell exclaimed, sweeping his hand toward his sister. "We can finally start!"

Ada could not force herself to offer even a fake smile, and Marjorie looked as somber as Ada felt. Her stepsister climbed the steps to the platform slowly, skimming her gaze over Ada and then settling it on Brothwell. When Marjorie's eyes did not grow warm and narrowed instead, Ada was certain the two must have been quarreling earlier. She found herself watching them with a spark of hope, even as Brothwell raised his hands to signal the beginning of the tournament, even as the three of them took their seats, and even as the warriors were called one by one to the front of the platform to show their respects.

Ada kept her gaze veiled under her lashes and trained on Marjorie and Brothwell. They whispered furiously at each other, clearly continuing whatever argument they'd not finished when last they'd seen each other. Perhaps this could somehow be used to Ada's advantage. Maybe Marjorie really was changed and ready to defy Brothwell…

Another competitor was announced, then came forward for Brothwell to greet and Ada to acknowledge. Both Freya and Hella growled as they had for each man who had been introduced before this one. Ada didn't bother to look at whatever devil thought to wed her for his own gain. Instead, she merely lifted her hand in a dismissive wave and continued to stare at her stepbrother and stepsister, her mind turning over Marjorie's actions of late. She had been reserved, colder to Brothwell, less ready to side with him, and less cruel to Ada. It had seemed to begin once Bram MacLean had come to their home. Ada was certain Marjorie cared for Bram, and the change had to do with him. Was it enough of a change, though, that Marjorie would aid Ada? Did she dare to ask or would that put Esther and Maximilian at risk?

"Where is he?" Marjorie hissed, so low Ada would have missed it if she hadn't leaned ever so slightly closer to Marjorie. She was certain they were speaking of Bram MacLean.

"I told ye," Brothwell replied in an angry whisper. "He is proving himself to me. And until he does, forget him. For if he dunnae—"

The rest of what Brothwell was saying was drowned out by the guard calling the next competitor forward. Ada paid no heed to the man's name, nor did she turn her head toward the newest competitor. She stared at Brothwell and tried to read his lips as she raised her hand in the acknowledgment she was supposed to give, but Brothwell suddenly stopped speaking to Marjorie and snapped his gaze forward, his eyes widening. When Marjorie did the same, except her mouth also parted, Ada found herself turning her attention to the warrior before them.

Oh heaven above...

Something deep in her belly fluttered. The sun cast a golden glow down upon the man, making him appear like a chiseled god. She blinked, sure the glare was causing her to see things unclearly, but no. Her vision was perfect. He was the most beautiful man she'd ever seen.

The dark slash of his brows arched in what appeared to be amusement. Even from the distance that separated them, she could see he had a square jaw covered by a shadow of stubble and inky locks that grazed his very broad shoulders. She inched her way back up his face, her pulse rising as her gaze did. He had sculpted cheekbones, a long straight nose, and lips curved in a half smile that seemed like an invitation to sin. A tingling danced across her skin, making her shiver as she slid her gaze to his eyes, only to find his own gaze riveted on her face. Her heart jolted as those perfect lips of his drew into a wickedly smug smile. One of his brows arched higher, and despite the cold, heat flushed Ada from head to toe.

"That's Bram's brother!" Marjorie cried, making Ada jump and thankfully breaking the odd spell under which she'd found herself.

Marjorie started to rise, but Brothwell's hand clamped

around her wrist and jerked her back to her seat. Freya and Hella immediately began to growl at Brothwell, and it was only then that Ada realized her hounds had not snarled at the warrior.

"Ye will either control yer tongue, Marjorie," Brothwell said, each word punctuated, "or I will control it for ye. Do ye ken me?"

Marjorie jerked her head in a nod, and anger stirred in Ada on her stepsister's behalf.

"Come forward, William MacLean," Brothwell commanded the man.

William's hand grazed the hilt of his sword for one brief moment before he started toward the platform. He walked with the long, easy strides of a warrior who was certain of himself and his abilities. With each step he took, tension seemed to build within her, and when he finally stopped in front of them, he looked straight at her.

Those eyes...

She swallowed hard. His eyes were every bit as extraordinary as his face. The blue was like a cold wave. For one moment, she felt as if she were floating in his endlessly deep stare.

"William MacLean," Brothwell said. "Do tell what brings ye here to my home to a competition for my sister's hand. Especially given ye were nae invited."

His home! His sister!

Ada clenched her teeth so hard her jaw pulsed. Despite her disgust with Brothwell, she found herself eager to hear what the man before them would say. "The king sent me," he said without a hint of fear.

Ada could not tear her gaze from the powerful and brave man before her. Why would he admit such a thing to Brothwell?

"King David sent ye here, ye say?" Brothwell's tone sounded civil, but his hand grasped the edge of the dais so hard, his knuckles were white.

"Aye. He got word of yer tournament and wished me to compete and win yer stepsister's hand so he would control the woman who can make a king."

William MacLean had a death wish or—Her second thought made her ill, but it was the most likely possibility: he had been sent on a secret mission by his king but William had decided to betray King David. Was he following in his brother's footsteps? Ada had never fully believed Bram was a traitor, but now…

"I see," Brothwell replied nonchalantly, which immediately made Ada suspicious. Brothwell did not possess a negligent bone in his body. He plotted every word, every gesture, every move he made. "Kill him!" her stepbrother ordered, and at once, guards poured forward with their swords raised at the warrior.

Ada found herself up on her feet, unsure how she'd gotten there, with her breath caught in her throat. "Nay!" she cried out, hardly believing she was defying Brothwell when Esther's and Maximilian's safety was at stake, but she would not sit by and watch Brothwell have a man killed and do nothing. Freya and Hella nuzzled her hands with their nostrils, as if they agreed with her decision. "He would have to be a fool to come here and say such things without another purpose, and he dunnae appear the fool to me," she pointed out. She broke into a frightened sweat as Brothwell's black gaze, unfathomable in its murky depth, landed on her. The anger radiating from him made her take a step back. She fisted her hands and summoned her courage. "Let him finish explaining himself."

"Why should I?" Brothwell clipped.

Ada's gaze immediately flew to William MacLean, who was looking at her with obvious incredulity. "Dunnae his brother serve ye?" she asked, grasping at what she hoped would make him pause and consider not killing this man.

Beside her, Marjorie shifted, and Ada could have sworn the woman hissed in a breath of pain. "Mayhap—" Ada hurriedly searched her mind for the right words to say, to persuade Brothwell to have leniency. "Mayhap he is here to do the same."

To her relief, Brothwell looked as if he was contemplating her words, and then he said, "Speak quickly."

"I ken, as does everyone, that my father and brother betrayed the king to serve the Steward and join forces with ye," William said, the rich timbre of his voice making her breath catch. "I have lived in the shadow of that shame for years." The pain that laced his words sounded so real that Ada did not believe he could be making it up. Her heart twisted for him. "I did everything in my power to oblige the king and make amends for what I thought were the dishonorable decisions of my father and brother. Yet in my time serving as one of David's enforcers, I have come to realize that he is nae the king that the Scottish people need. He makes vows he dunnae keep, he takes land and castles away from good men because they want to have a voice in how their country is ruled, and he has become unreasonable. I kinnae follow him any longer. I can now see why my father and brother turned from him. I only wish I'd realized it sooner."

Uncertainty flooded Ada. She didn't know what to believe about this man, but she was still glad she had spoken up.

Suddenly, William MacLean dropped to his knee and lifted his sword. Ada bit her lip in dismay and disappointment, knowing what was to come. "Laird MacQuerrie, I bend the knee to ye now and will do so to the Steward when I stand before him. I pledge my sword arm, my life, and my fealty as long as I draw breath."

If one wanted to gain favor with Brothwell, groveling before him and pledging oneself to him, a man who was hungry for respect and power, was the most certain way to do it. Disgust made her press her lips into a thin line.

"It will take more than a pledge of fealty for me to believe or trust ye, Wolf," Brothwell said.

The warrior glanced up sharply, and when Ada looked to Brothwell, a sly smile turned up the corners of his mouth. "Yer brother paid special heed to whispers regarding ye this past year, Wolf, and Bram made mention to me of yer exploits. He was verra interested in what ye were doing." Ada could see by the widening of William MacLean's eyes that Brothwell's words surprised him.

Brothwell rose and descended the platform quickly. "Rise," he said, motioning for the man to do so. When William stood, he was slightly taller than Brothwell, who had, up until this moment, been the tallest man Ada had known. Everything about William MacLean commanded one's attention, from the way he stood with utter confidence, his Viking legs spread firmly apart, to the easy look he wore on his face. The two men faced each other. A blade could not have been slid between them without the very real danger of cutting one of their noses.

"If ye are truly here to bend the knee to the Steward and pledge yerself to our cause, then ye will nae mind a task to prove yerself trustworthy."

Ada held her breath with hope that the man would decline, though if he did that, Brothwell would surely kill him.

"I'll gladly take on anything ye require, Laird, but will I nae miss the beginning of the tournament if I am performing this task for ye?"

"The tournament begins tomorrow, so ye can complete the assignment tonight, and if ye are successful, I'll allow ye to fight in the tournament for a chance to woo Ada."

Ada felt an odd mixture of emotions. On the one hand, she was angry that William seemed so willing to do Brothwell's bidding, but on the other hand, she was glad he would not die this day. Though she certainly should not be so happy that a man who was betraying the king would live another day to strike at him. What was the matter with her?

"What is it ye require of me?" William asked Brothwell, interrupting Ada's thoughts.

"Hmm..."

Just then, Connely came rushing through the crowd toward Brothwell and William MacLean. "Laird! Laird! I need a word with ye."

Brothwell motioned him forward, and Connely quickly whispered something in Brothwell's ear, to which he threw back his head and laughed. "Perfect!" he boomed. He clapped his hands, gave a quick order for the guard to gather some men, and turned back to William.

Ada had a bad, bad feeling about Brothwell's good cheer. It usually meant something unfortunate for someone else.

Brothwell sneered. "The perfect way for ye to show yer loyalty to me and the Steward has just crossed onto my land."

If Ada had not been staring at William's face, she would have missed the way his lip curled ever so slightly in what appeared to be disgust. But the expression was gone as quickly as it had appeared, replaced with a neutral one. Still, she vowed she'd seen it, and it gave her the tiniest bit of hope that perhaps William MacLean was not a real traitor.

"And what might that be, Laird?" William asked.

"Connely tells me that he spotted Thomas Fraser—an old friend of yers, I believe—on my land. He gave him chase and lost him. I owe Thomas's father a bothersome debt, and capturing his wayward son will be the perfect way to repay it. Track him down, bring him to me, and then—and only then—will I allow ye to compete in the tournament."

Surely no honorable man would bring his friend into the lion's den willingly? Ada stared at William, and without showing a hint of regret, he said, "I'm at yer service, Laird."

Either William was excellent at playing the part of a traitor or he was indeed disloyal to the king.

Five

Several hours later, after losing the guards that Brothwell had sent with William to find Thomas, William finally came upon the cave where the men who he and the king had gathered to aid in this mission were awaiting him. The first person he saw, standing just outside of the cave, was Thomas. The fool was bent down skinning a rabbit.

"Ye've been spotted," William said by way of greeting.

"What's that ye say?" Grant Macaulay asked, appearing at the entrance of the cave.

The king had contacted Grant because, of the men in the king's inner circle, Grant lived the closest to the MacLean holding, and time had been of the essence. Once William won the tournament and wed the lass, he hopefully would have the names of the remaining three lairds secretly plotting against the king, and then they could flee to take down those men and find his brother. He was unsure how Ada was to help him exactly with this gift she supposedly possessed, but the king was insistent that she would be of aid.

Grant, along with Lannrick and Thomas, who William had convinced the king could be trusted and of help, had been sent with him so that once he got away from Brothwell with Ada, they could assist him in bringing down

Brothwell and the other lairds. Likely, he would send the men in three directions to gather troops from the MacLeod stronghold, the Douglas stronghold, and the MacLean stronghold to join them in fighting Brothwell and the traitors, but he could not know for certain until he had the lass and the names.

Thoughts of the lass with hair the color of golden, glistening honey and eyes as intense as a threatening gray sky before a winter storm sparked his lust to life. And it *was* lust. There was no other way to describe how she made him feel. He'd not exchanged a single word with the watchful lass, but his body had responded to her as if they were long-lost lovers.

He'd felt an instant pull to her, and guilt tugged at him at how they were planning to use her. But with so much at stake, remorse was not a luxury he could allow when it came to her. Besides, there was the real possibility that she was conspiring against the king with her stepbrother. He needed to set thoughts of her away. He did not have time to dwell upon her. When he was standing in front of her again, there'd be time enough for contemplating how to proceed until he was rid of her.

"William?" Grant asked, snapping his fingers in front of William's face.

"Sorry," William responded and waved toward Thomas as he glared at his normally careful friend. "Thomas was spotted by the MacQuerrie's guard. Now the man is demanding I bring Thomas to him to prove my newfound loyalty to the Steward and the MacQuerrie himself."

"Christ," Grant growled, yanking a hand through his hair and glowering at Thomas. "I told ye nae to chase after that rabbit!" The jagged red scar that ran down the length of Grant's right cheek darkened.

"I told ye so, as well," Lannrick said, adding his own dark scowl to the ones already directed at Thomas.

Thomas rose, his razor-sharp blue eyes flashing with clear ire. "I made a mistake. If any man here has nae ever made a mistake, speak now and I'll wash yer feet because, surely, ye are a god."

William let out a breath of frustration and pressed his lips together.

"I've made two mistakes," Grant said. "The first was nae killing a man when I had the chance, which got me this." He ran a finger down his scar. "The second was trusting his duplicitous sister, who swore to God above that she was not aiding the Steward. Of course, that particular mistake landed me in captivity for a year." Grant's gaze locked on William. "Dunnae trust Ada. Heed me, William."

Before William could respond, Lannrick said, "I've made two mistakes that almost got me killed in battle, and both had to do with my brothers. The bond of brotherhood can lead us to do foolish things, things that will harm us, but we do them anyway—for our brothers." His gaze rested on William now, as well. "I ken ye took this mission for yer brother, as well as the king. I dunnae fault ye that. I'd have done the same. But keep yer eyes open when and if ye see yer brother again. He may nae have come here a traitor, but love does strange things to men's honor."

William nodded. He'd already been considering what it would mean for him if Bram was truly a traitor, if that was why contact with the king had stopped. What if Bram had fallen in love with Marjorie MacQuerrie and truly had turned in support of the Steward? William did not think he could bring Bram to the king to be beheaded as David had demanded if that was the case, and that would make William a traitor, too.

"Now that we all ken that nae any of us are gods," Thomas said, "what is the damage created by my stubbornness to catch the damned rabbit to eat?"

William took a long, slow breath, considering Thomas's question, what had happened, and how to respond. "If I dunnae take ye to Brothwell, he'll nae let me compete, and it will make it verra hard to get near enough to Ada MacQuerrie to snatch her, let alone wed her and bed her so that she is truly my wife. I was to woo her, wed her, bed her, get the information and flee all within a sennight. A difficult task, at best, made nearly impossible if I have to snatch her *and* a priest, and we all have to flee while being pursued."

Thomas nodded. "What do ye propose?"

William slid his teeth back and forth, listening to the grating sound as he thought about what to say. The only possible solution was for him to take Thomas to the MacQuerrie, but he was loath—no, more than loath—to tell his comrade that he should offer himself up like a foolish lamb to be slaughtered. William had little hope that the MacQuerrie would not subject Thomas to torture. Oh, he would not kill Thomas, as Brothwell himself said he needed to deliver Thomas to his father alive, likely to then be killed for betraying the man, but there was some dispute between Thomas and Brothwell. The desire for vengeance had dripped from the MacQuerrie's gaze.

"He's obviously nae going to answer ye," Lannrick said to Thomas, "but I will. Ye'll have to allow William to take ye to the MacQuerrie, prepare yerself for pain, and trust that we will rescue ye before ye are killed."

"Put most efficiently," Thomas said with an agreeable nod. "The MacQuerrie will nae kill me. I have nary a doubt that he wants to hand me over to my father. Just free me before then, and I should recover from whatever pain the MacQuerrie inflicts upon me."

William frowned. He didn't know much about Thomas's past, besides it being a dark one with twisted deeds inflicted upon him as a young lad that led him to align himself with his father and the Steward simply so he could seek vengeance against the MacLean. But apparently, the MacLean had broken through Thomas's hatred, and he'd seen the wrongness in what he'd been doing. Thomas had not given William a single reason not to trust him, so trust him he would until the man proved he did not deserve it. But this, this unselfish act, proved much in William's mind.

William clasped Thomas's shoulder. "I'm sorry, Thomas."

Thomas shoved William's hand off him, making William recall that the warrior did not like to be touched. "Dunnae be," Thomas said. "'Twas my folly, and now I will suffer the consequences willingly to keep the mission alive. Did the MacQuerrie say anything else regarding me?"

"Only that ye would serve to cancel a debt to his father," William responded. "What's between the two of ye, though? It seemed there was more."

"Seemed that way how?" Thomas tilted his head, waiting, watchful.

William motioned to his eyes. "He could nae hide his hatred for ye."

Thomas chuckled at that. "What's between us is a woman. I tell ye now, William, it always comes down to a lass. And what of yers?"

"She's nae mine," William answered automatically, though the clenching of his gut indicated he already felt possessive of her. Before even a touch. Before even two words had been exchanged. Before vows. Before the bedding.

That would not suffice. He had to be prepared to do anything to clear his family's name, and he could not do that if a lass had his attention. He needed to be focused on his mission and unaffected by Ada MacQuerrie, no matter how beguiling she was.

Six

Forced to endure the attentions of the warriors who openly hated King David, the midday festivities were a special kind of torture for Ada. No man was here for her. They did not even truly see her. She would wager they had not even noticed what color her eyes were, that she had a spattering of unattractive freckles across her nose, or that her cheeks had odd little dents in them when she smiled. Of course they could not. They did not know her! The afternoon was for Brothwell to determine who he wished to allow to continue in the tournament.

She had her noonday meal among men who laughed openly about how they would take glee in killing King David, and it took all her will to sit there calmly. She wanted to flee, but that was not a choice. The truth of her situation sickened her. How was she supposed to shackle herself to one of these men for life?

As conversations flowed around her, her thoughts drifted to the warrior William. She had immediately cast him as horrid when he'd agreed to hunt down Thomas Fraser, but she could not dismiss the memory of the disdain she'd seen on his face. Perhaps William had as little choice in what he must do as she had? Still, what sort of man could bring another to be tortured? She did not know, but if he returned, she needed to find out—and quickly. Mayhap he was her greatest hope if he was here under a ruse, or mayhap she was a wishful fool, making up things that were not true at all.

"I'm nae sure King David needs to be killed," said Darrington, the man who sat immediately to Ada's left. She looked up from her trencher of food, where she'd purposely kept her gaze, and turned to Darrington in time to see Brothwell direct a murderous glare at the man that sent chills across Ada's skin.

She swallowed, fear rising in her for Darrington, who had dared to voice compassion for the king that stood in the way of all Brothwell wanted. Her stepbrother's mouth twisted into a semblance of a smile that did not reach his eyes, and a hush fell over the group of men sitting at the table.

"I applaud yer compassion, Darrington," Brothwell said. "'Tis always good to have men who think of other ways to deal with problems. Tell me, as ye drink from my special stock of wine, what would ye have us do with King David once he is nae king any longer?"

Darrington grinned like a fool as a serving girl rushed forward with a fresh goblet for him and poured him wine from a jug Ada had never seen. Uneasiness stirred in her stomach, especially when she caught Marjorie's eye and the woman looked as tense as Ada felt.

"We could use him to bring all the clans who support him under our control immediately," Darrington suggested and then took a big gulp of his newly poured wine.

Brothwell raised an eyebrow. "Tell me, do ye nae think the men who support King David would still try to do so if we keep him alive?"

As Darrington made his case and Brothwell and some of the other men debated with him, Ada watched the man consume three more glasses of wine. His color slowly changed to a deep red, and by the time the meal was nearing its end, Darrington was sweating profusely and had begun to shake.

"I dunnae feel well," he slurred, reaching for the goblet of wine in front of him but knocking it over instead.

Ada's gaze flew to Brothwell. He did not look the least bit concerned. He motioned calmly for the serving wenches to aid Darrington as the men around him grew quiet. "Take him to one of the guest chambers to rest," Brothwell ordered two guards. He turned to Ada suddenly and patted her hand. "I'm so sorry, Sister. Darrington appeared to have especially captured yer attention."

She bit her lip. She had to be more careful around Brothwell. He was ever watchful. "Nay. Just listening to the conversation."

"Well, I'm afraid I kinnae allow a man who imbibes so much wine but kinnae tolerate the effects to compete for yer hand."

"Here, here!" came a chorus of agreement from the men at the table.

Ada shifted restlessly, and Hella licked Ada's right foot from where the hound lay beside her under the table. Not a moment later, Freya nuzzled her left leg. Her heart clenched with love. In her darkest hours, her hounds were always there for her.

The late afternoon drew on in the same fashion as the earlier part of the day. The men went through exercises in the rings, and Ada was ordered to walk with Brothwell to watch them. Any warrior who showed the slightest hint that he would be less than ruthless with King David, or not utterly loyal to the Steward and Brothwell, met with some sort of regrettable injury during the course of the waning sunlight hours that left him unable to compete in the tournament.

By the time the sun was setting and the sky held an orange glow, only fifteen of the twenty-five warriors who'd been called to compete remained able. Brothwell turned to the group of men who were gathered in the courtyard. "Who would like to participate in a friendly competition to have the chance to sit by Ada for supper tonight?"

Ada nearly groaned. She could only imagine what sort of competition Brothwell had concocted, and she doubted there was anything friendly about it.

"Grinnald, bring out the boy," Brothwell called loudly.

Ada's heart stuttered in her chest as she glanced around the torchlit courtyard for Maximilian. When Grinnald stepped out from the garden pathway with Maximilian in his clutches in front of him, Ada surged forward with a cry, but Brothwell's hand shot out and grasped her. When he did, Freya and Hella began to growl, and Hella snapped at Brothwell.

"Ada," he warned, backing away from her hounds.

God, how she wished she could allow them to do what they clearly wanted to do. Swallowing the desire, she said, "Down, girls," and both dogs immediately complied.

"Ada here," Brothwell said, squeezing her arm, "is most fond of this ragged boy who feeds her hounds. I'm certain she'll want to take him with her to her future husband's home. Will ye nae, Ada?"

"Aye," she answered, trying to ignore the throbbing of her arm where Brothwell was clutching her.

"The boy will need to be made into a warrior; therefore, he needs his first lesson in courage. Dunnae ye all agree?"

"Aye!" came the hearty replies.

Ada glared at the cowardly men surrounding her. She did not even want to contemplate what a future with them would look like.

Brothwell, who always enjoyed torturing others, chuckled. "Let's see how braw he is while each of ye take a turn shooting at an apple upon his head. The first man to split the apple in half wins the pleasure of sitting by Ada at supper. But ye all must line up at the other side of the courtyard to shoot."

Ada gaped. That was an impossible shot! Maximilian's life would be in danger! "Brothwell, nay!" she burst out, but he did not even glance at her.

"That's at least five hundred steps," one of the men complained.

Brothwell cocked an eyebrow. "If ye dunnae believe ye can do it—"

"I can make the shot," announced a deep voice. It seemed to be coming from the shadows near the stone path leading from the courtyard to the woods.

Ada's pulse spiked as she squinted into the darkness. Guards rushed toward the voice, one of them holding a torch, and when they raised it, flames illuminated the angry face of a complete stranger. Behind him, stood William, a bored expression on his handsome face and a dagger in his hand, which was positioned across the stranger's throat. The dancing flames flickered over the man's neck, showing a line of blood trickling from a cut. As she took in his appearance, she noted he also had a busted lip and nose.

She looked sharply at William, her mind whirling with the unanswered question of whether her instincts about him were right or if she was a fool. Considering the fact that he had hunted down a man and brought him to Brothwell like a prized sheep to the slaughter, she was starting to think she was being foolish.

"William," Brothwell boomed, "what a pleasant surprise. Where are the guards who were to accompany ye?"

William shrugged. "I could nae say, Brothwell. They were too slow and held me back. I had to leave them."

Brothwell scowled. Ada felt her mouth pull into a smile, which she immediately fought. Perhaps she was not all wrong about William. He shoved his quarry, who she could only assume was Thomas Fraser, forward toward Brothwell's guards. Thomas stumbled, righted himself, and then snarled as Brothwell's guards caught him by both his arms.

Brothwell released Ada to step forward, nearly face-to-face with Thomas, who looked boldly at Brothwell. "I have waited a long time for ye to come for me. Ye were coming for me, were ye nae? Since I had her?"

Thomas growled low in his throat. "Aye, Brothwell. I was coming for ye. Where is Lisette?"

"Dead," Brothwell replied, emotionless.

The only woman named Lisette who Ada had ever met was an Englishwoman whose father, Baron Gastillion, was one of the King of England's favored men.

Thomas surged forward and grasped Brothwell's neck, but his guards were quick and dragged the man back as he let out an inhuman cry.

"I did nae kill her, *ye fool*," Brothwell snarled. "She killed herself. Live with that, as I do. Take him away," Brothwell commanded. "I'll deal with ye later, Thomas."

The man sagged in the guards' grips as he was being dragged away, and Ada's heart twisted for him. She could not help but look to William with anger for bringing the man here, but the momentary flash of raw pain she saw in William's eyes, before his expression went blank, appeared genuine and heightened her confusion about what he was doing here.

"Now that we've dispensed with that," Brothwell said, clapping his hands together with a look of glee, "let us see who among ye can make the shot. Go line up at the other side of the courtyard." With those words, he clutched Ada's arm once more.

Dread filled her. Not only was it a long shot but they did not have the brightness of day to help keep their aim true. Terror danced across Maximilian's face. She jerked out of Brothwell's grasp and tried to run for Maximilian, but Brothwell stopped her easily with a hand around her throat.

"Ada!" Maximilian shouted and tried to wriggle out of the guards' grasps.

She coughed and sputtered and struggled to pry Brothwell's fingers from around her throat as Maximilian shouted from what was rapidly sounding like an increasing distance. Her hounds barked, and tears filled her eyes. Suddenly, William was before them both.

"Ye'll kill her," he said with a quiet but forceful calm. She could just make out his racing pulse at his neck, which was the only indication he was affected at all.

"Aye, ye're right, of course. I lost my temper," Brothwell said, his breath fanning the back of her neck, and then he released her.

Dizziness washed over her. She started to stumble forward, but William caught her in his solid, warm embrace and brought her into the circle of his arms. They were like bands of steel across her waist, but she didn't mind it. For one moment, she felt safe, locked there with the heat of his body seeping into her own cold skin.

Oh my…

His heart was thudding so fast it felt like a galloping destrier. Had he been scared for her? She glanced up and over her shoulder, and her gaze met his. There was an emotion there, in the depths of his hard blue eyes. It was one she was familiar with, for she'd seen it in her father's eyes for years: protectiveness.

"Release her," Brothwell commanded William, then to a guard he said, "Go fetch an apple for the target."

The tension that rippled through William at her stepbrother's command was visible and unmistakable, and it somehow made Ada feel better, as if he would do anything to keep her safe. But of course he would! He wished to use her as everyone else did.

"Dunnae fash yerself for yer wee friend," William said, giving her a squeeze on her upper arm before relinquishing her. "Brothwell," he said, stepping away from her, "I'd like to suggest ye allow Ada to decide who gets first shot. If we shoot all at once, the arrows could hit each other instead of the target."

"Aye," Ada hurriedly agreed. "An excellent point."

Brothwell eyed them both but then shrugged. "What do I care? 'Tis amusement all the same, and I suppose ye have a point, Wolf. Ada?" Brothwell looked to her.

"I choose William," she said to the protest of the other men.

"If he splits the apple, will we all get a chance?" one of the men demanded.

The idea of Maximilian being shot at multiple times made her feel as if she would faint, and just as she felt it, Maximilian did it. He dropped like a stone thrown hard in the dirt. Ada turned to start toward him, her heart jerking in her chest, but Brothwell bid her hold, and she feared going to her young friend would make matters worse for him. But William apparently had no worries of angering Brothwell and immediately went to Maximilian's side. As the giant warrior kneeled, his shoulder-length black locks fell across his face to obscure his features, but she could hear the concern in his voice and see it in the careful way he lifted Maximilian's head and cradled it in his hands. Long, sure fingers curved around the lad's sandy-brown hair, and an unexpected longing pierced Ada's chest.

She blinked, and her cheeks heated as she stole a quick glance to ensure no one realized the ridiculous wanting flowing through her. When she discovered all eyes were focused on William, she examined her feelings for one brief moment as William roused the boy and the other men—*swine, the lot of them*—jeered at him for his kindness. William did not appear to notice, or perhaps he simply did not care. He seemed to be a confident enough man that the latter could be true.

She tried to push away the longing. It was an impossible dream to be cradled and cared for and loved simply for herself, not because of the gifts the fae had given her. To wed for love. This was her secret desire that would never be fulfilled. A marriage of passionate love was what her parents had possessed, but it was not to be for her.

She glanced at the men around her. Not one of them cared a whit about her. They only cared about the power she possessed inside her. Not even her stepbrother. Her gaze skittered to the giant warrior now helping a lad he did not even know to his feet. Perhaps... No, not likely. Not even William MacLean. Yes, he was displaying honorable qualities, but even honorable men had desires that drove them.

A thought barreled into her. Maybe she had a bargaining chip she'd never truly considered: herself.

Seven

William mentally berated himself as he helped the lad, who was trembling with fear, to his feet. Curse it all. He had one task: persuade Brothwell to trust him. Coming to the aid of the boy that Brothwell clearly was going to take great pleasure in torturing was not the way to gain the coldhearted man's trust. But William's Achilles' heel had always been women and children in need. Presently, he was faced with both.

Ada might be supporting his enemy—or she might not, he did not know—but it was clear in every line of fear mapped on her face that she was petrified for the lad. And rightly so. The competition Brothwell had proposed was a dangerous one at best and a deadly one at worst.

Brothwell cleared his throat, interrupting William's thoughts. "Are ye going to join the others, William?"

William looked around him; he was the only one still standing there. The other men had crossed to the far side of the courtyard, and Brothwell's guard stood with them. "Pardon," he said, resisting the urge to reach out and squeeze the lass's shoulder again. Her eyes were bright with fear, but he could not keep showing such compassion if he wanted Brothwell to trust him.

"Brothwell, I beg of ye," Ada pleaded, as William forced himself to walk away from her. "Dunnae allow each man a shot at Maximilian."

When the lad whimpered, it took all of William's self-control not to turn around and put a stop to this nonsense, no matter the consequences to himself. But that was the problem—the consequences of this mission failing would affect far more people than just him. It would affect his brother, the King, all the people of Scotland if the king should lose his throne.

"I'm feeling generous toward ye, Ada, since by the end of this tournament, ye will finally choose a husband, so if William splits the apple, then the other warriors will nae shoot at it, but if that happens, they'll be sorely vexed, and I'll have to offer some sort of consolation as a generous host."

William was well aware that he was walking about as fast as a snail, but he needed to hear what was being said, and he did not like the direction the conversation was taking.

"What are ye proposing?" Ada asked, her voice tight with clear displeasure. The lass may support the Steward, but it was obvious she and her stepbrother did not particularly get along.

"A dance," Brothwell said. "It seems only fair if William wins the opportunity to sit by ye at supper and the other men dunnae even have a chance."

"Since when have ye cared about being fair to others?" Ada demanded.

"Careful, Ada," Brothwell warned, his tone laced with both amusement and a sharp edge to it. "Ye will wound my heart."

Ada snorted. "Ye'd have to possess a heart for me to wound it."

"Ye think bastards dunnae possess hearts?" Brothwell

asked.

The men gathered on the other side of the courtyard were giving William strange looks, so he forced himself to speed up, having to strain to hear the next words, which were little more than a whisper in his ear.

William turned, and disappointment touched him that he could no longer see Ada's face. She had kneeled down in front of the boy, her back to the warriors. She brushed a lock of hair from the lad's forehead and then cupped his cheek with her hand. Ada MacQuerrie appeared to be a woman of compassion.

Something softened in him as he looked at Ada's profile, and he did not care for it at all. Still, it was one thing to keep a wall between himself and the woman he would wed, and it was entirely another to allow someone else to hurt her or an innocent. She and everyone she cared for were his to protect now, whether she knew it yet or not.

With that thought in mind, William withdrew his bow and arrow, which Brothwell was motioning him to do. Once the apple had been placed on the lad's head, William inhaled a long, steadying breath, closed his eyes, and said a prayer for his aim to be true. When he opened his eyes, he focused on his intended target. He saw nothing but the glistening red of the fruit. He tasted sweetness. He could almost hear the terrified boy's heartbeat. But the lad would not die today. Not if William could help it.

The string of the bow cut into his fingertips as he drew it back taut. His heart thudded in his ears, drowning out all else. He counted the beats as he waited for the slight breeze that had picked up to die down.

One.
Two.
Three.

He released the arrow, tracking it as it sliced through the growing shadows, met its target, and carved the apple in two. To his surprise, a sudden *whoop* filled the silence, and when he searched for the source, Ada was grinning at him. She possessed the most blindingly beautiful smile he'd ever seen. It was like seeing the sun for the first time. Warmth filled him and his chest lurched, his lips tugging into a return grin. And then suddenly, chaos exploded.

The two massive white hounds by Ada's side took off at a gallop across the courtyard.

"Freya! Hella!" Ada bellowed, chasing after the hounds.

William watched in amused fascination as the hounds ignored her and thundered toward him and the other men, Ada running after them with her skirt flying and long hair fanning over her shoulders and off her face as she pursued the beasts.

"Halt! Halt!" she called, but the beasts would not be deterred.

As she approached, William realized that Ada feared for their safety, as did the other men if their uneasy exclamations were any indication. William darted his gaze from Ada to the hounds, who were now baring their teeth and barking. The men around him shuffled backward, some withdrawing swords, others bows.

"Dunnae harm them!" Ada called, but the men ignored her.

William did not know what had set off the hounds, but as a lad, he'd had his own hunting hound, Dithorn. He had trained Dithorn himself and loved him dearly. It had been years since he'd thought of his dog, who had disappeared on a hunt not long after his mother had left them. Ever since, he hadn't taken his own hound hunting with him, preferring to simply rely on himself. But he kneeled now to show the hounds not to be afraid of him and to meet them at their level as he'd once done with Dithorn. A memory stirred of the happiness Dithorn had brought him, but sharp upon the memory was another and his chest tightened with the pain of Dithorn's loss. Abandonment was more apt.

"Get up, man! Are ye mad?" one of the men called from behind him.

As the hounds grew nearer, their razor-sharp teeth glistened and their deep growls seemed to vibrate the very air. They did not even slow as they closed the remaining distance to him, and before he could react, both beasts launched themselves at him. Their paws connected with his chest and propelled him backward to the dirt with a thud.

For a beat, all he could see was white fur and teeth, but then a slobbery tongue licked him on one of his cheeks and a cold nose nudged him on the other. He groaned. "Get off me, ye great big beasties," he ordered, but the two hounds did not listen to him any better than they did their mistress.

Just as he gave one a gentle shove off and was about to do the same to the other, he heard Ada command, "Hella, down, girl," and the weight of the beast lifted off him. Ada appeared in his line of vision, and then she leaned over so that he had an enticing glimpse of the tops of her lovely, ample breasts. Blood surged to every part of his body, stirring his lust and making him all too aware that she was a woman made for a man's tender touch.

"I kinnae believe it," she said, her warm, husky voice snatching his attention to her face. A look of utter shock greeted him there. "Hella and Freya like ye." Her tone underscored the same skepticism her face held.

As if Hella knew she was being discussed, she flopped down beside him and laid her chin upon his chest. She almost appeared to be smiling at him. *Clot-heid*, he chided himself, even as he reached out to pat her head. Her tail began to thump, and she panted her happiness.

"Why would she nae like me?" he asked, giving Hella a gentle nudge off as he found his feet and stood up, coming face-to-face with Ada. He inhaled a sharp breath, air catching in his chest and the scent of wildflowers filling his senses. Ada MacQuerrie was not only so bonny it made him ache but she smelled like an invitation to tumble naked in soft grass under a blue sky, then laze away the day entangled in her arms. He frowned at his thoughts. The tumbling was not an unwelcome one, but there'd be no lazing away with her—ever. Theirs would be a marriage of convenience and nothing more.

Ada tilted her head to the side and back just slightly, her inquisitive silver-flecked gray gaze meeting his. "Neither of my hounds has ever liked any man besides my father."

"I used to have a hound," he said, forcing himself to respond, though he was utterly distracted by her eyes. A man could get lost in them.

"Used to?" she inquired.

He nodded, still staring at her eyes, and she met his stare unabashedly, the brazen lass. "He disappeared," he replied. He'd never seen eyes like hers. They were like mysterious clouds that appeared in the sky and commanded every bit of one's attention because one could not be certain if they were harbingers of a storm or simply an overcast day. Eyes like hers could cause a man to forget himself, and for a moment, William leaned toward her, tugged by something strong and invisible but undoubtedly, impossibly there.

Mesmerizing. That's what she was with those sooty lashes and the smattering of freckles that told him this lass was no simpering miss who spent her days hidden away in the castle with womanly pastimes. Ada had seen the sun enough to make her bonny freckles come out. He felt a stirring of gladness that he'd not be wed to a woman who preferred a drafty, dark castle to the bright outdoors. They could—

He killed the thought with a mental dagger through its nonexistent heart. They could *nothing*. Doing things with her was not part of his plan.

"And ye have nae ever gotten another hound again?" she asked.

He shook his head. "I dunnae care for the beasts."

Ada frowned and then whispered, "Yer actions dunnae match yer words, my lord. Either yer behavior is a ruse or ye are lying about how ye feel."

"Ada, come!" Brothwell boomed from across the courtyard. "Leave the men to train for tomorrow's tourney. I wish to speak to ye before supper."

A determined look flitted across Ada's face as she stared at William. "So are ye a liar or are ye hiding yer true self?"

He had no desire to lay himself open for this woman to examine, yet his gut told him there was much to be lost in this moment, that if he answered incorrectly Ada would not choose him as her husband. "I liked hounds," he said in a tight, low voice, "but then mine disappeared." He shrugged, discomfort settling over him. "I dunnae have time for that which I kinnae rely upon."

"Is there a great deal on that list?" she asked, genuine interest in her eyes.

Now was the time to lie, yet he wagered the truth would hold more weight. "Dogs. Most people."

She nodded, surprising him. "I dunnae agree with the hound bit"—she motioned to hers, which were now standing on either side of her—"but as to people, I heartily agree. Most of them will disappoint ye. I suppose I *can* count upon seeing ye at supper since ye wish to wed me because of the gifts the fae gave me." Her arched brows rose higher, challenging him, and she plunked her hands upon her hips. Her pink tongue darted out to lick her lips.

This lass was likely to be bold in bed, and the notion conjured up an image in his head of her naked, her slender arms and legs wrapped around his midriff. He hardened with distracting awareness of her.

"Aye," he said, his voice husky with his lust, "ye can be certain ye will see me tonight. I did win the wager, after all. However, it is yer loveliness that lures me to yer side. Of that ye can rely upon."

It was not a lie in this moment. He wanted to strip her naked and worship her, but the hope that painted her lovely features suddenly gave him pause.

"Do ye expect me to believe ye are interested in me simply for me?" she demanded.

He stiffened at the question. He detested liars, and now he would become the worst sort of one. Except it was not entirely a lie. He was undeniably attracted to her as he had never been to another, yet it was the gifts within her that would make him wed her. "I may have come lured by the gifts within ye," he said, forcing himself to speak, "but ye have beguiled me with yer compassion and yer boldness." It was the truth, though it did not change the circumstances of what must be done, nor how their marriage would be.

Her eyes widened and then she gave her head a little shake. "I am well aware I'm nae so enticing, my lord. There is nae a need to be deceitful."

It angered him that she did not seem to know her own appeal. Impulsively, he raised her hand to his lips, turned her hand wrist up, and pressed a kiss to the delicate skin. A sharp gasp escaped her, and desire nearly made him groan. Her skin was like the finest silk. "Ye are nae aware of yerself at all if ye dunnae ken that ye are dangerously alluring."

Her cheeks flushed, and she bit her lip, making him want to do the same. It was plump and red and begging to be kissed. The lass was going to make him a fool if he was not careful.

"Are ye trying to seduce me, my lord?" she whispered.

He was, because he was supposed to be. And because he wanted to. It was as complicated and simple as that. Guilt consumed him at twining truth and lies together, but he had to press on.

"Aye," he said, praying she would not demand more.

She frowned. "Ye make me think things I should nae," she grumbled.

"I can say the same of ye, Lady Ada." And that was the God's truth.

She opened her mouth, then clamped it shut as if she thought better of what she was going to say. Instead, she turned and fled across the courtyard, almost as if she were running from him. One dog followed her, but the other, Hella, stayed by his side. Halfway to her stepbrother, she abruptly stopped and swung around, her hair and skirts swishing.

"Hella, come," she commanded.

The dog looked up at him as if waiting for him to agree. "Go to yer mistress," he ordered the hound, and when he saw the open gazes of lust on the other men's faces, he added, "and guard her with yer life."

He could have sworn the dog gave him a nod, which told him Ada had already managed to make him a little daft. Dogs did not nod or smile.

"She'll be mine by tomorrow night," one of the men

said from behind him.

Possession strummed through William's veins as thick as his blood as he turned to face the light-haired warrior.

"Ye think so, do ye, Connor?" another man said.

"I ken so," the man replied smugly, which caused insults and boasts to be thrown back and forth.

William walked away from the men, noting and counting all the guards around the periphery of the courtyard who likely had been ordered to watch them. He pulled out his sword and began to go through his practice, alternately seeing the man Connor's face and imagining defeating him, and then seeing Ada's face and imagining touching her. He'd win. Of that much he had no doubt. What troubled him was that it felt like winning might come at a greater cost than he understood.

Eight

Though the great hall was noisy at supper that night and conversation flowed around her upon the dais, Ada felt the moment William's gaze landed upon her as surely as if he'd brushed his hand across her cheek. She looked up from the trencher of food she'd purposely been staring at, and when she gazed to the left, her eyes met William's. Her belly tightened as his gaze darkened, but then Brothwell said something from William's left, and he turned to her stepbrother.

She took a sip of her wine to calm her racing heart and order her thoughts. When he looked at her that way she almost believed he truly desired *her*, the woman. William had professed to be here to serve Brothwell and the Steward, so why was she questioning him or his motives? Why could she not just accept that he was yet another man who had come with the hope of wedding her to curry favor with the Steward?. She still held hope, that's why.

Music suddenly started, and Ada blinked in surprise as she glanced up once more from her trencher. She'd been so lost in thought that she had not even noticed that the tables and chairs had been pushed to the sides of the great hall to make room for dancing. Her stomach roiled as Laird Tidmore came to stand before her. "Lady Ada, I believe we each get to claim a dance with ye."

Ada wanted to protest, but she knew it was hopeless. Brothwell would force it no matter what she wished. She inclined her head and started to stand, inadvertently glancing toward William. As she did, she stilled, held in place by his burning gaze. There, again, in the depths of his eyes, she thought she saw hunger. Her breath hitched as their gazes held. There was something else there, too, something that looked like possession.

"Lady Ada, are ye coming?" Laird Tidmore asked.

Ada forced herself to look away from William, and then she quickly descended the dais and took Lord Tidmore's hand. The dance was as she had expected. Lord Tidmore spent the time showering her with ridiculous, untrue compliments.

The rest of the dances followed in much the same fashion until she was at the last laird she had to dance with, Laird Connor MacKinney. She had known him for years, but something had always seemed odd about him. He'd become bitter as the years passed and King David had taken some land from Connor's family and given it to others. Connor hated the king for taking away what he considered his by birth.

"Lady Ada," he said, offering a neat bow before her. When he came up, his dark eyes met hers. He was, by all rights, a handsome man with perfect lordly features. Many a lass would be thrilled to wed him, but she was not one of them. Not only did they believe different men should be king but her father had said time and again that the MacKinneys would kill their own bairns to get what they desired. She didn't believe for one moment that he intended to wed her and then do as Brothwell bade. That in itself would not be a bad thing, but she suspected his plan for her could possibly be worse than anything Brothwell might do, and that turned her blood cold.

"Laird MacKinney," she replied, taking hold of the hand he offered her.

"I've been wanting to get ye alone, Ada," Connor said, his husky voice surprising her.

She was saved from responding by the dance, which took them in separate directions. She was spun around the room multiple times, forgetting her worries for a moment and actually laughing and enjoying the dance. Guilt immediately besieged her, given Esther and Maximilian were being kept prisoner because of her. She danced down the middle of the line, feeling as if someone was watching her, and when she came to the end of the dancers, Connor was there. He grabbed her around the waist, which was not at all part of the dance, and jerked her close, pressing their bodies together.

Her breath whooshed out of her, making her feel trapped and overpowered. "What are ye doing?" she hissed, pushing on his chest, but the man was large, muscled, and immoveable. He lifted her off her feet just enough so that she could not stop him but his actions would not be noted by others, and then he carried her backward into the thick crowd of laughing, boisterous dancers. People swirled around them, dancing and paying them no mind.

"I wanted one moment with ye, Ada, to speak in private," he said, maneuvering them toward the outer edge of the dancers now, where she noted several of his men stood. His men parted, and he pushed her against the wall as the men closed around them in a semicircle, creating, she realized with fear, a shield so that no one could see her. How long before Brothwell noted her absence?

Gooseflesh swept her arms, but she refused to succumb to her fear. She cocked her head back to look at him and shoved, yet again, against his chest. "What is it ye wish to say, Connor?"

"Ye must wed me," he said, his grip tightening on her.

"Ye kinnae compel me, Connor. I must be willing."

"I've seen ye looking at the traitor, Ada. He is nae the man for ye."

She blushed at that, her jaw clenching. Men always told women what to do, how to think, and she was tired of it. "And ye are?" she asked, incredulous.

"I am. The Steward is nae fit to be king, and together we will see that he is nae."

She blinked in surprise. "Brothwell would kill ye for uttering such a thing."

Connor frowned at her. "Are ye going to tell yer stepbrother? I was under the impression that ye hated him."

She would not because Brothwell likely *would* kill Connor, and she did not want to be responsible for the man's death. But instead of confessing that, she asked, "And who in yer mind should be king?"

"Me, of course," he said with an air of pompousness that only a man born to privilege and whose life had been steeped in it could possess. He was so certain that she would wed him that she decided to let him think it, and then when the moment came to pick her husband, he'd most certainly *not* be her choice.

She smiled up at him sweetly. "If I wed ye, will ye make me queen?"

He grinned at her like the fool he was. "Aye, lass."

"I dunnae see how I can possibly say nay to that," she lied. "Just make certain to advance in the tournament so that I can choose ye to woo me. I best get back to Brothwell before he becomes aware ye have taken me away."

Connor nodded eagerly, and his men parted at an indication from him. Ada's blood coursed through her veins with irritation as she stepped out of the circle and into the even more congested crowd of dancers. She sidestepped one couple and then another, and that same feeling of being watched tickled her senses. She darted a glance over her shoulder, expecting to find Connor's gaze on her, but he was nowhere to be seen. When she turned back around, she gasped. William stood in front of her with a predatory gleam in his eyes.

His gaze was riveted on her face and then moved slowly over her body before returning to her eyes. Heat pooled in her belly, and when his fingers found her arm and he said, "I've come to claim ye, Ada," the heat in her belly moved swiftly to parts of her body she had not known could feel heat.

"Claim me?" she asked, her voice coming out in little more than a whisper. "For what?"

His finger stroked deliciously back and forth over the skin of her hand. His appeal devastated her senses. The music faded. The people disappeared. All she saw was the man before her. His smoldering eyes. The sinful smirk upon his full lips. The way his hair curled slightly at the ends that grazed his shoulders.

"For a dance," he replied, his voice sliding over her like warm water. He drew closer to her, his hand sliding up her arm, a whisper of flesh upon flesh. "Whatever did ye think I meant, ye wicked lass?"

✦

By Christ, he was losing his prized control. It had begun the moment he'd seen Ada. It had slipped a little more somewhere between watching the MacKinney crush Ada to him and then tracking her as the devil maneuvered her to the perimeter of the great hall. It had dipped further when the MacKinney's men had encircled her and cut her off from his view. His vision had momentarily clouded as fury choked him, and he'd excused himself from the conversation he had instigated with Brothwell in the hopes of learning the other traitors' names. He'd abandoned his plan, the mission he'd been sent on, and he'd pounded down the dais steps with his heart beating rapidly as he'd begun to weave himself in and out of the thick throng of clanspeople and competitors gathered in the great hall. The lot of them had continued to merrily dance and drink as he darted and snaked his way into a position where he could see not only the MacKinney's hands and face but see Ada's face, as well, so he could judge whether or not she was in need of him.

In need of him.

The four words mocked him and made him want to shake the beautiful lass. He'd read her lips as she'd talked to the MacKinney. She'd said she wanted to be queen. Lipreading was a very handy trick his father had taught him years ago and William had perfected over time. He had to be at just the right angle; sometimes he could read every word, sometimes just a few. Tonight, he'd read enough to know that Ada, by her own declaration, wished to be queen. And by the looks of MacKinney's face after she'd made the statement, he was only too happy to oblige her, which meant the MacKinney must plan to try to put himself on the throne.

The stakes had just become higher in this deception. He had to ensure Ada chose him over the MacKinney, and the only weapon he had at his disposal was seduction. There could be no mercy. He would employ every tactic of enticing a woman he'd ever known. He would ignite her lust and enslave her heart. Unbridled anticipation shot through him, and with it came concern that she could so stir him to desire. Everything he wanted was at risk, and the woman had unknowingly declared herself his enemy. There could be no missteps, no quarter given, no guilt allowed.

"Come," he said, the predator to the prey. "Let us dance."

Unmistakable worry flashed in her stormy eyes, but then she notched her chin up and smiled at him. It was an outwardly pure smile, a sweet one. The damned thing made his chest squeeze, but he was not a pup to be toyed with. He cleared his thoughts of all but one: she thought to be queen and would soon have the power to make it so. His instincts about her had been so very wrong.

They faced each other as the music began. Her long eyelashes fluttered upward, rosy color touching her cheeks. He wanted to run his fingers over the slope of her cheekbone. More madness. He needed to concentrate. She tilted her head, and then her chest rose with her full breath. "Why are ye trying to seduce me?"

"Because ye are making me crazed," he said, deciding to stay as close to the truth as possible. Her eyes widened, the music began, and they were pulled away from each other by the steps of the dance.

When they came together again several beats later, she spoke before he could. "What do ye like about the Steward?" she asked, pitching her voice under the music.

He circled her once as the steps demanded, and when facing her once more, instead of answering, he forced himself to say, "He's clever." He didn't like one damned thing about King David's deceitful nephew, but he could not say that, knowing now that Ada wanted to sit on the throne herself.

The dance took them apart again, this time for longer, and William watched her as she was twirled from man to man, her hair swinging, the color in her cheeks rising. Christ, she was lovely. It was a good thing she was treacherous. It would make it easier to keep distance between them once they were wed.

When they met in the middle once more, he spoke before she could. "How is it ye came to support the Steward when I ken yer father supported King David?"

Her eyebrows arched, and a crease appeared between her brow. "How is it *ye* came to the Steward's side?" she asked instead of answering.

"I simply followed my father's and brother's paths," he replied as the musical notes faded and loud chatter replaced them. People began to move about around them, looking for new partners, talking among themselves, or taking swigs of wine and mead from goblets to refresh themselves before the next dance.

William and Ada stood there, near the great hall door where the end of the dance had left them, neither moving. "So ye are telling me," she said, near a whisper, eyes searching, "that ye came to support the Steward based merely on the fact that yer brother and yer father did?"

Her incredulous tone surprised him, not only because she sounded irritated at him but he had long wished most people would not so easily think he was a traitor simply because they thought his family was. It struck him as funny and slightly bittersweet that Ada was the one to disbelieve it.

"Is that so hard to accept?" he asked.

She pressed her lips together for a moment. "Nay, but it is disappointing."

"How so?" He took her by the elbow and guided her

away from the path of the door toward the wall.

"Well, I would wish for a husband who had his own mind."

It was his turn to cock his eyebrows. "As ye do? Do ye support the Steward simply because yer father did nae? Was it a rebellion of sorts?"

"Nay!" She bit her lip. "I mean, I—" She pressed her fingertips to her temples. "It was nae a rebellion."

"Ada!"

William cursed at the sight of Brothwell waving Ada to him where he stood with the MacKinney.

"I must attend my stepbrother," she said, starting to move away. He caught her fingertips, aware he had made little progress in his seduction. She stopped and glanced back at him, frowning. "What are ye doing?"

He looked to where Brothwell was, and seeing the man waylaid by some of his clan members, William decided to use the gift to his advantage. He brought her fingertips to his lips, intending to press a kiss there and then release her, to entice her with what could be, but when his lips grazed her silken skin, he forgot himself. A jolt of awareness gripped him. He heard the sharp intake of her breath, watched her chest rise once more, and her tongue dart out to wet those full lips that would be his undoing if he did not taste them soon. Instead of relinquishing his hold, he slid his hand to her wrist, encircling the fragile bones, and increased his grip, his thumb pressing to where her pulse frantically beat.

She wanted him just as he wanted her. Triumph engulfed him, searing him from head to toe. The feeling, however, had less to do with the fact that his plan was working and more to do with the anticipation of touching her, possessing her, hearing what sounds she made in the throes of passion. A satisfied smile tugged at his lips, which he tried to stop, but it was as impossible as halting the need to breathe. She snatched her hand away and scowled at him. "Dunnae look so pompous."

Her injured feelings felt like a hand at his throat, squeezing. Devil take it. He was not supposed to allow guilt. *No quarter.* He repeated the phrase in his mind until the guilt subsided. "That's pleasure, *mo ghraidh.*"

"Yer love?" She shook her head. "Let us be honest, shall we, William?"

"Call me Will," he said impulsively, driven by some strange craving to hear her use the shortened version of his name that only his family and his closest friend, Brodee, had ever used.

"Will," she said, her tone petulant, but all the same, he liked hearing his name upon her lips, which was a potent reminder that he had lost his control. Or maybe he'd lost his senses? "Ye are seducing me to ensure I choose ye to wed. There is nae a need to pretend there will ever be love between us."

"I am seducing ye because I want ye," he replied, the words coming smoothly because, God help him, they were true. Yes, he had to seduce her to ensure things went according to plan, but he did want her, so much so he was having trouble thinking straight.

When she gave him a doubtful look, he went on. "Aye, I wish ye to choose me to wed, but—"

"So ye can become close to my stepbrother, gain his favor, and that of the Steward?"

In a sense it was the truth, so it was easy to nod. Her upper teeth pushed into her plump bottom lip once more, and all the blood he possessed in his body seemed to go straight between his legs. "If ye keep biting yer lip like that,

I'm going to throw all proper decorum to the wind and kiss ye right now," he blurted.

Her eyes went wide, and her lip released from her teeth immediately. A spark of pleasure lit her eyes, making them lighten a shade. "I dunnae believe Brothwell would like that," she said.

"I dunnae, in this moment, believe I give a damn what yer stepbrother would like."

"Ada!" Brothwell's voice came from their right, and one glance said he was fast approaching and irritated.

"That is a verra odd thing to say for a man trying to curry his favor," she said, her gaze boring into his, questioning. "Unless," she continued, surprising him by stepping nearer to him and grabbing his forearm in a hold that felt urgent, "ye are nae really here to gain his favor." The last was said in a whisper, and William got the strange notion it was to protect him.

"And if that was true?" he asked, his words just as urgent as her hold with Brothwell only a few steps from being upon them. Had he misjudged her? Misunderstood somehow what she had said to the MacKinney?

But before she could even open her mouth to answer, Brothwell was there, taking her by the elbow and sweeping her away toward the treacherous MacKinney, whose open look of lust toward Ada made William want to kill the man.

Nine

If Ada had held any doubt that William would advance in the tournament, by midafternoon she harbored it no more. He fought with a skill she'd never seen before. It seemed almost otherworldly the way he parried blows and struck down man after man like a warrior on a mission who refused to let himself tire as a mere mortal would. She watched each of his fights on the edge of her seat upon the dais outside, thrilling a little every time he won.

As she sat, and while she broke her fast, and even when Brothwell or Marjorie spoke to her, Ada could hardly draw her thoughts from William to the conversation at hand. She thought upon their conversation in the great hall last night over and over, his good deed for Maximilian, the way Hella liked him—the hound had greeted him this morning by bounding up to him and sitting beside him until he petted her—the way he made her feel he wanted her more for her than the gift from the fae that she possessed, and his odd word choices last night.

It was the last two she kept returning to. She could not shake the feeling that William did not really support the Steward or her brother, and if he did not, then surely he supported the king. After all, she knew he'd worked with the king's right hand over the last year to crush traitors.

Brothwell obviously believed William had turned traitor as his father had. She was still unsure about William's brother Bram. She'd told Esther as much one night. The man had done much that indicated he was indeed a traitor to the king, but she'd never quite believed it. Like William, Bram had shown a very compassionate side to others in need, and she'd seen him show disappointment and hide it—more than once—when the Steward had a victory over the king's forces. The man had disappeared suddenly, and Ada did wonder if he was on a mission for Brothwell or if Brothwell had discovered Bram was actually sent by the king to spy on him. And if Bram was a spy, then...

She glanced sharply toward William where he now stood beside Connor in the middle of the arena that had been created for the tournament. Sun glistened down on both their heads. Connor's golden locks and William's dark ones contrasted as much as the rest of their physical appearance. Whereas Connor was light skinned, William was bronzed by the sun she felt sure he constantly trained in. William was a head taller than Connor, but that did not make Connor a short man. William was just uncommonly tall, and broad shouldered, and muscled everywhere.

He wore only braies, which hung low on his hips, leaving his abdomen, legs, chest—nearly all of him—exposed. She swallowed hard, heat sweeping through her. As far as she could tell, William did not possess a smidge of spare fat, but he did have an abundance of sinewy muscle. His arms were lethal weapons the way they bulged, and his legs appeared to have been crafted to carry him an endless distance.

Both William and Connor had won all their matches, so they would be the two allowed to woo her tonight. She took a deep breath. That left her less than a day before her fate was irrevocably sealed.

She studied William as he stood there, eyes alert, hands gripping the hilt of his sword, posture tense. He was not at ease among these people he claimed to want to join forces with. She was as certain of it as she was her own name. Would he admit the truth if she asked? She did not think he would. Not yet anyway. Perhaps he was uncertain he could trust her. If she told him that she supported King David, would that make him open up to her? Was it foolish to admit such a thing based on a feeling deep in her gut?

There was one last consideration. The heat of a blush covered her cheeks and neck just thinking about it. Ever since she'd failed to escape Brothwell and he'd imprisoned Esther and Maximilian, she had resigned herself to the fact that she'd have to wed one of Brothwell's men and have a marriage without passion or love. But now… Her attention was drawn again to William's powerful form, and promise and desire flared hot. If the attraction he felt for her was true, as well, then what if—Her breath caught in her throat, the fear of even considering something she had long hoped for choking her. What if passion could lead to love?

She bit hard on her lip, suddenly feeling as if she was being watched, her thoughts being read. She glanced to her left, where Brothwell was paying her no heed, but when she turned to her right, Marjorie's probing gaze was on Ada. Marjorie arched her red eyebrows, and a knowing smile turned up the corners of her mouth.

She leaned close to Ada. "I see ye," she whispered. "Ye have a look about ye when ye stare at William. I ken that look. It's hope." She paused, as if considering her words. "Be careful, Ada. I too have hoped, and I can tell ye now, to find hope and then to lose it is worse than nae ever having hope at all."

Marjorie looked and sounded so genuinely sad that Ada felt the walls she normally had up around her stepsister lower. She suspected Marjorie was referring to Bram. Ada had watched them laugh together, exchange looks of desire. She had even seen them locked in each other's arms one night in the gardens when they thought no one was around. She'd kept their secret. Why would she not?

"Ye speak of Bram?" Ada asked quietly.

Marjorie's eyes cut past Ada to where Brothwell sat on the other side of her. Ada heard him speaking, and Marjorie lowered her lashes as if to hide the fact that she was looking at him. For some reason, she didn't want her brother to see.

"Ada." Brothwell suddenly rapped his knuckles on the table beside her. When she turned to him, he was standing and staring down at her. "I'm going to speak with the MacLean and the MacKinney to decide who may spend time with ye first, and then I'll come to fetch ye. Dunnae move."

"Nae even to blink?" Ada said, unable to stop the snarky remark.

Brothwell's gaze narrowed upon her. "Ye test me, Ada, ye do. Ye dunnae want to do that." He motioned to Marjorie. "Take a lesson from Marjorie and be a good, biddable sister."

Aware that her actions could have repercussions for Esther and Maximilian, Ada forced herself to nod.

"That's a good lass," Brothwell said, before descending the dais.

The moment he was out of earshot, Marjorie said, "Ye should nae prod him." Ada turned quickly to Marjorie as she continued. "'Tis like poking a wild boar. His teeth are sharp and his hits painful."

It struck Ada that she had done a grave injustice to

Marjorie. She had not looked past the woman's jealousy and cruelty to understand why Marjorie acted the way she did. Ada finally realized that part of it was fear of Brothwell. The other part might well have been jealousy that Marjorie did not have someone who loved her as much as Ada's father had loved her. The thought of him brought a wave of fresh grief over Ada. She sucked in a pained breath.

Marjorie did not seem to notice. Her eyes had taken on a faraway look. "I did nae ever think to find love," she said, tears pooling in her eyes. "I've kenned my entire life that I'd be wed to a man Brothwell deemed useful, just as ye will be." Marjorie eyed her. "But then Bram appeared here. Brothwell liked him, and I hoped, perhaps, Brothwell would let me wed him." A tear slid down Marjorie's cheek, and she quickly wiped it away and shrugged. "The point is, Ada, hope is a dangerous thing. Relinquish it. William MacLean could disappear tomorrow, just as his brother did, if he displeases my brother. And if ye allow yer heart to become engaged, ye will be just as alone as I am, for ye dunnae have yer father to give ye solace or protection any longer."

Marjorie had never opened up to Ada, let alone revealed a soft side to her. Why now? Was it the appearance of William? Ada thought perhaps it was. "Do ye ken where Bram is?"

Marjorie shook her head. "Brothwell will nae tell me."

Ada wanted to ask if Marjorie thought Bram truly supported the Steward, but if she questioned Bram's loyalty, Marjorie might question William's. Ada did not want to cause undue problems for William.

"Mayhap since Bram's brother is here and proving himself to Brothwell, he'll trust Bram once more." Marjorie grasped Ada's hand. "Will ye choose Bram's brother to wed?"

Ada could not see the harm in saying yes. She did not have to explain herself. "Aye."

Marjorie smiled. "I thought so. There is something special about them. I hope...I hope he is nae taken from ye and that yer marriage brings Bram back to me."

If William was for King David as Ada was beginning to suspect and hope, her marriage to him would not bring Bram back to Marjorie, even if Bram truly was a traitor. Brothwell would never trust Bram again if his brother was the king's man.

Ada swallowed. "If ye had to choose between Bram and Brothwell, would it be a difficult choice, Marjorie?"

She didn't know why she'd asked it. She'd never suspected Marjorie might have a different opinion than her brother. But now she wasn't so certain. And if William was the king's supporter and there was an opportunity to escape Brothwell, they could take Marjorie with them.

"There is nae a choice there, as far as I can see. Bram has my heart, but I'd watch ye tortured before ever admitting I said it, so dunnae think of using my words against me."

Before this conversation, Marjorie's threat would have angered Ada, but she understood her stepsister a bit better now. She squeezed Marjorie's hand. "I will nae ever tell Brothwell something to bring his anger upon ye. I vow it."

Marjorie looked at her with surprise, but then she nodded. "I have wronged ye," she admitted. "But ken this: I am sorry."

"I am, too," Ada said.

"Ada, come!" Brothwell called from the tournament ring. "We will retire to the solar so the men can have time to speak with ye."

As Ada started to rise, Marjorie tugged her back. "Ye

can ken an awful lot about a man by the way he kisses ye." Ada felt her mouth slip open, and Marjorie laughed. "I'm nae suggesting ye kiss them both, but if I were ye, I'd prod William to kiss ye, though I dunnae believe it will take much effort. He stares at ye like a wolf stalking its prey." Ada could not stop the smile that came to her lips, to which Marjorie gave a knowing nod. "If there's going to be great passion between ye, ye will feel it all the way through ye with a simple kiss. I felt Bram's kiss everywhere, even in my fingertips. But here—" she placed a hand on her heart "—is where I felt it the most."

"Ada, now!" Brothwell boomed.

Ada jerked at his irritated tone. "I'll bear that in mind," she said, then quickly departed the dais.

As she started toward the three men awaiting her in the center of the tournament ring, edged with all the warriors who had fought and lost, and the clanspeople who had come to watch, she looked to William, drawn to him as if there were no one else there.

She was not surprised to find him staring back at her. She was getting used to it, but as she moved closer and could read his expression more clearly, her heart jolted. He looked at her as if he was memorizing every detail of her, as if he were ravenous and she were his meal. She was going to get William to kiss her when they were alone if it was the last thing she did. Then she would know for certain if her hope was foolhardy or the beginning of something wonderful.

***

It was all William could do to keep himself seated in the antechamber and not storm after Ada, who was disappearing into the solar with MacKinney close behind her. The man turned, gave William a smug smile, and then shut the door with a soft click. William briefly imagined his fist connecting with MacKinney's nose, but Brothwell turned a searching gaze upon him. William focused on the man, forcing thoughts of Ada, and his concern for her, to the back of his mind. Instead, he concentrated on trying to ascertain what had happened to Bram.

As William was considering how to broach the subject without raising suspicion, Brothwell spoke. "I must admit I'm surprised ye have nae inquired about yer brother. Dunnae ye wonder where he is?"

William's gut clenched. He inhaled a slow, steady breath to calm his nerves. "I assumed ye would tell me if and when ye trusted that ye could."

Brothwell inclined his head at William's words. "Ye are more patient than yer brother," he said. "And a more skilled warrior, Wolf. That was a surprise."

The man was testing him. "Was it?" William asked. "I did lay siege to castles on King David's behalf for the past year, as I'm certain ye're aware."

"I'm aware. I ordered yer brother to kill ye and the king's right hand Blackswell who ye laid sieges with."

Willian stilled at the revelation. Was that why Bram had been sent away? He'd refused Brothwell's order? Had Bram risked his own life to protect William and Brodee's?"

Brothwell splayed his hands, as if in apology. "I could hardly have imagined one of the king's favorites would turn traitor."

"Could ye nae?" William asked, forcing himself to control his rising anger. "Many of the nobles have turned on the king for disregarding their counsel and giving away their land to commoners. Why should I be any different? My father was once laird of his own clan and castle, and then he was relegated to a lesser role, promised land by the king that he did nae deliver."

"Aye, I ken it all, but why now? Why did ye finally decide the king would nae ever keep his promise to yer family?"

"Because after a year of faithful service and vow after vow, he gave the land he'd promised me to another," William lied. "I thought my father and brother perhaps too rash, but now I see they were nae."

A serving wench scurried in and placed two wine goblets before them. Brothwell raised his to his lips and took a long drink. "There were whispers that yer brother was nae truly for the Steward."

William had to clench his teeth on a curse. It was as the king had suspected and as William had suspected. "Whoever whispered that was simply jealous. They must have wanted to be rid of Bram," William said, thinking it could perhaps be true. "Everyone knows Bram turned against King David. He fought alongside ye in the Battle of Kirldine, for Christ's sake."

Brothwell set his goblet on the small table between them and leaned forward, setting his elbows on his knees. His eyes bore into William's. "Aye. I believed as ye did, and some of the men did nae trust him. They said he did nae kill some of the king's men when he had the chance."

"That dunnae mean he still supports the king," William argued, feeling as though he was arguing for Bram's life. "Did he stop these men he did nae kill?"

"Aye."

"Then maybe he did nae see the value in killing them."

"The value, Wolf," Brothwell said, his voice tight, "is that those men he injured will heal and rise again to take up arms against us. And I did nae send him away simply on the grumblings of my men." Brothwell's gaze searched William's. "'Twas when Ada questioned his loyalty that I kenned I was ignoring signs simply because he had become my friend. Ada has nothing to gain by questioning if he is truly for the Steward, unlike some of my men."

William was too stunned to respond. *Ada* had questioned his brother's loyalty. *Ada* was the one responsible for Bram's life being in danger. Anger swept him. Ada could not possibly be a supporter of King David in light of what she'd done. She had to have known her doubt about Bram could well get him killed.

"Aye," William finally choked out, his head throbbing with the effort to hold back his rage. "It makes sense now why ye sent him away. Or did ye imprison him?" William asked as casually as he could.

Brothwell's fingers drummed the goblet he had once again picked up. "I imprisoned him," the man said. "I offered him the chance for freedom or death once I got him to Trethway Island. All he had to do was kill one of the king's guards whom I had captured, but he would nae do it. He's set to die in a fortnight." Brothwell's gaze turned cold. "I befriended yer brother. I dunnae ever do that, and this has reminded me why. He'll die at Trethway. Do ye ken the place?"

"I do," William said, picking up his goblet and drinking down the entire contents. He feared if he spoke too soon, he'd reveal himself. He wanted to wrap his hands around Brothwell's throat and squeeze the life out of him for so casually and emotionlessly saying Bram would die at Trethway. But at least he was alive, and William had a fortnight to save him.

"How do ye ken Trethway?" Brothwell asked with a

frown.

"I trained with the Dark Riders," William replied, suspecting Brothwell already knew this and that the man was once again testing him.

Brothwell nodded. "I had heard rumors, and when I saw the way ye shot an arrow, I suspected the rumors to be true. So, ye ken Trethway belongs to the Order? The Dark Riders dunnae care for the Order."

They didn't care for the men in the Order; they were unfair and powerful, which was a dangerous combination. The Order was a group of six lairds from border area between Scotland and England who used the island to unjustly imprison any men who opposed their rule of the borders. Any man taken to the island was left to be killed or tortured until they submitted to their captor's commands. The king knew of it and intended to do something to stop them, but it was a delicate situation. The men of the Order supported him, and he needed their support while he opposed his nephew.

"I ken it."

"Have ye been? To Trethway, that is?"

William shook his head, his thoughts pulled between this conversation and Ada. She was his enemy. She was the king's enemy, and he would have to wed her. He desired her, but he would need to control that desire and guard himself around her.

"Yet ye ken it? Why?"

"My debt to the Dark Riders for their training me was five missions. One was to free a prisoner from Trethway Island."

Astonishment touched Brothwell's face. "An impossible task. The guard towers that face out to the water are manned at all times, and ye have to cross the water to reach the island. Dunnae tell me ye fulfilled the mission?"

William considered how much to reveal. He'd fallen ill and never completed the mission. Should he say that? It was the simplest explanation but made him look weak and would lead to more questions. The truth was that Brodee had come searching for William at the king's behest, found him, and completed the missions for him. It was why William was indebted to Brodee. He wanted to serve his friend as Brodee served the king as his right hand.

"I did nae free the prisoner. He died before I reached the island. After that, they sent me on other missions, which had naught to do with Trethway."

Brothwell chuckled. "'Tis a good thing. Ye would have died there."

William forced a small smile, his mind turning with what Brodee had told him about the waters and how he had survived. The information would be most useful when he went to free Bram. And hopefully, by then, Ada would be useful with her gift activated.

The door to the antechamber suddenly opened, and the MacKinney emerged with that same smug smile still on his face. He inclined his head to Brothwell and cocked his eyebrows to William. "She says she will speak to ye now, but I dunnae believe ye should bother. She'll choose me."

"Ye're verra certain," Brothwell said, before William could speak.

The MacKinney nodded. "I beg pardon, but Lady Ada was quite passionate with me—"

Another bout of rage exploded inside William. He had his dagger to the MacKinney's neck before the man could even move his hand to his weapon. "Are ye telling me that ye touched the woman that will be my wife?" William seethed.

"I think ye best answer the man," Brothwell said in an amused tone.

The MacKinney's face was red with his own rage. "She kissed me, MacLean." The words were a triple punch to his gut, and he despised that it bothered him, that hot jealousy seared through his veins, that all he could see were Ada's plump, lovely lips on this scoundrel's face. And just like that, reason fled him, and without a care for the consequences, he whipped his fist backward and then drove it into the MacKinney's nose.

Ten

Scuffling and yelling drew Ada to the antechamber. When she stepped into the room, she could do no more than gape at the scene before her. Both Connor and William were being held by Brothwell's guards. Connor had blood running from his nose, and William had a murderous look on his face—and a dagger, which the guard was demanding, clutched in his hand.

Brothwell's gaze fell upon her. He arched his eyebrows and gave her an amused and slightly censuring look. "It is hardly befitting of a lady to kiss a man," he announced from across the room, bringing everyone else's attention to her.

"I did nae kiss him," she said through clenched teeth, turning her attention upon Connor accusingly. *"He* kissed *me."*

The man had the audacity to look at her innocently. "But ye said ye wanted passion."

She ground her teeth at that. She had, in fact, told him she would not wed him because she did not think there was passion between them. That was but one of the hundreds of reasons, but she'd not felt inclined to give the man the rest. Then he had surprised her by kissing her. Before she could say more, William broke free from the guard who was holding him and ascended upon Connor like a violent storm.

She gasped as he reared his fist back and punched Connor. "That," he bit out, "is for taking without being given permission."

"Wolf!" Brothwell roared. "Hold yerself."

William whipped his head toward Brothwell, and Ada's breath caught, wondering if he would listen. For a moment, time seemed to stretch, and then slowly, he lowered his fist. But he did not move from where he had planted himself in front of Connor, even though a guard was tugging at William's arm. He shoved the man away, seemingly without much effort. "I will kill ye if ye ever touch her again."

"Ye are nae yet her husband, MacLean," Connor snarled.

"Ada," Brothwell interrupted. "Take Wolf into the solar and make yer decision. I tire of this back-and-forth."

Her heart thundered as her gaze locked with William's, and she frowned. His actions were protective, those of a man who wanted her, yet he looked at her almost with disdain. Was she imagining that? She stared, trying to decide, and his face seemed to change before her. The disdain disappeared, and in its place was a neutral expression, a mask, she thought, of his emotions.

It was time to be truthful with William. She hoped she was making the right decision and that he was the man she believed him to be. With that in mind, she simply nodded to her stepbrother, turned back to the solar, and moved into the room. Behind her, William's footsteps sounded, and then the door swished and clicked shut.

She turned, her breath hitching at how near he was to her. She expected him to pause so they could talk, but he stalked toward her. She scrambled backward, feeling as if she had somehow unleashed something wild within him, given the determined, ruthless look in his eyes. By the time he reached her, she had her back pressed against the wall. He splayed his hands against the wall on either side of her to cage her in. "So ye desire passion in yer marriage, do ye?"

His taut tone and rapidly beating pulse at his neck told her that he was struggling to hold back, but she was not scared. She was intrigued. This had to be jealousy. She'd not planned to make him jealous, but if she provoked him just a bit, would he kiss her or would she truly rouse the beast? Would she feel his kiss everywhere as Marjorie had said she had felt Bram's? She'd not felt Connor's kiss, except for the annoying pressure of his lips upon hers.

"Ada," he demanded, her name a warning from his lips. "Answer me."

It was his own fault, she decided. He was prodding her, so she had to poke back. "I do want passion. If I'm to wed without love, I will at least have passion."

Which will, God willing, lead to love.

A wicked grin came to his lips and a spark of danger to his eyes. "I can promise ye passion, Ada. Of that ye can be certain."

A thrill shot through her, and before she could even think of how to answer, his lips were upon hers, hot, possessive, and awakening every part of her body like a jolt of lightning. Desire poured through her, curling her toes and sweeping gooseflesh over her skin. She groaned with the rush of it, as did he. His tongue touched the crease of her lips, demanding she open her mouth, and she did so eagerly, wantonly.

He slid into her mouth with his tongue, hers meeting his and then tangling as his hands traveled up to her breasts, which had become heavy, her nipples tight and aching. His palms skimmed over her breasts, making liquid fire and a pulsing need spring at her core. Dear God! She would melt from how much she wanted his touch.

His lips trailed a fiery path down her neck, which shot an odd tension along the nerves within her body. Something was building in her, and quickly. Something she had never imagined, never before felt.

Down, down, down trailed his sinful mouth, and then he gave a hard tug to her gown. She gasped as cool air hit her breasts. But there was no time to protest, not that she wanted to or even could have formed the words, because as quick as he had tugged her gown over her breast, his mouth claimed the right one, drawing her nipple into his mouth.

Oh, the sensations! Dear heavenly Father above, the sensations!

Warmth and softness and wetness surrounded her nipple, and he sucked and pulled upon it with lavish strokes that surely the devil himself had taught this man. Her senses spiraled and collided, and the tension in her continued to build, her core now throbbing painfully.

A sudden pounding at the door jerked her from the sensual frenzy, and her gaze flew to the door, which rattled. For a moment she feared that Brothwell would barge in, but then she realized the door was locked. She stared at William, who looked at her with complete and utter triumph and possession. She didn't mind. Not one small bit. She felt the same way about him.

"Ye locked it," she said simply.

"Aye," he replied, swirling his tongue around her nipple one more time, causing her knees to go weak, but he caught her and crushed her to him, her bare chest to his hard one. Never had she been intimate with a man like this, never had she wanted to.

"Ye will be mine," he said.

"Aye," she agreed. But he would be hers, too. First in passion and then in his heart. She'd not felt so hopeful in a very long time.

~·⋅⋅⋅~

She'd known Brothwell would move rapidly, eager to get her wed and bring her gift to life within her, but she'd not expected to be wed before the morrow like this. She stood, anxious, facing Father Dorian. William stood on one side of her and Brothwell on the other. There had been no time to talk with William, to tell him she supported King David, and to hear for certain where his loyalty lay. Brothwell had not left her side since he'd entered the solar, demanding her answer as to whom she would wed, and then sent a servant to fetch the priest. She stood there, fearful and wary, but reminded herself that if she was to be forced to wed this day, she would wed at least where passion existed.

The only things keeping her somewhat calm were Freya and Hella. Freya had positioned herself in front of Ada, and Hella had positioned herself in front of William. It was that show of love for William by Hella that made Ada confident she was making the best decision she could, given the situation. Some might think she was mad to trust a dog's instincts, but she did when combined with her own. On top of that, she'd caught William gently petting Hella's head mere moments before.

As Father Dorian cleared his throat and then began the ceremony, she stole a sideways glance at William. His shoulders appeared tense, his jaw tight, and there was a tic at his jawline. Her gut clenched. He did not appear at all happy to be wedding her. Mayhap he was just nervous. When Father Dorian told William to face her and he did, she started to smile, but the look he gave her was dispassionate, not at all like the desire that had been burning his gaze in the solar not long ago, and her smile faded. Worry set in. He seemed cold, as if he'd reined in all his emotions and locked them away.

When the priest asked for her to say her vows, she could not seem to form the words. Her heart raced. Her mouth was too dry, her tongue too thick. She took a step back, and William frowned at her as both Freya and Hella began to whine.

"Ada, what are ye doing?" Brothwell demanded.

An excellent question. What *was* she doing?

Perspiration dampened her brow, her underarms, her scalp. She was scared. She looked to William, hoping for a glimpse of understanding in his eyes, but if she didn't know better she'd swear he looked angry at her. She had the overwhelming urge to run, but not only did she have nowhere to run to but she had Esther and Maximilian to think about. Not to mention she doubted she'd even make it to the door before Brothwell hauled her back in here.

Freya bumped her from behind, shoving her straight into William. He caught her with his large, sure hands, and she grasped onto him, feeling almost faint with fear now. He sucked in a sharp breath. "Ye're clammy and cold and trembling."

"Och," Brothwell said. "She'll be fine." He narrowed his eyes at her. "Dunnae tell me ye have changed yer mind, Ada. Ye ken what's at stake."

She bit her lip on his not-so-subtle threat and nodded, catching William studying her.

"Say yer vows, Ada," Brothwell demanded.

"Aye, lass," the priest added, "ye must willingly say yer vows."

Hella and Freya whined louder. She knew she had to say the vows. The part of her that hoped for something special to come from this wanted to say them, but the rest of her needed a sign from William. Something. Any small sign to show he would be caring, warm, and not the cold man standing before her now.

Suddenly, he squeezed her hands. "Dunnae fash yerself, lass. I will protect ye with my life and nae ever harm ye."

That was hardly the declaration of love she had once dreamed would come from the man she wed, but she supposed it would have to do considering the circumstances. Still…

"I would have yer vow," she said. If he was honorable as she hoped, he would never break his vow once given.

He took her hand and placed it on his thundering heart. Her mouth slipped open to feel his own nervousness, and his mouth began to move. He was giving her his vow, but all she could hear was her own thumping heart in her ears, and all she could think was, despite how detached and unaffected William may look, he was just as hesitant as she was to bind himself to her. Knowing that gave her the courage she needed. She curled her fingertips into his chest, not moving her hand and holding his gaze as she said her vows. As she spoke, she would have wagered her life that longing glimmered in his eyes. It was not love. Of course not. They barely knew each other, but it was most definitely a start.

Curse it all. William clenched his jaw as Ada said her vows, her palm on his heart, her luminous eyes locked on his. *This woman.* Why did she affect him so? He'd known her for two days, and already she'd made him feel searing desire, as well as burning rage. And that kiss... Just recalling it made him hard as stone.

He'd kissed her to ensure she chose him, but he'd be a fool not to acknowledge that he'd forgotten himself when their mouths had met and he'd tasted her. He found himself staring at the long column of her neck that led to her chest, and he recalled in vivid detail the feel of her smooth flesh against his lips, the erotic sound of her moans in his ears. What he needed to recall, however, was that she was responsible for his brother's life being in danger. So why had he taken her hands just now? Why had he given his vow to protect her with his life and never harm her?

Devil take it. He knew why. Because it was true. She would soon be his wife, and whether he liked her or not, he'd guard her with his last breath. He may wish to lash her for her hand in his brother's current problems, but he wouldn't. He'd never laid a hand upon a woman, and he was certainly not going to start now with his wife. The word *wife* made him uneasy. He had not wanted one, but in a few more breaths, he'd have one.

He swept his gaze over her beautiful, delicate body and then back to her gaze, which no longer glittered with fear but with something that looked suspiciously like determination. What was she determined to do? Rule him? Bend him to her and Brothwell's will? It didn't matter, though, because Ada was about to discover who he really was, who he really supported, and what he really wanted.

"Ye may kiss yer wife," the priest announced, jerking William's attention back to the present.

The words hit him like a punch in the gut. Kiss her? He feared if he kissed her, he'd not stop. He could see why poor Adam had taken a bite of that apple—damned Eve. William tried to pull his gaze from Ada's lips, but his body would not cooperate. Kiss her? He could not very well decline. He needed to get her alone, so he could instigate the second part of the plan. With that in mind, he looked down at her, intent on giving her a peck on the lips, but he stilled, surprised by the eagerness in her eyes as she stared not at him but his mouth.

Ada was like the snake in the Garden of Eden—too tempting to ignore. That look in her eyes ignited his blood and set his inner warning bell to ringing. With no hope of avoiding it, William leaned down. He planned to quickly brush his lips to hers, but he was only human, for God's sake, and the minute he touched her warm lips and tasted her seductive sweetness, he knew, with every finely honed instinct that had kept him alive thus far, that he was in trouble.

Instead of pulling back, he tugged her near. How in God's name had his hands ended up around her waist? Her mouth parted and invited him to sin, and he wanted to imbibe in wickedness with her until he was drunk with pleasure. God help him, he did. The little sigh she gave nearly tipped him over the edge. Except then Brothwell said, "Enough," and William luckily found the strength and sense to end the kiss.

He broke the contact, feeling her loss acutely, physically, painfully. His gaze went to her despite telling himself not to look at her. Her lips were swollen from his kiss and her cheeks were flushed, but it was her eyes—those stormy silver-specked eyes—that nearly sent him back to kiss her once more. She had a pleased look in her eyes—and a lustful one.

When Brothwell stepped between them, facing Ada, and grabbed her by the arms, William had to clench his fists not to haul Brothwell away from her. Ada's gaze went wide with obvious fear. "Ye're wed now, Ada, and willingly. So tell me, does the king ken of our plan to attack his forces in Glen Brittle Forest in a sennight?"

William stiffened at the news of the impending attack, even as his focus went to Ada. She bit her lip and shook her head. "I dunnae ken."

"What do ye mean ye *dunnae ken?*" Brothwell bellowed. "Ye are wed now! Ye will tell me, or I'll kill that damned scruff boy and old companion ye hold so dear."

"I kinnae tell ye what I dunnae ken," she said, her words halting.

"Tell me, now!" Brothwell demanded, shaking her, and when she cried out, William reacted instinctively. He grabbed Brothwell by the arms and jerked him away from Ada. He would have thrown the man against the wall and sent his fist into Brothwell's face but the man's guards surrounded William, swords drawn and pointed at him.

Yanking his arms away from William, Brothwell narrowed his gaze. "I'm pleased ye would protect Ada. She's a prize to be sure. I allowed her to wed ye, as I kenned ye would keep my prize safe, but she is just that: *my prize.* Dunnae ever think to protect her against me again or I will kill ye."

Before William could respond, Ada said, "I'd nae do that if I were ye. I believe I dunnae feel any different yet because, well…because the marriage has nae yet been consummated."

William gaped in shock at Ada's words. A vivid blush swept her cheeks. Damn the lass. Why did she have to say such a thing and look so appealing? Now all he could envision were her legs wrapped around his body, her breasts bared for his touch, her hair fanned out for him to feel, and her lips parted for him to taste her once more.

The reasonable, warrior side of his brain almost disappeared under the deluge of desire, but with the force of his will, he brought his thoughts to his brother and the task at hand. If his wife needed to be bedded for her gift to come to her, then bed her he would. It was the perfect opportunity to finally get Ada alone and make their escape. *After* she aided him in learning the remaining three traitors' names. This would not be a joining of lust but a detached one of necessity.

He glanced at her, and his treacherous body hardened even more, an ache to make her his coursing through him in the most primal way.

"Then bed the lass now," Brothwell ordered, looking from William to Ada and back again.

William frowned, an unwelcome suspicion rising. "Ye dunnae mean here."

"Aye, I'd witness—"

"Nay!" Ada cried out, and William was in perfect agreement with her. He despised the custom of men observing the consummation of a marriage. He'd never understood why any man would allow others to view his wife naked.

"Brothwell, I dunnae hold with that custom," William said, not giving a damn if his protest irritated the man.

"I need proof," Brothwell said, his tone unbending.

"Then ye shall have it," William replied, taking Ada by the hand. "I will give ye the sheet from the bed."

Brothwell narrowed his eyes at William. "I will be outside her door with guards. I need an answer tonight."

William nodded, knowing that no matter what transpired, he could not allow Ada to aid Brothwell and the other traitors in killing the king's men. He also had to keep a distance between him and Ada.

He started the process of detaching himself as he followed her to her bedchamber, Brothwell behind them. Remembering who she truly was and the role she had played was made easier by Brothwell continuing to talk about the different questions he wanted her to answer when her gift awakened. He did so until they reached her bedchamber door. Brothwell nodded to William, and he and Ada entered.

When the door was closed behind them, William locked it, then turned to face Ada, who stood in the center of the room with an uneasy look on her face. He stiffened at the protectiveness that surged within him. She did not need his protection, though. It was he who needed to guard himself from her.

"William," she said, stepping toward him, so close that her wildflower scent swirled around him. "In truth, I dunnae have any notion if consummating our marriage will awaken my gift."

"Then why did ye say such a thing?" The moment the question was out, he cursed himself. No doubt she'd make up some lie.

"I thought to—"

"It dunnae matter," he interrupted. "Do ye or do ye nae feel any different than ye did before we were wed?"

"I feel the same," she said.

"Then we must consummate the marriage. Yer gift must be awakened."

"William, I—"

"I'm going to have my guards bust down this door if ye are nae out shortly and presenting me with the sheets," Brothwell bellowed. "I want an answer to my question, Ada."

"Come," William said, catching her by the hand. "I, for one, dunnae wish an audience for this."

When he felt her trembling as she stepped toward him, he could not stop the rise of concern for her. He may wish to be detached, but he did not wish to hurt her, and he did desire her. "Dunnae fash, *bean bhàsail*. Remember, I vowed I would nae ever hurt ye."

"Ye think me a temptress?" she asked, her tone shy.

"Aye," he replied. What else could explain the near insatiable urge he felt to possess and protect her in this moment?

He needed to keep the joining dispassionate, but the moment he touched the bare flesh of her chest and glided his fingertips along her collarbone to slide them under the material of her gown, reason fled and yearning replaced it. Slowly, he pulled her gown over her shoulders and down her body until it puddled at her feet. She moved to cross her arms over her breasts, which could be clearly seen under the thin material of her léine, but he stopped her, his heart threatening to beat right out of his chest. She was just a woman. He repeated it and repeated it, trying to temper the lust blazing within him, but it would not be tempered. It would not be stopped. It was consuming him like a fire burning out of control.

He circled his finger over the peak of one of her hard buds straining against the linen, and his lust ripped his control from his grip. With an urgency he'd never felt, he divested himself of his clothing and her of her undergarments as she boldly stared at him. Then, he swept her into his arms, her softness against his hardness, and carried her to the bed. He wanted to take hours to worship her, but there was not time for that. He laid her down gently, nudged his knee between her thighs, then ran his palms up the length of the silken skin on the inside of her legs, to spread them gently apart.

She did not protest, but she sucked in her lip and her breathing had become jagged. Was it fear or lust? He wanted lust from her. He may not have her honest words, but he'd have her unfettered desire.

He meant to use the skill he'd learned to pleasure a woman. He intended to wield it like a weapon, but all his intentions slipped away as he slid his fingers between her legs and found her hot and ready for him. "Ye want me just as much as I want ye," he blurted, catching her shy gaze.

"Aye. 'Tis likely sinful how much I want ye. I'll need to make a quick prayer of forgiveness for my wanton nature when we're done."

He laughed at that. "God has better things to concern himself with than yer wanton nature," he replied. "Besides, 'tis nae sinful to yearn for yer husband."

"But Esther says—"

"Who's Esther?" he asked, gently stroking over the nub that was the center of her pleasure. When she moaned and arched her back, he grinned. He rubbed the nub again, his own need growing tenfold. "Esther?" he gently reminded. "Who is she?"

Ada opened her eyes, which she had squeezed shut, brought herself up onto her elbows, and her eyes widened as she looked at him. "My companion. She—Ah!" Ada's head had fallen back to the covers when he'd stroked her once more.

His grin widened. His wife was a passionate woman, and the way she responded to his gentle touch was making him crazed. "I want to put my mouth on ye."

"Wh-what?" Ada brought her head up again.

"My mouth. I want to taste ye." He circled her nub in

slow, tantalizing strokes, making her squirm. "Here." He bent his head between her thighs as she started to protest.

"William, I—"

He parted her and slid his tongue up her center, a growl of pure, unadulterated lust escaping him. He'd died. He'd died and gone to Heaven. She no longer spoke but whimpered. Her hands had come to his head to press him closer, which made him chuckle with triumphant pleasure as he licked and lavished her with only one thought in his mind.

Claim her.

Her fingers tangled into his hair, her nails raking over his scalp as he suckled at her center, driven now by the need to bring her fulfillment. She thrashed beneath him and her motions drove him to move his tongue quicker, stroke her more intensely. "William," she moaned, his name a soft cry of need from her lips. "William, please, please," she begged, her hands coming to his shoulders, trying to tug him up.

He paused only long enough to say, "Trust me, Ada."

She nodded, her eyes glassy, her expression dazed, and he bent his head to attend her more, even as he slid his hands over her taut belly and found his way to her nipples. He took each between his thumb and forefinger, gently stroking, lightly pulling. Her thighs suddenly pressed together, a pant escaped her, and then she tensed around him as her climax took her. She throbbed beneath him, her body pulsing with her desire—and his own desire, his need for this woman claimed him completely now.

He rose between her thighs, glanced down at her, and stilled for one moment, drinking her in. "God, ye are beautiful." A strange ache took hold of him, squeezing his chest. What was that?

A pounding came at the door. "My patience is nearing

its end," Brothwell boomed, and William cursed the man to a thousand slow deaths. Ada stiffened under him.

"Push him out of yer head, Ada, or this will hurt more."

"I kinnae. I—"

William took her nipple into his mouth, suckling until she once again was squirming, and then he released her bud to claim her lips as he claimed her innocence. He delved his tongue inside her mouth as he gripped her bottom, hoisted her up, and slid into her with one quick, sure stroke.

When she sucked in a sharp breath, he released her mouth and stilled, wanting to soothe her. He kissed her forehead, her nose, her lips, then locked his gaze to hers. "Tell me when ye feel ye are ready."

She nodded. "'Tis a strange feeling to have ye inside me. It hurts."

"Aye, I'm sorry, lass, but—"

"The sting is gone," she interrupted. "I... Well, I want ye to move."

"Ye're certain?"

She grinned. "I *need* ye to move. I need...I need...something..." She trailed off.

He knew what she was after even if she didn't, and he drew all the way out of her almost to his tip before sliding back in. He watched her, holding himself in check with iron control. His own body demanded release, but he held himself back, waiting, wanting to please her, to give to her. The moment bliss sparked in her eyes, triumph flowed through his veins. He increased his pace as she ran her fingertips tenderly along his back.

Her touch, gentle yet urgent, made that same strange ache grip him, but satisfaction flooded his mind as her body tightened around his and began to contract with her release, which gave him his. The way her body pulsed around his intoxicated him and filled him with sweet agony. Waves of warmth pounded him as he pumped into her, giving her not only his seed but all of him.

That was it, he realized with sudden, shocking clarity. The feeling in his chest was desire, but it was the desire to give all of himself to her and take all of her. Not just the lust. Not just the yearning.

As his pleasure subsided and she collapsed against the bed, smiling up at him, cold fear gripped him, washing away the searing warmth of seconds ago. He could not be so foolish as to let lust be his downfall. His body wanted her, but he could never allow himself to need her. She was deceitful.

"I will have my proof now!" Brothwell ordered.

Ada's eyes widened, then narrowed with irritation. "William, I—"

"Get dressed," he ordered, desperate to take control of himself and the situation once more. He rolled off her and stood, glancing down at her.

Her confused frown, followed swiftly by a hurt look, struck him like a blow, but he'd been hit before, physically and mentally, by men who wished to kill him, by men who he'd trusted, by his mother who'd left him. He could take those powerful hits and decimating betrayals and still keep going. He had to stay detached because that's how one proceeded, even when one had been shredded by others.

She scooted off the bed, and he scooped up her gown and handed it to her. "Ye will do as I say from this moment forward," he told her.

She nodded, and it seemed almost absentmindedly as the door began to rattle. "William, I must tell ye—"

"Save yer breath. I ken ye are responsible for my brother being sent away," he growled, filling with anger at himself for all the control he'd lost when she was in his arms.

"What?" Her frown deepened as Brothwell started yelling.

William ignored her feigned confusion and concentrated on the most important matter. "I've wed ye and I've bed ye, so tell me now, Wife, who are the traitors to King David and how can we save my brother? I ken ye told Brothwell that my brother was a traitor. I ken ye are responsible for Bram being sent away. Brothwell told me so."

The color drained from her face, revealing her guilt, but then, for a breath, she looked scared. It took every bit of control not to reassure her, soothe her, and the fact that he wanted to made him livid.

She stared at him for a moment. "This was all a game? It was all a ploy? All of it?" Her voice held a ring of incredulity.

"Aye. Of course. And ye are going to help me whether ye like it or nae, or so help me God—"

Her palm connected with his cheek—hard. Surprisingly so for such a delicate-looking woman. Her eyes danced with anger. "Ye are a beast and a fool," she whispered furiously. She turned from him, marched to the door, unlocked it, and swung it open.

Brothwell and two guards immediately poured in. "Ada?" Brothwell was asking an unspoken question and came to a halt in front of her.

William could do no more than stare. He'd not even considered that Ada could betray him. It was a grave error. One he would have never made before meeting her. She was his wife. Surely, her powers were given to serve him.

She swept a hand toward the bed. "There is yer proof that the marriage has been consummated, and there—" she turned to William, giving him a cold look "—is the key to defeating King David."

William moved toward his sword, which he'd foolishly not picked up, but Brothwell's guards were upon him. He could have fought but he'd never escape. He'd not live to help Bram, Thomas, or the king if he died here and now.

Brothwell grinned as he moved to Ada's side. "Ye have yer powers," he said, looking down at her with a pleased expression.

"I do, Brother." The smile she gave Brothwell made hatred flare brightly inside William. "And I dunnae have to use it, it seems, to serve the man I've wed, nor who he serves, so ye best take a care."

Shock slammed William in the chest.

"Take a care to treat me well, Brother, lest I decide nae to serve ye and the Steward," Ada threatened.

William clenched his hands into fists.

"I will lavish ye with all ye desire," Brothwell vowed, making William's gut twist.

"Oh, I ken," Ada replied, a smug smile coming to her treacherous lips.

"Do ye?" Brothwell said. "What's it like? How does the power work?"

She cocked her head, turning her gaze to William once more. His flesh prickled with a searing physical memory of what they had just shared, even as her eyes seemed to sharpen like shards of ice. "'Tis a gut feeling," she said, "an intuition of what must be done. My gut tells me to lock William up. He is for King David. Oh—" she turned and bestowed a sweet smile upon Brothwell "—and dunnae attack Glen Brittle. I have a feeling it will nae go yer way. Ye must hold."

William shook with his rage as the guards gripped his arms tighter.

"Take him to the cave and chain him with the others," Brothwell demanded, never taking his gaze from Ada.

As William was dragged toward Brothwell and Ada, her focus once more returned to him. "Dunnae kill him, Brother. I'm certain we can use him."

"I'll nae kill him," Brothwell said, an anticipatory expression sweeping his face as he looked at William, "but I vow to ye that he will suffer."

Ignoring Brothwell, William dug in his heels when he was face-to-face with his treacherous wife. "I underestimated ye," he bit out.

"Aye," she said, her tone like jagged ice. "Ye did."

Eleven

Nausea gripped Ada as she paced her bedchamber with Hella and Freya on either side of her. Their nails clacked against the floor as she tried to be patient and let enough time to pass that most of the inhabitants in the castle would be asleep. Whether the swirling feeling in her stomach was from the strong urges to aid William in his quest or from the way William had duped her, she did not know. Or mayhap the nausea was caused by exhaustion from Brothwell badgering her with questions or even from her time in William's arms.

The horrid liar! To purposely make her think he truly desired *her*... She clenched her teeth in frustration. Despite the fact that his betrayal felt like an open wound, she felt compelled to help him. Even if she'd wanted to strike back at him, just the thought of doing so made the nauseated feeling within her grow.

She paused at the window, as did Hella and Freya, and she smiled grimly. She may not be able to hurt him as he'd hurt her, but she'd at least struck a small blow, even if it was with a lie and he'd soon know the truth. It had felt wickedly good in the moment to allow William to think she was for the Steward and that she was using her newfound powers to betray him.

"He deserved it," she murmured, glancing down at her

hounds. Freya licked Ada's hand, but Hella seemed to frown at her.

Ridiculous. Dogs do nae frown.

"He used me, Hella." The dog whined in response, as if defending him. "He's a scurrilous beast," she muttered.

Even now, hours later, shame heated her cheeks and bitterness soured in her mouth when she thought of the hope she'd felt thinking he'd truly wanted her and the promise she'd convinced herself was in his touch. How foolish she'd been. How naive! How wanton and wicked! If it had been true she would not have regretted it, but it all had been a lie, and regret weighed heavily upon her. He'd not desired her; he'd desired to use her, just like all the others.

She stared out at the bright moon, unshed tears blurring her vision. She knew perfectly well why he wanted to use her. The truth of who he really was had filled her senses the moment they had joined. He was King David's man, and her gift was meant to be used to keep the king on the throne. She did not even question this. It was a fact as unchangeable as the color of her eyes. King David was the rightful king, and William was the king's man.

Beyond that, she did not know. She had no sense of him personally, no intuition on his thoughts and feelings. In fact, all the instincts that had overwhelmed her since joining with William were directly related to keeping King David on the throne. So that was why he had wanted to use her, to wed her. That was why he had seduced her. Why would he believe Brothwell's lies that she had betrayed Bram when Brothwell was William's true enemy?

Another feeling hit her like a smack in the head, and her nausea increased. She fell to her knees, palms against the cold wood floor, and sucked in sharp breaths. Beside her,

Hella and Freya both whined. Bram's name rolled through her mind, followed by his image. Bram was King David's man, just as she'd suspected, but she'd never told Brothwell that. She would not have put Bram in such danger. She cast her mind back, trying to recall any conversation she'd had about Bram, but there had only been one with Esther.

Oh heavens! She'd told Esther that she felt as if Bram was hiding something, and after she'd said that, she'd heard a noise outside of her room and found Brothwell passing. He'd said nothing to her then, but he must have heard her and become suspicious of Bram himself. Brothwell must have twisted that incident to William. There could be no other explanation, and William had simply believed Brothwell and thought she'd done this horrid thing.

The knowledge did not lessen her hurt, but it did take the edge off her anger just a bit. William clearly loved his brother, and that was an admirable quality, even if he was a beast. A sigh escaped her. She'd hoped passion would lead to love. Now she laughed at that folly. Freya nudged her, and Ada reached out and patted her. "I'm wed now, Freya. I'm wed with nae any love and nae any passion and nae any promise, but I have my gift from those bumbling fairies."

Freya whined louder, and Hella barked. "The gift is odd," she murmured. "I ken well I'll use it to aid King David, but then what?" The future stretched bleak before her. She shook her head. No, she had to concentrate on the present.

What did she need to do exactly, though?

William *had* asked for the names of the traitors to King David, and she assumed he meant what lairds and lords had joined forces with Brothwell and the Steward. She'd had her suspicions based on the men who had come here and dined with Brothwell and who sent troops at various times, but names rang in her head now, making her skull ache and the nausea… She swallowed and swallowed again, but it would not be kept at bay.

Her stomach tightened, and she doubled over, retching as one name after the other became clear and certainty seeped into her. Beside her, Hella and Freya whined as the names became louder. Laird Bard, Laird Lindsey, and Laird Stone. Lowland chiefs. Traitors to the king. They felt discounted, stripped of the power they'd once held. King David did not give power to the lairds as they wanted, and the Steward would.

She swiped a hand over her mouth and sat up on her knees, shaking. Laird Bard, Laird Lindsey, and Laird Stone had joined forces with the Steward and four of his sons, John, Walter, Alexander, and Robert, to rebel against David.

She forced herself to rise as she took long, calming breaths. Freya and Hella rose with her. They needed to escape, a possibility made easier now that Brothwell thought her fully on his side. He had not stationed guards by her bedchamber door as he normally did, and with her naming William a betrayer, she'd effectively learned where Brothwell was keeping Esther and Maximilian. The trick now was to make her way to the cave without being seen.

But then what? A guard would no doubt be at the cave, and she had no weapon, except herself. She glanced down at her rumpled appearance and decided grimly to follow William's lead. She would try to seduce the guard to distract him and somehow get his weapon, and if that didn't work— Fear rose inside her, but she shoved it down. It *had* to work.

Brothwell had commanded her to present herself at the solar when the sun rose, and he'd told her in plain terms that he intended to have her help him decide his plan of attack on the king. Brothwell was canny, and she did not think it would take him overly long to discover that she was lying to him, and then he would undoubtedly kill Esther or Maximilian. Determined not to let that happen, she strode to her dressing table and prepared to seduce.

William jerked awake at the feel of something touching his forehead. Disorientation flooded him as he blinked in the darkness, trying to get his eyes to adjust. Something sharp poked into his back, and a rushing sound—water?—filled his ears. A cool breeze blew, swirling the smell of salt and sand around him. The cave. He was in the cave by the ocean.

"He's awake," a man's voice murmured low.

Instinctually, William tried to bring his fists up to defend himself, but he couldn't. He pulled on his arms, realizing they were bound in front of him. *Tied?*

Another tug.

Definitely tied.

At the wrist. He tried to touch a finger to the rope to no avail. Questions exploded in his head at the same time as pain. "Christ," he growled, recalling suddenly the hit on the back of the head he'd received from one of Brothwell's guards. The man had not appreciated William's efforts to escape.

"Shh," came a woman's command from his left.

He jerked his head that way, nausea roiling in his stomach, and he squinted into the darkness. "Ada?" William croaked.

"Nay, MacLean. 'Tis her companion. Where is the lass?"

"Thomas?" William swept his gaze around the cave, starting to finally make out faint outlines. Rock. More rock. A blob. He moved past it only to go back. The blob was big.

"Thomas?" he asked again.

"Aye, and lower yer voice," Thomas whispered. "The guard assigned to watch me loves to give me a hit when I wake."

"Where is Lady Ada?" a young lad asked, the voice very close, making William jerk instinctually. He scanned at the space around him, seeing no one, but when he tilted his head up, there above him, on a rock appeared to be someone whose face he could not see. Whatever had been touching his head disappeared and returned with a sharp kick. A foot.

"What did ye do to her?" an irate young lad demanded.

Images of Ada slid into his mind. Ada naked. Ada in the throes of passion. Ada naming him a traitor. "I did nae do a thing to her," he said, his anger vibrating in his tone. The minute the words left his mouth, he clenched his teeth against the realization that he'd not spoken the entire truth.

"Filthy liar!" the lad accused, then kicked him in the head again. The throbbing pain at the base of his skull reverberated through his entire head and down his body. He hissed with the excruciating agony.

"Maximilian," the woman chided. "Dunnae kick the man. Recall what Thomas told us. He is for the king."

"Oh aye," the lad, Maximilian, said, his tone sarcastic. "He's for the king, but he's here to use Lady Ada just as all men wish to use her."

William was having trouble keeping up with the conversation because of the torturous throbbing in his head, but he could keep up enough to realize that Thomas had been divulging secrets. "What the devil, Thomas? Why are ye revealing things to our enemies?" William gritted out between waves of pain.

Thomas snorted. "Lady Ada's companion and the lad

that feeds her hounds are nae our enemies."

"If they are her friends, they are nae to be trusted," William growled, only to get kicked in the head once more. "Dunnae kick me in the head again," he bit out.

"I'll kick ye if I want to kick ye," the lad challenged. "For one thing, ye're tied up good. For another, ye are speaking lies about me and Esther, and—"

"Lies?" William bellowed, to which all three of his cave companions hushed him. William took a breath to calm his temper. "Lady Ada," he whispered fiercely, "is the reason I'm in here! She named me a traitor and told her brother I was a supporter of King David."

"Ye must have done something terrible to her," the lad said, matter-of-fact. "Either that or it's true."

"Maximilian speaks correctly," the woman, Esther, agreed, her tone disapproving. "Thomas, I thought ye said ye and this man were for King David."

"We are," Thomas said. "MacLean, what did ye do to the lady?"

An image of him kneeling between Ada's lovely thighs and then hovering above her came to him, hardening him everywhere. "I wed her," he said thickly.

"Oh!" Esther exclaimed. "Then has her gift—"

"How the devil am I to ken?" he snapped irritably. "She told Brothwell about me immediately, and I was hauled off. If yer lady supports the king, then why she would have told her stepbrother that I am the king's man?"

"I suspect ye hurt her, and she reacted in anger," Esther said. "And I can assure ye that Ada does support the king. We are in this cave, sir—"

"William," he interrupted.

"We are kept in this cave, *William*," she went on, "because Brothwell used us to force Ada's hand in choosing a husband. The three of us tried to escape several times after her father died, and the last time, when Brothwell stopped us, he informed Ada that she would either willingly select a husband from the warriors he was assembling for a tournament or he'd kill us."

"Still, how do ye explain why Ada told Brothwell my brother was for the king?"

He ducked at the swish of air behind him, and he glanced over his shoulder to glare at the lad. "If ye are untied, ye devil, why have ye nae released yer companions so ye could escape?"

"He's nae untied," Thomas answered. "His feet are nae bound, and Esther and I are chained, nae tied. The guard has the key. Ye, however, are tied, which is why we were trying to wake ye, so ye could try to stand. Maximilian tried already to reach yer wrist but could nae with how ye were positioned."

"Why'd ye nae say so immediately?" William whispered. With considerable effort, he rose slowly to his feet. The room swayed, but he remained standing. "Now what?"

The lad jumped off the rock that he must have climbed upon and came quickly to stand in front of William.

"Put out yer wrists, ye swine."

"Ye have the manners of a goat," William grumbled.

"Ye smell like rotted swine," the lad retorted.

William thrust his wrists at the boy, who turned his back to William, making William realize the lad's hands were tied behind his back. The lad fumbled, trying to find the rope, and after a minute, he finally did and set to work trying to loosen the knots. "Lady Ada would have nae ever have told Brothwell that Bram was a supporter of King David," the lad said. "She liked him, and she detests Brothwell."

"'Tis the truth," Esther said. "If Brothwell told ye that, he lied. He must have overheard Ada telling me her suspicions that Bram was nae who he presented himself to be. We were in her bedchamber one day when she said it, and we heard a noise in the corridor, only to see Brothwell pass."

As Esther's words sunk in, William stiffened. Christ, if that was all true, then all his anger at Ada was unfounded. Immediately, he thought of how coldly he'd treated her right after they'd joined, and how he'd flatly and unemotionally told her he'd wed and bedded her simply to use her. He had wed her to use her, but the joining had been solely about his desire for her, his burning need to touch her.

He was repelled by how he'd acted and wary at the tide of strong emotion he felt for Ada. He was a fool—a fool for believing Brothwell's lie, and more the fool for allowing himself to feel for Ada. And if he had such feelings now after only just meeting her, how strong would they become in time? Too strong. Unacceptably strong. A vivid image of his father weeping in his bedchamber because William's mom had left came to William. He never wanted to be hurt like that because of a woman. He did not want such attachments. He would take back the hurt he'd caused Ada if he could, but perhaps it was best if she now despised him. It would make it easier to keep distance between them.

"I still come back to why Ada would have named me a traitor to Brothwell if she intends to aid King David," he said.

"Because, ye scurrilous beast," came Ada's voice, "I had to gain Brothwell's trust so he'd call his guards off me."

Twelve

"Ada!" Esther and Maximilian exclaimed joyously. With Hella and Freya on her heels, Ada rushed into the cave, heading toward the direction of Maximilian's voice. "We must hurry!" she said, touching the lad's head, then pressing a kiss to it while trying to ignore William's large presence near Maximilian. It was nearly impossible. The man had not said a word since she'd made her presence known, but even in silence, she was utterly aware of him. She could feel him as if he touched her. She could hear him breathing as if each breath was for her. And she could smell the power he caged and possessed like a wild animal. Power he had unleashed on her and that had left her deliciously spent and equally as foolish.

"How did ye get here, Lady Ada?" Maximilian asked.

"I'll explain later," she hurriedly replied, Freya at her side while Hella moved close to William. "Are ye bound or chained?" she asked Maximilian.

"Bound behind my back by my wrists," he said.

"I'm chained," Esther said, "and my ankles are tied together."

"I'm chained, as well," a voice she did not know said. It had to be William's acquaintance Thomas. "I dunnae suppose ye have the key?"

Ada pursed her lips. "I suppose I do." She was not yet

getting a feeling one way or the other about Thomas.

"He supports the king," William said, his voice reaching out like fingers to wrap around her heart and squeeze it. Devil take him. She wanted to despise him, but apparently her foolish heart felt otherwise. The instinct that Thomas was meant to aid them in helping King David suddenly swept through her, as if William's words had triggered her intuition. She swayed with the feeling for a moment, fighting back the nausea.

Once it had passed, she said, "And I'm to believe ye because...?" She allowed the full ire she still possessed to seep into her tone.

"I am nae lying to ye," he said.

"Ha!" she barked and released Maximilian from his ties. She walked away from the lad, Freya by her side, to release Esther.

"I told ye I was here to seduce ye," William said testily. "Well before ye wed me, I told ye that."

"There is telling, and then there is *telling*," she said, setting Esther free, who gave her a quick hug before Ada disengaged herself and moved to stand before Thomas. She hesitated in releasing him only because she wanted to hear what William would say in return to her.

"Ada, dunnae punish Thomas because ye are vexed with me," William urged her from across the cave. "I'm certain ye have a good plan, but I would think the guard would be a concern."

Ada snickered. "He would be except I knocked him on the head with a chalice, and he fell straight out."

"Ye killed him?" Thomas asked from in front of her.

"Nay. He's just taking a lovely little sleep."

"My," Thomas said slowly, "aren't ye the dangerous lass? I like that in a woman."

"Thomas," William growled, "if ye banter with my wife anymore, I will punch ye when I am untied."

Hope that he might truly care tried to niggle at her, but she quashed it with her anger. The man did not care about her; he was simply possessive, like a spoiled child with a favorite toy. "Dunnae pay him any heed, Thomas. We are wed in name only." With that, she started to release Thomas.

"Make no mistake, Ada, ye are mine," William said. "Ye belonged to me the moment ye said yer vows, and when—"

"That's quite enough!" she hurried to cut him off, her neck, face, and ears burning with embarrassment. How dare he! How dare he use her, make her feel so wanted, tell her so cruelly he did not really desire her, and then think to lay claim on her? The unfairness and awfulness of it burned her eyes with unshed tears.

Suddenly, Thomas touched her face with his fingers. "Lass, nae any man is worth yer tears."

"Thomas, dunnae touch my wife!" William roared, and everyone, including Ada, shushed him.

She gently pushed Thomas's fingers away from her cheek. She felt a sudden liking for him, but his touch unsettled her. She suspected it had everything to do with the fact that her body wanted William's touch and no other man's. "I would have to care about William to shed a tear for him. The salt in the air burns my eyes."

Thomas leaned in and whispered, "A verra good story. I shall keep yer secret. Now scoot over and release him, as I'm certain ye ken ye need him, and I'm equally certain time is of the essence in order for us to escape."

She nodded and moved toward William because what Thomas said was true. Freya ran ahead of her, and Hella was still at his side where the disloyal hound had stayed since they'd entered the cave. When Ada stood before him, his heat invading her and his power engulfing her, desire tightened her core. Devil take him. He'd made her a wanton with one joining.

She pressed her lips together on speaking, not trusting herself to successfully hide her tumultuous emotions, but William bent his head toward her. "Ada, I'm sorry."

She struggled to ignore how his breath tickled her neck and made her feel as she untied his wrists and then bent to untie his ankles.

"Ada?"

"What are ye sorry for? For using me or for lying to me about desiring me?" she asked in low tones.

"For both," he whispered. "I'm sorry for both. I did what I had to for the king and to find and save my brother."

Her breath hitched painfully in her lungs, and she grimaced at the ground. She supposed there had been the tiniest part of her that had hoped he would deny that he'd lied to her, that he might say he truly did desire her. A tear slid down her cheek, and she swiped it quickly away, eternally grateful she had turned her face down.

"Ye did what ye must, I suppose." A sudden horrendous thought occurred to her. "Did ye have to sacrifice much? Were ye set to wed a woman ye love?" God above, would he take the woman as his leman, his mistress, keeping Ada as his unwanted wife simply because the king wanted him to control her?

"Nay," he said, his voice tight. She undid the ropes at his ankles, and he shrugged out of them. He started to step away, then turned toward her and grasped her fingers with his own rough, sure ones.

"What are ye doing?" she asked, surprised he would take her hand. The gesture seemed intimate, meant for someone who loved another.

"Keeping ye near, lass. Ye're too valuable to lose," he replied, tugging her toward the cave exit.

His words pricked her pride and slashed at her heart. She jerked her hand away and batted at his when he attempted to reach for her once more. "Have ye stolen many a woman's heart with those flowery words?" she snapped.

"Nay," he said, his tone now equally as terse as hers. "I dunnae have any interest in possessing a woman's heart, Ada."

As his revelation hit her, she bit her tongue on her acerbic reply and turned from him, taking a step toward the cave exit. But he stopped her forward progress with his hand on her arm. "I'll go first to protect ye," he said.

"I dunnae need yer protection." She tried to tug her arm away and frowned. His grip had become unbreakable.

"Ye do," he answered, his voice brooking no argument. "How did ye get close enough to the guard to disable him?"

"I kissed him," she slung out, perversely happy to be able to say that to this man who'd just wounded her so. "And then I hit him on the head, which knocked him out, and then I tied him up and stuffed his mouth with cloth."

William's fingers twitched around her wrist. "We will talk about the kiss later," he growled, moving in front of her to tug her out of the cave, but when he reached the entrance, he stumbled on the guard she'd left there, who now was awake and moaning into the cloth. William released his hold on her as he righted himself, and when he turned to her, his face was illuminated by a slash of moonlight and she could see that he was glowering at her. "Ye might have told me ye left the man at the entrance."

She scowled back as she felt Freya rub against the side

of her leg to come to stand by her. "What did ye think, William? That I picked up the guard twice my size and carried him? Mayhap I slung him over my shoulder."

"Cheeky wench," he growled.

Thomas, Esther, and Maximilian came out of the cave. "We need to flee," Thomas said, almost as if scolding the two of them for bickering.

"Aye," William agreed. "They took my sword."

"Mine, as well," Thomas said.

"These swords?" Ada asked, grinning and motioning to the pile of weapons it had taken her two trips to bring down to the cave.

"I could kiss ye!" Thomas declared.

"Thomas," William said, the one word a lethal warning.

Thomas grinned, bent down, and picked up his sword. "I said I *could*, nae that I would."

And then, quite unexpectedly, William turned to her and pulled her close, his lips descending upon hers. Warmth infused her. Her belly tightened, her heart fluttered, and her hands went to his neck of their own volition, and just as yearning gripped her, he set her away, leaving her feeling adrift in a sea of longing and confusion.

Why did Ada have to be so alluring? And now that he knew she supported the king and had not purposely sent Bram to his doom, it was hard—so hard—to keep a distance, but that's exactly what he needed to do. The king had said William's mother had left his father because he was always off on missions, and William's life would take the same path. Would Ada one day leave him? He shoved the thought away. Not only did he need to concentrate on escaping and what needed to be done but wondering if Ada would one day flee meant he was forming an attachment, and he did not want that. God, but he wanted her. She was worse than the apple in the Garden of Eden; she was the Garden if the whole thing were forbidden and dangerous.

Concentrate. He forced his gaze from her lips, which were beckoning to him to kiss them again, and met her confusion-filled eyes. He supposed he'd caused that. He suddenly felt like the worst sort of scoundrel. He had told her that he didn't desire her, and then he had kissed her. He needed to keep his hands and his lips to himself. "Ye did nae get my bow and arrow perchance?"

She smirked at him and motioned to his left. "Perchance, I did."

He glanced down to find Hella with his bow clutched in her mouth. He laughed and patted the hound's head before relieving her of his bow and picking up his arrows to stash them. "How did ye come to get the weapons?" he asked, looking around for the best route of escape, which appeared to be to the left of the cave where the land rose to the woods. That would set them in the direction of the cave where Lannrick and Grant were waiting for him and Thomas to return.

"I snuck past a sleeping guard into the weapons chamber," she replied, pride in her voice.

"Ye should nae have taken such a risk," William said, fear for her gripping him.

Esther snorted. "That is like telling the lass nae to think of the dangers to herself. All her life—"

"We need to go. Now," he interrupted. It was true, but he also did not want to know any more personal details about Ada. They made her seem ever more real, ever more alluring.

"Aye, of course," the woman replied, looking hurt.

Regret rippled through him, which annoyed him. Now he was having soft emotions for some woman he did not know at all? What in God's name was wrong with him? It felt like some box that'd he'd locked away inside him had been unlatched. He mentally slammed the box shut. "Ada, I need to get the names of the other three lairds who—"

"Laird Bard, Laird Lindsey, and Laird Stone," she said, as if she had read his thoughts.

"How did ye—"

"'Tis a gut feeling—an overwhelming, nauseating gut feeling."

He pressed a hand to her cheek without realizing what he was doing until the deed was done. The thought that he should pull away occurred to him, but he wouldn't. He sensed her need for reassurance, and everything in him compelled him to offer it to her. "Does it hurt ye, this feeling?"

"Nae too much."

He wanted to cup her face in his hands and brush a gentle kiss across her lips. Instead, he allowed his palm to linger upon her soft, warm skin for a moment before pulling away and looking to Thomas. "We'll have to split up once we get to Lannrick and Grant."

Ada swayed beside him, and he slipped an arm around her waist, pulling her soft body against his.

"My lady!" Esther exclaimed.

Maximilian, who'd been quiet, rushed over to them. "Lady Ada, are ye all right?"

Ada shuddered, but nodded.

"Did ye get another feeling?" Thomas asked before William could.

"Aye. Someone is coming."

William shoved Ada behind him while he drew his sword, but she stepped around him and swung to face him. Placing her hand on his chest, she looked at him, her gaze boring into him. "Ye will nae make it out of here alive if ye dunnae let me go into the woods to meet who comes. They seek me, and if I meet them, they'll nae come to the cave, and ye can—"

"Nay," he said flatly, the very notion of allowing her to endanger herself to protect him turning his blood to ice.

She tilted her head back, her eyes pleading. "Ye will save me because ye must do so to save the king. I ken it...here." She placed a hand on her heart.

"I dunnae give a damn what ye ken—"

"Thomas," she said, releasing William and turning from him. "Thomas, ye must heed me. Aid me. Ye are the only one who can stop the Steward, the only one who can get close to him and his sons, and if ye die here—"

"Go!" Thomas ordered.

William recoiled at the betrayal, and it cost him precious seconds. He reached toward Ada, but she had gotten just far enough away that his fingers only brushed her skirts as she fled. "Freya, attack!" she called as she moved.

Thomas bounded toward him, and William had every intention of knocking the man down with all the murderous rage he felt, but suddenly Freya plowed into his legs with such shocking strength that he was propelled forward into Thomas, who swept William's legs out from under him. He landed hard on his back, all the air rushing from his lungs. For a moment, he lay stunned, listening to Hella whimper and feeling her lick his face. When he finally managed to shake off the daze, he turned his head to glimpse Ada disappearing into the woods above them with Freya fast on her heels.

Thirteen

Ada raced up the hill, her side cramping and breath coming in short gasps. She didn't know who was waiting for her just beyond the crest. Her gut feeling had not told her that, but she did know someone was waiting for her, someone who was not good, someone who wanted to use her. But if she had not come, she had known for certain that Thomas would die, and that he was the key to stopping the Steward. What she didn't know, though she had lied and said she did, was what would happen to her. She had no feelings or instincts about herself. She could be racing to a horrible fate, for all she knew. Maybe she'd already played her part. Those bumbling fairies clearly had not considered that just because Ada was wed and suddenly had instincts about how to aid the king and those who served him, didn't mean that her instincts would protect her from evil men who sought to use her.

Freya barked coming up on Ada's right. Ada glanced down at her loyal hound as she ran, intent on putting distance between herself and William so that he, Thomas, and the others could escape. Just as she reached the top of the hill and the edge of the woods, five men poured onto the path from the left and the right, all holding weapons. In the dawning light, she easily recognized Connor.

"Ye've made things easy for me, Ada," he said. "I was

coming for ye. Who are ye running from?"

Freya barked beside her as Ada answered, her heart pounding so hard that her chest ached. "Brothwell," she automatically said.

Connor nodded. "Ye always have hated him… Now…where is yer new husband? He must die."

Ada sucked in a fearful breath. "He's already dead," she choked out. "Brothwell killed William the moment the vows were said. I'll nae serve Brothwell," she finished, knowing Connor would believe that.

"Then wed me, Ada. Serve my cause. *Our cause.*"

Ada nodded, fearing at any moment that William would come bellowing over the hill and get himself, Thomas, Esther, and Maximilian killed. "We should ride now. Brothwell is on my heels."

"Father Lockeby!" Connor called.

Ada's gut clenched and her pulse quickened as a tall, lithe man she recognized stepped forward. "I thought he was one of yer warriors," Ada said.

Connor smiled. "He is a warrior, but he's also my priest from my castle. I brought him with me, just in case I had need if things did nae go my way. I'm always prepared, Ada."

Dear God above! Was he planning on wedding her now?

"How fast can ye wed us?" Connor asked, as if he reached into her head and snatched her thought from it.

"If there are men coming for the lass," Lockeby said, "we best ride and do the deed once we're away."

"Aye," Ada agreed, dizzy with fear. "Ye have me. Ye're nae going to lose me."

Connor gave a swift nod, then raised his hand and swirled it around, an obvious signal for his men to retreat.

They faded quickly into the woods as if they had never been there. Connor turned to Ada and held out his hand. "Come, lass, ye'll ride with me. My horse is just through the trees."

"Where are we going?" Ada asked, fear rising in her. She had no sense of what would happen to her, but the intuition she had about Connor was not at all good.

"We'll ride to my home, wed along the way, and gather the rest of my troops. Then, with yer help, I'll kill the king."

Freya nuzzled her hand, and Ada glanced down, knowing the hound would not be able to keep up once they rode, though Freya was an excellent tracker and could likely follow her scent if she did not fall too far behind. Still, Freya would also likely be in danger when she tried to protect Ada, which she did not doubt her loyal hound would do. "I'll just say goodbye to my dog," Ada said, bending down before Connor could protest. She hugged Freya to her and whispered in her ear, "Go to William."

"Come!" Connor demanded from above her, impatience in his voice.

Ada stood, nudging Freya with her foot, and the dog reluctantly and slowly started away from Ada. Connor made a grab for Ada when she did not immediately take his offered hand. As his fingers closed around her wrist, a wave of gut feelings hit her: Thomas would lay siege to the Steward's castle, four of the Steward's sons would be locked in a dungeon, and finally, William would fall from a great height. The feelings stopped, and she began to shake. If William reached Connor, William would die.

Her instincts urged her to run with Connor, to put as much distance as she could between him and William, but dizziness suddenly overcame her, nausea striking and bright specks of light appearing in her vision just before everything went black.

"I should kill ye!" William said, shoving Thomas roughly off him and bounding to his feet.

"Kill him later if ye must," Esther snapped. "We need to go after Ada!"

Beside Esther, Maximilian sniffled and looked as if he was fighting tears.

William glanced in the direction in which Ada had disappeared. "If she is hurt—" He stopped, having to swallow back a tide of emotions and clench his hands into fists. There was no time to waste. He locked his gaze on Thomas. "Go to the cave. Take Esther and the boy with ye. Leave them with Lannrick to take to his home to be kept safe. Send Grant after me." Grant was an exceptional tracker and fighter, and if anyone could aid William, it would be Grant. "Then make yer way to the MacLeod holding and get aid in laying siege to the Steward's castle."

"I'm sorry, William," Thomas said.

"Ye should be," William growled. "Ye may have just sacrificed Ada for the king."

William's eyes widened at his own words, as did Thomas's. Hella started barking, and Esther grinned as did Maximilian.

Thomas nodded. "Ye'll save her. I ken it."

He would, and nae simply because he must for the king. And that scared him more than any enemy he'd ever faced. They moved up the hill together, Esther and Maximilian behind them, Hella by William's side. They got to the crest, and William felt as if a hand squeezed his chest when Ada was nowhere to be seen but Freya trotted toward them.

Hella immediately began to howl, as did Freya, and the dogs shot toward each other. A sense of terrible foreboding twisted through William, and at the look of fear on Maximilian's face, that feeling of doom increased. Thomas put a hand on William's shoulder. "I can come back with Grant and send Lannrick to—"

"Nay," William interrupted. "I'll nae allow Ada to have put herself at risk needlessly. Go now."

With a nod, Thomas turned. Maximilian fell immediately behind Thomas, but Esther hesitated. She came quickly to William and grabbed his hands. "I was there the day the fae gave Ada the gift, closest to them when they tried to right the mess they had made."

William's brow furrowed. "Tried to right the mess?"

Esther waved a hand. "'Tis a long story for another time. But I ken something that nae anyone else does, nae even Ada. I told her father, but he made me vow to keep it secret until the day I thought I had met the man that would make it so."

William frowned, unsure what Esther was trying to tell him and impatient to go after Ada. "Make what so?"

"To set the gift to rights. The fairies' arguing mucked up the gifts they gave Ada. They said so that day, but I was the only one who heard it."

A bad feeling took hold of William. "Are ye saying Ada's gift is nae working properly?"

"Aye, 'tis exactly what I'm saying," Esther replied. "Two sacrifices must be made for the gift to be fully activated—one by Ada and one by the man who thinks to hold her heart. Until this happens and the love is true, the gift will nae have the power it is supposed to."

"By all that's holy," William said. "What sacrifice? I dunnae wish for her heart."

Esther arched her eyebrows. "Dunnae ye? I suggest ye look within yerself." With that, she fell into step behind

Thomas and beside Maximilian, and the three of them hurried in the direction of the cave.

Resisting the urge to rush headlong in a direction that might be the wrong one, William kneeled to see if he could track the path Ada—or whoever had been waiting for her—might have taken. He scanned the dirt and grass, looking for signs of someone having passed this way. He moved down the path, anger rising with each passing moment that he saw nothing, and then a footprint in the mud caught his attention. Then another. And another. Until he counted six sets of footprints. Five of them were much larger than the other. Five men and a woman.

Ada.

He scampered over the ground on his hands and feet, following the six sets of prints up and to the right. But then the prints disappeared into the leaves and grass. Frustration choked him as he scanned the ground. It would be much harder, much slower, to track them over the leaves and sticks. Nearly impossible, unless he was an expert, and he wasn't Grant.

Suddenly, a stick cracked behind him, and he jumped to his feet, swinging around with his sword drawn. He gaped at the sight of Marjorie, dirty, disheveled, and grasping a dagger. "Connor took her," Marjorie said, matter-of-fact. "I was hiding when he and his men came by."

"What were ye—"

"Bram," she interrupted. "I was coming to free ye so ye could rescue Bram, but it seems Ada got to ye before I could. I thought she'd betrayed ye."

William nodded. "As did I." He eyed Marjorie. "It seems nae anyone is quite who they appear to be."

"I love yer brother," Marjorie said, her voice unapologetic. "For him, I will do anything."

"Then he's lucky," William said, meaning it. "Do ye ken where the MacKinney was going?"

"Aye. To his stronghold—Castlerock. He means to wed her."

The notion pumped anger through William's veins. "Well, he kinnae. She's my wife."

"Aye," Marjorie agreed. "But Ada told Connor that ye were dead, that Brothwell killed ye."

Panic rioted within him. She'd offered herself as a sacrifice to protect him. She had to have known that Connor would wed her the first chance he got, thinking to use her and keep her with him. "We'll have to make haste. If ye kinnae keep up, I'll come back for ye."

"I will keep up. I'm fast," Marjorie said, determination vibrating her words. "But, William, ye should ken that Connor has a priest with him. He'll likely—"

"Stop and wed her," William bit out. The anger and worry hit him so intensely that he bellowed his rage as he began to shake. The MacKinney would bed her, thinking Ada had willingly wed him, unless William reached her first.

Fourteen

A sense of disbelief descended upon Ada as she said marriage vows for the second time in three days. She was beyond weary from the nonstop galloping across the countryside, and her body ached all over. She also had a gnawing worry that Freya might have simply decided to follow her, and the knowledge that she needed to find a way to escape Connor pressed on her. She had a very strong sense that the opportunity to run would present itself soon, so she had to maintain the pretense until then. If she did not, Connor would be so livid that he would very likely kill her.

She fought a tide of revulsion as the priest instructed Connor to kiss her and he pressed his mouth to hers. His kiss was nothing like William's and did not sweep her into passion as William's had. *William.* Just thinking his name shot a deep pain to her heart. He would come for her. Of course he would. He needed her to help him save his brother and the king. She wished her gift had nothing to do with why he would come for her. She wished that the possibility she had felt for them had not been a lie.

"Ada, come."

She blinked, staring at Connor's outstretched hand. She did not know what Connor had said to her because of her pondering over William. "Are we riding again so late?"

The desirous look Connor gave her made her stomach dip with anxiety. She could just kick herself for the words that had suggested she wanted to stay here in the woods, to sleep here beside him, giving him the opportunity to—

She could not even think it. Her marriage to William may be one that was forced upon her, but she was wed to him, and at least she desired William. She wanted Connor's touch like she wanted leaches upon her body.

"Nay, we'll bed down here for the night and consummate our marriage." With that, he grabbed her hand and tugged her past his men, who were all snickering. The ill sensation roiling within her became greater with each step she took away from the others and toward the trees. This was her chance to escape! If she could get away from Connor, she could run.

She slid her gaze over the landscape and listened. In the distance, she could hear water rushing. She'd follow the water west, which would take her in the direction of the Iona Nunnery. That was the only place she knew where she would be safe, and the sisters would aid her.

"Connor, do ye have any wine?" she asked, hoping he would leave her to get some. "I'm anxious, and—"

"I brought some with me, Ada." He stopped suddenly and swung her to face him. "Here," he said, reaching into his sporran and bringing out a wine skin, which he opened and offered her. "I thought ye might want some."

That gave her hope. Maybe she could appeal to his softer side. "Connor, I'd rather nae consummate our marriage on the ground. A bed would be so much nicer."

Connor's eyes narrowed upon her. "Ye will bed me, Ada. Ye will nae shame me again."

"Again?" she asked.

He nodded. "Ye chose MacLean, who is nae even a

laird, over me. I've been shamed enough by ye and my mother."

"Yer mother?" She had no notion what Connor was talking about.

"Aye. Do ye think that yer stepbrother is the only bastard of the Steward?"

Ada's mouth slipped open.

"Now ye see," Connor said, his words heavy with sarcasm, "I'm a bastard, too. And ye are my only hope to deal my father the blow he so richly deserves for refusing to acknowledge me. He bed my mother, left her with child, and did nae give a care what happened to her or me. He's nae ever even seen me!"

Pity blossomed inside her. The Steward, it seemed, was a man with much lust and no care for the consequences of that desire. "Connor—"

"Nay!" He cut her off and grabbed her shoulders, his fingers biting into her skin and making her wince. "We will consummate our marriage tonight, and ye will use yer gift to help me become king. Ye are the King Maker! And when I'm king, I'll imprison my father and he'll endure what I had to endure all my life at the hands of the man my mother wed because he was actually willing to pretend I was his. But the lie had a price, Ada. He hated me. Beat me. Until I could nae take any more. I finally killed him, but now it is my true father's turn to pay."

"Connor..." Ada swallowed. She'd not truly seen the pain in Connor, and she regretted that. She touched her free hand to his cheek, the instinct rising in her that she should offer him honesty in this moment, because that is what would save her—and possibly him—but what she needed to say was a hard truth, one she herself did not care for. Unfortunately, that didn't make it any less true. "Without being legitimate, most Scottish lairds will nae ever support ye."

"Ye will make them support me," he said.

She shook her head. "I kinnae. I support King David. I—"

The hit stung like a hundred bees, and the shock of it vibrated down the length of her body. Connor drew back his open palm, his mouth parting with obvious shock at his actions, but then his lips pressed into a thin, hard line. "I am sorry, Ada, but ye kinnae say such things. I kinnae tolerate disloyalty from ye."

A strong sense of fear swept over her, leaving gooseflesh across her skin. She clenched her teeth on the desire to scream her frustration. Those fairies had given her a faulty gift—or mayhap it was just her. But whatever was wrong with her power, all her instincts were screaming at her to run, and she was going to do just that the moment Connor released her wrist. She had to get him to lower his guard.

"Do ye forgive me, Ada?"

She nodded. "Aye. It's just that my father supported King David, and—"

"Ye wish to follow yer father." Connor smiled. "Ye are a good person, Ada, and ye will make me good."

The strange wistfulness of his tone filled her with unease. It seemed he had imagined a great deal about what she would do for him, *could* do for him. Pity for him battled with her fear as he raked his gaze over her. "Come," he said, tugging on her so that she had no choice but to follow. He led her along a meandering path through thick woods, and as they walked, the rushing sound of water became louder. A chill had set in the air as the sun was mostly gone from the sky, and she shivered from concern as well as cold.

"I used to hide out here," he said suddenly, breaking the silence.

She frowned. "Are we on yer land?"

"Close. 'Tis Furquart land."

She knew enough about where things were located to know that the Furquart holding was about a sennight's journey from Trethway Island where Bram was being kept prisoner. Her stomach clenched with the knowledge. "Why did ye hide here?" she asked, curious and hoping if she got him talking about his past he'd become distracted and she could somehow get away from him. She'd succeeded in protecting Thomas, William, Esther, and Maximilian from certain death, but she'd run directly into the arms of trouble for her efforts.

Connor led her through a break in the trees to a space that overlooked a cliff that dropped to the ocean below. To the right of them, in the distance, she could see a waterfall. That must have been the rushing water she'd heard. He started to pull her toward the edge of the cliff, and uneasiness coursed through her. She was going over that ledge. Very soon.

A chill gripped her and made her shiver. She had to get away from Connor. His hand came suddenly to the back of her neck, his fingers curling tighter. "Look down," he ordered.

Her heart thundered with the tip of her feet upon the edge of the cliff. The wind began to blow, making her hair flap around her face and her gown flutter. She reached a trembling hand to grasp her hair as she looked down, hoping that if she did as Connor bid her, he would release her. Her breath caught as she took in the drop to the churning sea below. The sheer span of it sent her spinning. A storm was brewing on the water, which seemed to match the turmoil swirling around and within her.

"What is it ye wish me to see?" she asked, her voice

shaking.

"I stood here many a times as a lad, crying, shaking, trying to find the bravery to simply jump and end the pain, but two things kept me from jumping, Ada: my mother's love for me, and ye."

She frowned. "Me?"

"Aye. My mother was at yer home the day the fae gave ye the gift, ye see, so she kenned ye could make me king. Every night before bed, she would tell me the story of that day and remind me that, one day, when I ruled the land, I would make both my stepfather and my real father suffer, and I would lift my mother to the status she deserved. I bided my time waiting for yer father to announce he was accepting suitors for ye, and when he fell ill and Brothwell took his place, I despaired. But I also began to plot to simply steal ye. I sensed we were meant to be."

Connor's mind was twisted. The surety of it hit Ada in the gut.

"But then Brothwell announced the competition," he went on, "and I kenned all would be well. Except ye surprised me, wounded me, angered me—"

"Stop! Ye're hurting me!" she cried out as his grip on her neck became like a vise.

"Aye," he replied, his tone as chilly as the wind. "As ye hurt me when ye chose MacLean. Why did ye nae want me?"

Her mind raced with what to say. She had to convince him she wanted him. "I do want ye," she said, wincing at how false she sounded.

"Liar!" he roared. Sliding his hand quickly from her neck to her wrist, which he encircled, he maneuvered her forward so that she was leaning over the ledge of the cliff, looking at the ocean below. "I should drop ye for picking him over me!" he bellowed.

She screamed with fright, the overwhelming sense that someone was about to die consuming her. "Connor, please!" she cried. "If ye drop me, how will I help ye become king? Think of why ye wed me. Think of what ye truly want."

"Attack! We're under attack!" a man's voice called from the woods they had just passed through.

Connor's grip grew even tighter. Ada looked over her shoulder to catch his gaze, but he was focused on the woods. She felt a slight tug as he started to pull her toward him, but then William and another man broke through the clearing, and Connor stilled. "Ye lied to me," he said, his tone accusing and hurt flashing across his face. Her gift may not have been working well, but in that moment, she knew exactly what was going to happen. A scream ripped from her throat, her very soul, as Connor released his hold on her and she began to fall toward the water.

"Ada!" William bellowed as the MacKinney loosed his hold on her and she fell over the cliff. He ran toward the devil, Grant on his heels.

"I've got the MacKinney," Grant yelled as he raised his sword, already bloodied from the five guards William and Grant had just battled through. "Ye go after yer lass!"

William lunged left as the MacKinney barreled toward him, and Grant flew into the man. William did not glance back to see who was winning the fight. Instead, he ran to the ledge and threw down his sword. He scanned the water for Ada, and seeing her tossed up by a wave, gasping and arms flailing, he dove for her.

The air whistled by, stealing all thoughts but one: *save her*. His hands sliced through the cold water, and when it covered his head, chest, and legs, it stole not only his breath but his ability to place himself for a moment. Panic tried to edge in, but he willed it away. He'd done this before— fought his way out of a restless sea. As a child, as a lad, and as a man training with the Dark Riders.

He stilled as much as he could, allowing the sea to claim him so he could become one with it. The waves pulled at him as the need for air burned his lungs and dizziness claimed his head. He clenched his jaw in an attempt to focus. The dizziness and the burn would subside the closer he got to the surface. But where was it? The tug was to his left, and without hesitation, he swam that direction, breaking the surface to gulp in air just as a wave crashed over his head and tossed him back under. He was propelled backward, his legs scraping against the rock of the cliffside, and then he was yanked violently forward. His body collided with something, and instinctually, he grabbed it so as not to hit too hard. And then he realized he had Ada.

She wasn't fighting him or clinging to him. She was simply limp.

Christ...

Desperation burrowed into his bones as he wrapped an arm around her waist and fought his way back to the surface. When he broke through, he gulped in a breath, located the shore, and turned them in the right direction. This time, instead of being tossed back under, he rode the wave into the shore until his feet touched the bottom. He clasped Ada to him, sweeping her off her feet and up against his chest. He trudged through the water, enraged at the slow progress.

"Stay with me, Ada," he pleaded, shoving back clumps

of wet hair from her forehead, only to discover a cut. "God above," he muttered, glad the wound did not look severe. When he reached the shore, he picked up his pace and ran the rest of the way out of the water. He laid her down on dry land and tilted her onto her side before he pushed into her stomach and chest several times, as he'd once seen a desperate mother do when her child had gotten caught underwater.

He did it again and again, his fear for Ada making him tremble violently. "Ada, come on, lass!" He slipped her onto her back and straddled her hips so he could press both his hands into her chest over her heart. He did it three more times, bellowing his rage, and then she began to cough, water spewing from her mouth.

He laughed with relief, and without thought, he leaned down and pressed urgent kisses to her forehead, nose, and cheeks. "Ada, are ye all right?"

"I will be when ye get off me, ye big Scot," she said through her coughing. "Ye're crushing me!"

Laughing more, he scooted off her, but as he did, he heard the distinct sound of a voice calling his name. He jumped up, moving his hand to where he sheathed his sword, only to remember he had thrown it down to go after Ada. "Get behind me," he ordered, reaching out to clasp her arm and yank her up. "I'll die before I let MacKinney touch—"

"Ye think I did nae take care of MacKinney?" Grant interrupted, emerging from between two rocks in a slash of moonlight. "I'd be offended if I was nae so weary."

"He's dead?" William asked, feeling Ada sagging against him. He pulled her near. She was so cold and she trembled so intensely that he wrapped his arms around her, half expecting her to protest, but she buried her head against his chest and let out a sigh.

"Aye, he's dead. Shall I hold this?" Grant asked, indicating William's sword, which he must have gone to reclaim for William.

As much as he did not want to loosen his grip on Ada, he needed to have his sword in hand. "Nay." He reached out and took the sword as Ada looked up at him, then to Grant.

"Who are ye?" Ada asked, the suspicion in her tone making William smile.

"Grant Macaulay," Grant replied.

"He helped me track ye here," William explained.

Suddenly, Ada tensed. "Connor's other men?"

"Dead," William and Grant answered at the same time.

Ada sucked in a breath, shuddering against William. The need to protect her had been constant since he had met her, but a new feeling sprang up—the wish to comfort her. That was a desire he absolutely should not allow, and once he was certain she was recovered from her fall, he'd stop the comforting and the holding. Though holding her, so soft, did feel good.

Ada set her palm against William's chest and tilted her head back to look up at him. He could just barely make out her worried expression in the moonlight. "Esther and Maximilian?"

"They are being escorted to the safety of the Kinntoch holding by Lannrick Kinntoch, son of the Kinntoch laird."

"How—"

"Lannrick was awaiting me in a cave near yer home," he replied, thinking he knew what she had been about to ask. "As was Thomas, before I was forced to retrieve him to prove myself to Brothwell, and Grant here."

Ada's nose wrinkled with what appeared to be confusion, but then she asked, "What of Thomas?" The concern in her voice was clear.

"Safely away," William replied. "He should be at the MacLeod holding by now to seek aid in taking down the Steward and his sons."

Ada nodded. "Hella and Freya?"

William shook his head, his gut tightening with worry. "Freya came back to us, but we had to ride and could nae go slower for them."

Ada nodded. "They will find us. They are incredible trackers."

Relief washed over William, making him scowl. Why in God's name did he care so very much that the dogs would find them?

"MacLean was like a man possessed to reach ye," Grant said, filling the silence.

"Aye," she said dryly, "of course he was. He dunnae wish to lose me because of my gift."

He wanted to dispute her, but he clamped his jaw shut. Her gift had nothing to do with why he had come after her, but it was best for them both that she thought it did. She stiffened in his arms, and he knew he'd likely hurt her, but if he was to keep a barrier between them, then he needed to maintain his silence in such matters.

"Ye may be interested to ken," she said, extracting herself from his embrace and stepping away from him, "that I believe my so-called gift is nae working properly. So, ye scurrilous beast—" They were back to that, were they? She poked him hard in the chest. "I dunnae ken how much good I will be to ye. What think ye of that?" she demanded. "Ye may have just risked yer life to save me and I'm nae worth it."

Her words infuriated him. He cupped her face, ignoring

the fact that they were not alone. "Ye have worth far greater than the gift," he told her, shaking with his struggle to hold back from saying more. "Hear me now—" her eyes had gone very wide, but she nodded "—I kenned when I came after ye that yer gift dunnae yet have the power it was intended to, and that it likely will nae ever have it."

"What?" she said, her voice filled with an odd mix of confusion and wonder.

He'd honestly not meant to tell her. Grant already knew. He'd told him after Grant had caught up with him and Marjorie—

"God's blood," he muttered, just then remembering that they'd left Marjorie by the rocks marking the border of the Furquart land with only the horses and her dagger. "We have to go fetch Marjorie," he said, turning. He expected Ada to follow him, but for a small lass, she was surprisingly good at digging in her heels. She did not budge. Oh, he could have moved her with force, but he did not wish to do that to her unless she became too stubborn.

"Did Marjorie come willingly?"

The way Ada phrased the question made William think she'd known about Marjorie and Bram. "She came willingly. Did ye ken about my brother and yer stepsister?"

"I had my suspicions, but Marjorie only confirmed them the day of the tournament. I'm glad to discover her love for Bram is true and deep enough to risk Brothwell's wrath. Hopefully yer brother feels the same way."

"We will nae ken until we rescue Bram, so come—" He tugged her a little, but she shook her head at him.

"Ye still need to explain how ye kenned my gift dunnae have the power the fae intended, though I suspect they simply bumbled it." She did not look overly surprised with his revelation.

"What alerted ye that something was off?" he asked.

"Well, my instincts dunnae seem quite as clear as I'd expected they would be—or should be."

"Well," he said, but then halted, the cut on her forehead catching his attention when the moonlight shone there. He reached for his plaid and ripped off a strip of it, and then he raised his arms to bind her head.

She leaned away from him. "What are ye doing to me?" she asked with a suspicious lilt.

Grant chuckled at that, to which William scowled. "I'm simply binding yer forehead, lass. Ye've a cut."

Frowning, she raised her hand to her forehead, touched the wound with her fingertips, and then hissed. "I've a cut."

"Is that nae what I just said?" he asked, incredulous.

"Aye," she replied, "but I've learned nae to trust ye."

He supposed he deserved that, so he did not respond. Grant, however, did.

"Ye can trust him," Grant told her.

Ada simply harrumphed, snatched the piece of plaid from William's hand, and tied it around her own forehead. She looked quite simply, piercingly lovely, even with a strip of his plaid tied around her bleeding head. He wished he did not find her so very bonny.

"Ye were saying about my gift…" she nudged.

"Actually, I was nae because ye keep interrupting me," William said, rolling his shoulders and then his neck.

"I'm all silence now," she assured him. He snorted, given she'd just talked. She scowled but did not speak.

"Esther told me there was a second requirement for yer gift to truly activate. Nae anyone ever kenned it but her because she was standing so close to the fae when they quietly said the words the day of yer blessing. She confessed it to yer father, but he made her vow her silence."

"What was it?" Ada asked, her voice little more than a fearful whisper.

He reached toward her and gently grasped her shoulders, hoping it was a comfort, and squeezed. He had to get a hold on this incessant need to reassure her. It kept driving him to do things before his mind caught up to remind him not to. Part of him wished he'd said nothing now, considering what he knew, but he could not let her feel she had no worth beyond the gift. He took her by the elbow and led her away from Grant, who had been blessedly and wisely silent. "Two sacrifices must be made," he said, keeping his tone low even though Grant already knew it.

"What do ye mean?" she asked.

"I would assume the fairies meant acts of sacrifice for another. One by ye…" He stopped, the realization that she'd made a sacrifice already stealing his ability to speak for a moment. "Ye ran straight into danger to protect Thomas."

"And ye," she blurted, then promptly bit down on her lip.

"Me?" He winced at the amazement in his voice. "Why would running to Connor have protected me?"

"Because," she said, her eyelashes veiling her eyes, "I had a vision of ye falling from a great height and I thought to protect ye from it, but—"

"It was ye that fell," he said. "I…I dove."

"To save me," she finished softly. Then she gasped. "Do ye think my gift will now work as it's meant to? Were ye the other person that Esther said would need to make a sacrifice?"

"Nae me," he said, the two words coming out clipped, strained.

"Then who?"

He slid his teeth back and forth, loath to tell her, but he

would not lie. He could not be so dishonorable.

"Who, William?" she demanded, her voice louder.

"Does it matter?" he asked, fumbling around for a way out of the mess he'd made.

She cocked her head and plunked her hands on her hips as if she were disassembling his inner thoughts by staring at him. The last thing he needed or wanted was Ada in his head. Releasing her, he started to turn away, but she caught his forearm. "William?"

His name was a quiet plea. How the devil was any man supposed to resist a plea from Ada?

He swallowed hard. "The man who wishes to hold yer heart," he said.

She recoiled as if he'd hit her, and then her lips pressed into a thin line. "I see," she said quietly. "Then my gift most definitely will nae work as it should yet. More's the pity for ye. Or should I say for yer brother?"

"Are ye trying to provoke me?" he asked, stunned.

"Of course nae," she said, then spun on her heel and marched toward the woods.

Grant shook his head at William. "Ye are in trouble with that one. She'll have ye around her wee pinkie sooner than ye realize."

William made a derisive sound from his throat, though he'd already had the same thought. Now he was more intent than before not to allow himself to become close to her.

Fifteen

Ada heard Hella and Freya before she saw them or Marjorie. The joy that exploded in her chest that her hounds were safe and had found her sent her running the remainder of the distance to the dogs. When she reached them, she offered a stunned-looking Marjorie a faint smile and fell to her knees to hug both Hella and Freya. The hounds bounded into her, knocking her onto her back and licking her face, most specifically her head that was bandaged. She groaned as leaves and ice crunched underneath her, her banged up body protested, and her teeth began to chatter as a chill started to set in.

"Hella, Freya, off!" William ordered, and to Ada's astonishment, both dogs immediately complied.

When William bent down to help her up, though, the hounds barreled into the back of his legs, pitching him forward so that he barely missed landing on her. Instead, he caught himself with his right palm, but it slid right out from under him on the icy ground. He landed with a grunt and a thud on his side, facing Ada. They stared at each other for one long moment, and then burst out laughing, reaching toward each other at the same time. William plucked some leaves from her hair, and she, in turn, snatched a twig from his. When she looked up, Grant and Marjorie were standing over them, staring as if William and Ada were cracked in the head.

Grant was the first to speak. "We should make camp for the night," he said. "We'll need rest for our journey to rescue Bram. Do ye think we can chance a fire?"

"Aye, we're far from the stronghold and deep in the woods," William replied. "Besides, if we dunnae keep warm, we will all freeze to death."

"We'll need to eat, as well, seeing that we've nae eaten a thing in two days," Grant added.

Ada's eyes widened. "Two days! Heaven above, why nae?" Connor's men had fed her, albeit quickly and not much.

"MacLean would nae stop; he said there was nae time. I'll go hunt some food." Grant smiled, though she could tell he was trying not to.

"I'll help," Marjorie piped up, scrambling behind Grant.

Ada wanted to speak with Marjorie, but it would have to wait. She glanced swiftly at William, who avoided her gaze, and her heart gave a little leap. She would have tried to suppress it so as not to, once more, have hope where none likely existed, except she could not. William had raced into danger, tracked her for days, without food, and without sleep, by the bleary-eyed look of him. All the while he also had known her gift was not working fully. And he had dived headfirst into the rough water for her! It was a sacrifice, to be sure, but he did not want her heart.

Did he?

God's blood, she was a foolish lass. Of course he didn't. He'd told her as much, and though they were wed and had—She blushed with the memory of the joining. Still, they were strangers, even if their bodies had joined as if their souls had waited an eternity. She pressed her lips together on her fanciful thoughts and smoothed her wet gown, giving herself an excuse to look away from William. When he stared at her with his probing eyes, it felt as if he could read her thoughts. She blew out a long breath. She was beyond foolish. She had such a grand imagination. Her father had always said so. Of course William could not read her mind!

Forcing herself to look at him, she froze. He was most definitely watching her intently, and well, it looked like yearning lit his eyes. Was she seeing what she wanted, or was desire actually there? His gaze moved slowly over her body, making her belly tighten, and when their eyes met once more, a definite primitive expression had settled on his face. Her heart jolted as he stiffened and made to sit up, but then Hella bounded on top of his chest and pushed him back down to the ground. She tensed, thinking he might become angry, but he let out a hearty laugh and hugged Hella's neck. A joyous laugh escaped Ada.

He grinned, his gaze coming to her once more, but this time soft as a caress. "Ye have a lovely, enticing laugh."

She cocked an eyebrow. "Enticing how?"

He waved a dismissive hand. "It dunnae matter."

He'd raised his guard, like a true warrior. She couldn't see it, but she could feel it.

"I should gather wood and make a fire," William said.

Ada eyed him as he remained there, lying prone under Hella. In the moonlight, he looked content, as if he was in no hurry. Suddenly Freya licked Ada's hand, and it almost seemed like Freya's way of letting Ada know she agreed. But that was impossible and ridiculous. Nevertheless, her gut told her it was so. She patted Freya and could not resist teasing William. "Then I suppose ye should pry yerself from under that mangy—"

Hella barked, interrupting Ada. William gave Hella a

vigorous rub. "Dunnae speak ill of my hound."

"Yer hound?" Ada said, excitement coursing through her. He'd claimed not to like dogs, but it was more than clear he had a developed a fondness for Hella, and if he could develop an attachment for Ada's hound so quickly, could he not develop one for her? She bit her lip. There she went again, being fanciful. Even so, the idea lodged in her heart like a fragile flower.

"I did nae say *my* hound," he denied, quite like someone who did not want to form attachments to anything. Ada had to bite her cheek not to grin.

"Ye most certainly did say *yer* hound," Ada happily informed him.

"A reasonable slip of the tongue," he replied, though his voice held concern. She watched, trying to contain her growing, likely unreasonable hope, as William gave Hella a gentle nudge to move her off him, then got to his feet and extended his hand to Ada. She grasped his large hand, and his warmth made her sigh. How could he be so warm when it was so cold out?

He grasped her other hand with his free one, and then captured both her hands between his own. He brought them up to his lips and then blew onto the tips of her fingers. Spirals of pleasure danced up her fingers, over her palms, and up her arms to her heart. She had the sudden wish for him to take her fingers into his mouth and suck on them much the way he had her breasts. Good heavens, William MacLean really had made her wanton! She bit her bottom lip on the wish to smirk, because she realized she did not at all mind being wanton if it was with him, her husband. She restrained a groan. She was not only fanciful, she was daft!

"Ye're freezing, lass," he said, his voice low and holding

a sensual promise. Did he know how he sounded? She doubted it.

"Aye," she admitted, her numb toes curling in her slippers when he blew on her hands again.

"Stay here," he said, his tone now rough, as if he was struggling to contain something within.

He released her hands and strode through the shadows to his horse. A moment of silence ensued, and then he came into bleary view again. When he drew near, she realized he was holding a blanket. He came behind her, his heat circling her and her senses jumping at his nearness. He laid the soft blanket on her shoulders, and then his hands rested there, so reassuring and comforting. Before she knew what she was doing, she had leaned back against his chest.

A rough groan rumbled from deep within him, and then his hands skimmed lightly over the dip in her waist to encircle her. His arms settled around her midriff before he pulled her flush against the length of his body. Even if she had not felt the proof of his desire pressing into her, she would have known it by his lips, which came to the back of her neck as he brushed her hair away.

"God's blood, Ada, ye are too much to resist."

"Then dunnae," she said, boldness coursing through her thicker than her blood. She yearned for him. It was a hot, frightening thing to feel so much for a man who may never give her his heart or even want hers.

She gasped as it slammed into her that she *wanted* his heart, wanted to give him hers in return. It seems she'd not yet given up her dreams of love, desire, and children.

His lips blazed a fiery path down her neck, and his hands slid up between her breasts to cup them. Rational thought fled as his fingers tweaked her buds, circling them, rubbing them, making them ache, making *her* ache all over for more. It was the most inappropriate time, and of course they could not… They were not alone, after all.

"Ada?" It was a plea of absolute need matched by his hand sliding low to press between her legs. She hissed her need as he yanked up her wet skirts and settled his fingers to where she throbbed while his other hand continued to blissfully torment her breast. All the cold that had seeped into her was now consumed by the heat of desire for him. She wanted him to touch her, to take her as he had before.

"MacLean!" came Grant's voice from the darkness.

William dropped her skirts and set her away from him so fast that her head spun.

"I've caught a rabbit!" Grant continued, his voice growing closer as he approached. "Get the fire started."

Ada could not see William's expression as his face was cast in shadows, but she was glad because that meant he likely could not see hers. She was grinning, no doubt looking like a fool. A fire had been started, all right, but it would not cook a rabbit.

William sat purposely across from Ada as they all ate the rabbits Grant had caught. He finally felt under control again, as if he could stop himself from touching her, kissing her, pleasuring her, but the shock of how very much he had wanted her, how he had leaped across the distance he was supposed to be putting between them, lingered.

Grant said something to Ada, and she turned her head to listen. Then she laughed. It was lyrical and from her belly and made William want to get up and sit beside her. He scowled into the flickering, popping flames. If he could not control his desire for Ada, how was he supposed to control any attachment to her?

He ground his teeth, contemplating the day and what had happened. Finally finding her and then watching her fall off the cliff had felt as if a hand had been driven through his gut to twist his insides. He'd not considered any danger to himself when he had dived into the water after her, and desperation had consumed him when he'd realized she was not breathing. One who possessed no attachment to another would not feel that way.

Esther's words came to him as Ada, Grant, and Marjorie's murmured conversation faded almost completely. *Two sacrifices… One by Ada and one by the man who thinks to hold her heart.* Ada had sacrificed for him, and then he had sacrificed for her. But he did not want to possess her heart. Did he? Was he such a fool? Was he so weak to need the affection of another, even knowing people one trusted, people one loved, always seemed to leave?

The last memory of his mother sprang into his head. She'd sat beside him on his bed, brushing her hand through his hair and singing him a song to help him sleep. Then she'd kissed his forehead and whispered that she'd see him the next morning. It had been so easy for her to tell the lie, to leave him without looking back, without even saying goodbye. Even if there was a small part of him that might want Ada's heart, that might long for affection, he had to lock that part of him away.

With that in mind, when they were all finished eating, he threw himself into creating shelters for each of them to sleep in. If Grant or Marjorie thought it odd that there were four shelters instead of three, both of them wisely kept any comments to themselves. By the time he was done, the day had caught up to him and he was exhausted. After bidding the others a quick good night—and specifically avoiding

Ada's gaze, which he could feel on him—he left the three of them chatting by the fire and he made his way into his shelter.

He expected sleep to come quickly, but his body ached for Ada, and that kept him awake, along with the occasional sound of her enticing laughter. It didn't help that the ground was like ice, and he'd given his only blanket to Ada. The thought that she might be cold tonight, with the dropping temperatures and the threat of snow, had him sitting up, but he forced himself back down. He could not lie beside Ada and offer her warmth. He'd never keep his hands to himself, and until he could control the weakness that was making him want to let her in, he could not touch her.

Once they rescued Bram at Trethway Island, he would take Ada to the king and then to the home the king had promised to give him where Ada could live in and be kept safe. After she was settled there, William would depart. He stared up at the sliver of moonlight he could see through the branches he'd fashioned around him and above him. Once he was separated from Ada for a time, he was certain that controlling his emotions would become easier, so when he saw her again, they could enjoy the carnal side of their relationship without his risking her seeping into places he could not allow her to be. It did not escape his notice that his decision did not fill him with warmth but a chill that matched the iciness of the ground upon which he lay.

Sixteen

William awoke with a start, something cold hitting his nose. And then his cheeks. And lips. And forehead. He swiped a hand across his face, his stiff body protesting the movement. Opening his eyes, he rubbed his freezing, wet fingertips together. It was snowing. The realization had him on his feet and out of his shelter in a breath. But with one step forward, he tripped over Hella, who was sitting right in front of his shelter, barely visible in the night with her coat that matched the snow. She stirred, lifting her head, her eyes seeming to glisten like steel as she looked at him.

"Were ye standing guard for me?" he asked, shaking his head. Dogs, even one as smart as Hella obviously was, could not understand him. As if she had heard his thoughts, Hella sprang to her feet and jumped up to put her front paws on his chest. After he gave her a quick pat, she got down and, turning, strode straight over to another shelter. Ada had to be in that one because Freya lay outside of it, but when Hella reached her, Freya rose and both hounds started to whine.

"Shh, ye daft dogs," he ordered, closing the distance between his shelter and Ada's. As he strode across the space, he noted the fire was dead, and a quick glance toward the other two shelters in the distance confirmed what he had suspected would happen. Grant was sitting up, legs crossed in front of him and arms crossed over his chest. The man was asleep against a tree beside the shelter that must have housed Marjorie.

William hesitated outside Ada's shelter when he saw that her gown had been hung over the two closest tree limbs he'd driven into the ground. It was serving as a makeshift door. If her gown was hanging there, though, that meant she was inside in only her léine. The mere thought of her clothed in only her undergarments stirred his lust. He inhaled a long, slow breath, battling the desire back, and then he looked between Hella and Freya. "I'm only going in to ensure she's nae freezing." Even as the dogs both seemed to answer him with a lick to his hand and a nuzzle against his leg, he had to chuckle at his inability to stop talking to the hounds.

He shoved back the gown, which had chunks of ice clinging to the material. The light from the moon was mostly blocked by the branches fastened above the shelter, which made it too dark to really make out Ada's form until he kneeled beside her, and his heart jerked.

The top curve of one bare, delicate shoulder peeked out from the blanket she'd wrapped around herself, but other than that, all he could see was her nose, eyes, and forehead. The strip of cloth she'd tied there was gone, and her glorious hair fanned around her. And then he realized she was trembling badly, and her teeth were chattering.

"Ada?" he whispered, not wanting to wake her if she was asleep.

She stirred, turning from her side onto her back. In the moonlight, she looked as white as the snow falling from the sky. "Aye?" she managed through her clacking teeth.

Worry overcame him, and he set a hand to her forehead, thinking mayhap she'd caught fever. "Ye're freezing," he said, relieved.

He must have sounded it, too, because she said, "Th-th-that is a verra odd thing to b-be glad about." She paused, shivering uncontrollably. "Wh-what are ye doing in here? I k-k-ken ye dunnae wish to be anywhere near me."

Even with all the stuttering, he could discern the hurt in her voice. But he did want to be here with her. Too much. And that was the main problem as he saw it. So instead of addressing the truth of the matter, he assessed her and made a decision. She needed him to keep warm this night, so she didn't truly get a chill and then a fever, and it was his duty as her husband to protect her. He would have to simply restrain himself.

"Open up the blanket for me," he said, praying she'd not demand he answer her question.

"What for?" she said, suspicion in her tone.

He found the edge of the blanket in the dark and tugged it out of her grasp.

"Oh!" she gasped. He suspected the freezing night air had hit her skin. "Why did ye do that, ye big Scottish beast?"

Somehow her insults did not bother him in the least. "Because," he replied, pulling the blanket all the way back on one side and down on the other so he could lie on it facing her and then wrap them both in it. "I need to do this." He made quick work of situating himself, rewrapping them both in the blanket, and then pulling her body flush against his so that her cheek was pressed against his bare chest, her hair tickling his nose, and her breasts—ah, God above, her breasts had been created to tempt a man to ruination—were also snug against his skin. Through the thin material of her léine, he could feel that her buds had hardened into twin peaks.

"Dunnae move," he growled huskily, his control feeling as taut as a bow about to be shot.

"Oh," she moaned, squirming against him, "but ye are like a fire!"

"Ada, hold still," he bit out, the friction of her nipples rubbing against his chest, making desire explode within him.

She did still, for one breath, and one of her hands pressed against his chest while she shoved the other between his thighs, perilously close to his bollocks. He instantly became hyper aware of her hand so close to his shaft. He hardened, and she gasped. "Oh! Should I move?"

Good God, no. "Aye," he croaked, his blood rushing through his veins so loud that his ears rang.

"Is my hand too cold? It's just ye are so verra warm." She wiggled her fingers, and they brushed his bollocks.

A groan of need ripped from his throat, and before he could stop himself, he had skimmed his hand over her hip to her backside and pressed her more firmly against him, against his shaft. And when she sighed a sound of distinct pleasure, his control snapped.

William's mouth claimed hers in a kiss that was anything but gentle. It was ravenous, possessive, desperate. The heady sensation shot from her mouth directly to her heart. He sucked and tugged on her lips while his hands divested her of her léine and himself of his clothing, but she didn't mind. In fact, her own desperation was stirring. At first, she had thought only to tease him because while she knew he may not want her heart, it was obvious that in this moment he desired her. But her attempt to tease him awakened her own lustful yearning to repeat what William had introduced her to the day they had wed.

He set her mouth aflame sliding his tongue along hers, and then he torched her neck with fiery kisses that led straight to her—ah! She raked her nails across his back as his mouth suckled her breast in long, maddeningly magical pulls. And when he flicked her sensitive, swollen bud with his tongue, she wanted to scream with pleasure, but somehow she managed to contain it. His touch was light and painfully teasing, causing a throbbing sensation deep in her belly and between her legs.

"I love yer breasts," he murmured, cupping them both to kiss one and then the other. "But I especially love yer perfect nipples." He took one in his mouth for a long suckle, making her arch against him, and then the other, which made her grasp his thick hair and tug at him.

"I want ye," she said, breathless and not caring how she sounded.

"Do ye?" His tone was slightly proud and definitely possessive. "Do ye want me more if I do this?" Suddenly, he parted her at her core and his fingers pressed gently to her sensitive spot.

"Aye," she gasped, feeling nearly mindless.

"What if I do this?" He rubbed that same spot in slow circles, which grew faster with each pass.

"Aye. I want ye more," she panted, sliding her hands daringly over his tight buttocks. Her fingers moved over muscles that were tensed with his control of his body. She wanted to make him lose control as he did her. "What if *I* do this?" she said, her voice shocking her with how husky it sounded as she moved her hands to his shaft jutting hard against her belly. She circled the tip of his cock, and he hissed. "Does that make ye want me more?" she asked, mimicking his words from moment ago.

"Aye," he grunted. "Careful, lass, or I'll be spent before we begin."

She curled her fingers firmly around his shaft, reveling in the warmth of him, the slickness, the raw masculinity. "Then we will just," she said, running her hand up and down his shaft as he groaned, "have to begin again."

"God's blood," he muttered, claiming her mouth once more in a savage kiss. When they broke apart, he said, "ye are most definitely my Eve."

"Who?" she asked, stilling as fear and shock surfaced.

"Eve," he repeated, his voice thick with need and what sounded like amusement. "Ye are like Eve in the Garden of Eden. Ye offer to me, and I kinnae turn away."

"Oh!" She began to stroke him again. She rather liked that analogy and the feeling of power it gave her. "Could I make ye spend yerself as ye made me before?"

"Aye," he said. "Most assuredly." A heady, very new sense of control consumed her, and recalling how his mouth had brought her so much pleasure, she released her hold on his staff to scramble to her knees so she could bend over him.

"Are ye certain—"

His words died when she took the tip of him in her mouth. Guided by his grunts and the way his hands fisted in her hair, she offered him the pleasure he had given her. As she did, her own need built and built, and when he finally found his release, shuddering against her and pulling away at the last moment to spill his seed, she felt as if she had been tied into a thousand knots. She pulled her knees up to her chest and wrapped her arms around herself, suddenly feeling the cold. Her body vibrated and hummed with the wish for him to take her, but she was too embarrassed to say anything, and honestly, she did not know how soon a man could do such a thing again.

"Will ye return to yer own shelter now?" she asked, her voice small in the quiet.

"Lass," he said, sitting up beside her, "there is nae a force on Earth that could drag me away from ye at this moment, including my good senses." With those words, he gently undid her arms and encircled her ankles with his hands to slide her legs down from her chest. When she gave a shiver at the cold, he said, "Straddle my lap."

She frowned. "What for?"

With a chuckle, he jumped to his feet, then swiftly leaned down and hoisted her up with a tug to catch her under her bottom. Her thighs spread automatically, and he brought his face close to her, his whiskers tickling her cheek. "Put yer legs around my waist, *mo bhean mhaiseach.*"

She sucked in a sharp breath at his calling her his beautiful wife. It wasn't even that she cared if he found her beautiful, though it was nice. It was hearing him call her his wife in that rough voice of his that made her heart race and her body flush. She wrapped her legs around his waist, as he instructed.

"There are many ways to join, Ada. And this way," he said, lowering himself to the ground while still holding her, "will keep ye as warm as possible." When he was sitting on the ground, he scooped up the blanket that had fallen when they stood, and he draped it over her shoulders before he lay back. "Now…" He slid a hand over her belly, which quivered at his touch, and then up to glide his fingers between her breasts, where he splayed them. He brought his other hand to her hip. "Straddle me."

She did not hesitate to comply. "Now what?" she asked, her body tingling with awareness of him. He smelled of smoke from the fire, and the tension in his body radiated toward her. He was like a coiled snake waiting to strike, and she was his willing victim.

His other hand came to her left hip, and he lifted her bottom slightly until she was hovering above his hard staff. "Now ye take me in as ye wish. At yer pace. At yer pleasure."

Her eyes widened at what he suggested, but she set her hands on his chest, surprised and thrilled to feel his heart thundering under her touch, and then slowly, she inched her way down over his hardness. He filled her completely as she took all of him in. Her heart even felt as if it stretched, too. It thundered with the need to give and receive more—more than just this physical joining, which was wonderful, but she needed a foundation of hope.

She settled fully on him, his hands beginning to rock her hips. "I want—"

Her words stuttered to a halt as she discovered the rhythm he set for them, and as they moved together, passion pounded the blood through her body and straight to her heart. Tension built, which she recognized from their first joining and there was an ache deep within her that she knew only he could fulfill. Her body started to tighten around him, and she felt him grow rigid, as well. As waves of ecstasy crashed through her, he clutched her, groaning with his own release.

"Is this what ye wanted?" he growled, pumping into her one more time.

"Aye," she said, near mindless, but then she added, "Nay," thinking of what she had intended to say.

He stilled immediately, and his hands came to cup her face. "What did ye want? Tell me and I'll give it to ye."

"I want..." She swallowed, fear of revealing her heart to

him almost keeping her silent, but she knew there could be no keeping silent if there was to be any hope for them. She cupped his face now as he was cupping hers. The shadow of stubble on his cheeks was scratchy against her fingers. How long did it take for him to grow a beard? The thought was an errant one, but it was exactly the kind of intimate detail a wife should know about her husband that Ada wished to discover.

All her hopes spilled out of her in a rush. "I want to ken ye. Come to love ye. Have lots of bairns with ye. I want yer heart, and in turn, to give ye mine."

Ada's words, her offer, was the best and worst thing he'd heard in his life. He was filled with pleasure and horror at once, the emotions colliding like a violent storm inside him. To become so entangled with her… The temptation was strong, the fear stronger. He released his hold on her lovely face, glad he could not see how his refusal might hurt her. He gently pushed her hands from him and set her off him and onto the ground.

He did not miss her sharp intake of breath, likely from hurt as well as her arse meeting the freezing grass. His heart thumped wildly as he stood, his blood rushing through his veins as if he'd just fought a great battle. He suspected the greatest battle of his life was about to come, and he'd be battling himself. His need for her. His desire for her. His weakness, so great already that it was a frightening thing.

Reaching down, he grabbed his braies and pulled them on as he spoke. The need to put distance between them was as urgent now as his desire was moments ago. "I kinnae give ye what ye ask for."

"Why?" she demanded, showing a surprising bit of stubbornness. Or maybe he ought not be surprised. She'd run from him to protect him, Thomas, Maximilian, and Esther after all.

"Because I dunnae wish to," he said. It was not entirely a lie. He didn't wish to because when someone was inside your heart, when they put a piece of themselves in you, they left a hole of pain when they disappointed you and left you. He never wanted to feel that again.

"Nae even to make my gift work properly?" she flung out, her words lashing with their repressed hurt.

"Christ, Ada," he said, almost trembling with the need to spill his secret, which would reveal he was weak and fearful. Warriors could not be those things. "I dunnae give a damn anymore if yer gift works properly or nae." That was the God's honest truth. One way or another, he'd save his brother and help keep the king on the throne.

"Then ye simply dunnae think ye could care for me in that way?"

The hurt in her words, the brokenness, was worse than any anger she could have slung at him. He turned from her, shoved back her gown, opening the makeshift door to escape all the emotions boiling inside him. But she grabbed him by the arm and asked, "How can we live together and nae ever become close? Will ye bed me coldly? Expect bairns?"

Her questions infuriated him, but the ire was solely directed at himself. He'd not thought things through. He could never bed her without emotion. It would be impossible. He swung his body around toward her, surprised at how close she was. Her warm breath hit his chest when she exhaled, and every muscle in his body tightened with the wish to pull her into his arms and never let her go.

"Do ye ken what ye are?" he growled, having to curl his hands into fists so he'd not touch her face. "Ye're a fever." Her scent tickled his nose, teased him, tormented him. "Ye make me burn and burn. I feel weak from ye. Vulnerable."

Christ, the truth was escaping him. He had to get away from her and stay away. No touching. No joining. No bairns. No giving and taking of hearts.

"William," she said, sadness in her voice. The moon slashed across her face and revealed trails of tears making their way down her cheeks. "Whoever hurt ye—"

He jerked back as she reached for him. "I need to be cold to survive," he ground out. He turned on his heel and stormed away, feeling as though he were trying to outrun the devil at his heels. But what if the demon he was trying to escape was himself? What then?

Seventeen

Ada did not sleep again that night, so when morning came, at first she was glad for it, but then she was loath to leave her shelter and face William. His words of rejection resounded in her mind. She had been foolish to think he would ever want her for her. No one ever had. She pressed her fingers to her throbbing temples as all the things he'd said to her last night ran through her head for the thousandth time.

Freya whined beside Ada and stuck her paw on Ada's leg as if to say things would be all right. Tears burned her eyes as she patted Freya's head. They dripped one by one onto the dog's pure-white coat, and Freya stuck her snout under Ada's hand.

Ada's thoughts tumbled one over the other as she absently scratched Freya. She was humiliated, and she did not want to see William, but what choice did she have? He was her husband. But what was his intention for their life together if he did not want them to know each other? Did he plan to ignore her? Leave her at a castle and never return?

The thought had her on her feet and out of her shelter in a flash. Ire boiling, she stomped through the snow, spotting William, Grant, and Marjorie across the way packing the horses. If William intended to soon deposit her somewhere to live her life alone, childless, and loveless, she would hear it now. She would prepare herself for what was to come. Both Marjorie and Grant stopped what they were doing and looked at her with matching shocked expressions.

"What?" she demanded, her fury and humiliation mounting. "Have ye nae ever seen an angry wife?"

"We'll just let the two of ye have a moment of privacy," Marjorie said, and when Grant did not respond but continued gawking at Ada, Marjorie elbowed the man. Ada frowned. Why was Grant acting as if he'd nae ever seen a vexed woman?

Before Ada could thank Marjorie, William turned toward her. "Nay, dunnae leave. The two of ye mount the horses. They're ready."

"Afraid to be alone with me?" she challenged. "Dunnae tell me a fierce warrior such as yerself kinnae control yer lust?"

A tic started at his jaw, and his gaze glittered dangerously. "Dunnae push me, Ada."

Out of the corner of her eye, she saw Grant take Marjorie by the elbow and lead her to the horse they were to ride, which he then moved away. "Or ye'll what?" she bit out. "Humiliate me? Ye've already done that."

He flinched. "I am sorry I hurt ye. Ye forced me to be truthful. I did nae wish to—"

"I ken it well," she interrupted, the blood in her temples pounding with anger that he could not see she had worth beyond her stupid, ill-working gift. She crossed her arms over her chest. "What do ye intend to do with me?"

"I intend to help ye mount after ye fetch yer gown and don it."

She sucked in a sharp breath and glanced down at herself. She quickly covered her breasts where her nipples were straining against the thin material of her léine, but she did not retreat for her gown. She would have her answers. "Ye ken what I mean. What do ye intend to do with me when this mission is over?"

She could see him working his jaw back and forth, as if he did not want to answer her, and part of her mind warned her to leave it alone. But the other part, the part that would know the hurt to come to prepare for it, demanded she push forward.

"Go dress, Ada. Let us leave the future for another day." His emotionless voice answered her where his words would not.

"Do ye intend to leave me in some remote castle to live alone? Was that yer plan all along?"

His eyes darkened with some emotion she could not name. A long silence stretched, and the word *aye* finally ground out between his teeth.

Her face grew hot with her shame. "Well, I'm certain it will be a great relief to ye when the mission is over," she said, not caring that she sounded churlish.

His jaw tensed, and for a moment she thought he would not respond, but he finally said, "Aye," again, and that agreement made her throat tighten with unshed tears.

Swallowing, she shoved back her shoulders, gathered the tattered remains of her pride, and turned on her heel without a word. Never would she allow him to hurt her again. She made her way to where her gown was hanging and took the cold, stiff material in her hands to dress. As she adjusted her gown, she considered everything. Maybe she would flee to Iona Nunnery as she and Esther had planned before William had appeared. Her mother had been raised at that nunnery, and Esther had come from the nunnery to be Ada's companion after her mother's death. The nuns knew this. They would accept her, shelter her. Ada knew it was not far from the MacLean holding. All she needed to do was escape William once they were close to his home.

"Ada?" Marjorie said at Ada's back, startling her.

She glanced behind her to look at Marjorie, who set her hand upon Ada's shoulder. "Are ye all right?"

"Aye." She sniffed. "'Tis nae any less than I should have expected. I kenned well I was only ever to be wed for that stupid gift."

"Oh, Ada," Marjorie said, pity in her tone. "I believe William is being cold because he cares for ye and he dunnae wish to."

Ada snorted at that, and before she could even reply, a wave of sensation swept through her and nausea sent her to her knees in the snow. She began to retch, her gut clenching into knots. Stars peppered her vision, and the very ground seemed to tilt.

"Ada?" William's voice sounded so concerned, almost loving. But it was false. A lie.

She squeezed her eyes shut. "Go away!" she moaned, hating how much she longed to have him truly care. Another convulsion took her, and she doubled over, her hands sinking deep into the snow. Her hair hung down either side of her face, perilously close to where she had just been sick. She wanted to care, but she felt too awful to move it.

Hella and Freya appeared to her left, whining and barking, and her hair was swept back off her face. She knew without looking that it was William. She could smell his manly scent and feel the heat only he radiated.

He leaned close to her. "I'm here, lass. Tell me what ye need."

She breathed deeply in and out her nose as she fought

the nausea. When she was sure it was over, she scooped up a handful of snow and pressed her face into it, reveling in the cool relief. When she shook the snow off her hands, she croaked, "Quit pretending ye care."

She thought she saw him flinch, but sparks of silver still blocked her vision. Suddenly he was on his knees facing her and offering her his wine skin. Her pride made her want to smack it out of his hand, but the more sensible part of her reached out to take the offering. Yet her hand trembled so badly that he ended up pressing the wine skin to her lips and tipping it up for her. She drank slowly, the wine sliding down her throat to her belly to calm and warm her. When she was done, she nodded and he lowered the wine skin. He stared at her for a long, silent moment. Why did she think she saw yearning in his gaze? What was wrong with her? She squeezed her eyes shut and willed herself to see what was truly there, but when she opened her eyes once more, she could have sworn he was looking at her with yearning. She was so daft. When he motioned to her lip, she cocked an eyebrow at him, vowing not to speak to him for the remainder of the day. Maybe longer. Maybe never again.

"Ye've wine on yer lip," he said, his voice husky.

She started to raise her hand to wipe it away, but his thumb was already pressing on her lip gently, rendering her immobile with shock. He glided the pad over her sensitive skin, causing her to shiver, and then he withdrew his hand.

"Why did ye do that?" she asked, breaking her vow in no less than two breaths. She'd have to do better with the next vow. Two breaths was shameful. There it was again—yearning. And there, blast it all, was hope once more.

"As I said, ye're a temptation to me," he replied.

She clenched her teeth on the desire to scream at him for making hope wiggle in her yet again. She willed her hope to die a swift death.

He assessed her with seeming concern that she knew was likely only in regard to if she had felt anything useful. So when he asked, "Did ye feel anything that might aid us?" she snorted even as disappointment slashed through her. Why could she not quit allowing herself to think there was something more between them when there simply wasn't?

She wanted to say that she had felt nothing that would help him, but instead she found herself saying, "Aye. Brothwell. He's coming. I feel it—here." She touched her gut. Good God, could she not lie about her instincts to William because he was her husband or because he had her heart? Both thoughts terrified her. Could she lie to him at all?

William nodded, as if he had expected her to say such a thing about Brothwell. "He'll be going for Bram because he kens I will be attempting to rescue him."

"Aye," she agreed, and then she decided there was no moment better than now to test whether or not she could hold something back from William. She pressed her lips together on the words that would alert him to the part of her intuition that made her feel Brothwell was first and foremost coming for her. William surely knew that. Brothwell would want vengeance upon William for duping him, of course, but her gut told her he'd sacrifice his revenge if it meant having her and her gift in his clutches once more. Suddenly, William swooped his arm under her legs and hoisted her against his chest.

"What are ye doing?" She squirmed in an effort to get out of his hold.

"Carrying ye. 'Tis it nae obvious?"

"I dunnae need ye to carry me," she growled, angered that her foolish heart tightened just from his touch. When he did not release her but his hold grew tighter and her heart beat harder, she became desperate for him to leave her be. She had to protect herself from him now. "I dunnae need ye!" she thundered.

She felt him tense under her and pause in his steps, but then his eyes met hers. He cocked his dark eyebrows, sardonic amusement flickering in his gaze. He brought his lips to her ear, and said, "Quit trying to seduce me. We have to make haste."

She gasped at his outrageous words and the way his warm breath fanning her ear and neck made her body feel aflame. "I'd nae try to seduce ye again if ye were the last man alive," she forced through clenched teeth, even as the warmth of his flesh against hers made her feel as if she'd imbibed a good deal of wine. And then, because she really had to get out of his hold before she became a quivery mess, she wiggled more while pushing her palm against his chest.

"Ada," he said, his tone now a warning, "ye may nae be aware of this, but every time ye wiggle yer sweet bottom, the movements sends a message to the part of me that makes me a man. And that message tells me to take ye, damned the consequences."

She sucked in a sharp breath at his words and the thrill they made spiral through her, which caused her to squirm again.

"Ada!" he growled.

"It was nae on purpose that time," she snapped. "Yer breath on my ear and my neck makes me wiggle." And his hard body. And his words, which should have angered her but instead filled her with lust. Her mood veered sharply to anger at him and herself. "If ye insist on keeping me near, dunnae breathe on me and I will nae wiggle against ye, ye scurrilous beast!"

He chuckled at that and swung her up onto their horse. "We're back to me being a scurrilous beast, are we?"

"Aye," she gritted. "We are. That should please ye."

William mounted the saddle behind her, his powerful thighs encasing her, his chest pressing against her back, and his breath tickling her neck. "It dunnae please me to hurt ye, Ada."

"Ye're breathing on me again," she said, feeling spiteful and lonely, though William was so very close.

The journey to Theondor Forest, which faced Trethway Island, was fast, hard, and uncomfortable—physically, mentally, and emotionally. Ada's bottom ached, but her heart ached more. It was exhausting trying to ignore William. He commanded space and attention naturally, and though he had not touched her again, except the occasional brush of his leg against hers on the horse, or when he set his hands on her waist to help her dismount, he had done other things that seemed contrary to his claim that he did not care for her. He'd given her his blanket each night, going without himself, and he'd given her his rabbit when she'd commented that she was still famished. She caught his gaze on her constantly, and she suspected he sacrificed sleep to guard her as she slumbered. When she went to sleep, he was awake watching her shelter from a distance, and no matter what time she awoke, be it the middle of the night or before dawn, if she glanced out of her shelter, he was sitting in the snow outside his, eyes wide and focused on where she was.

Why did he guard her if he didn't care about her? In the hope that she would get another feeling that would provide more insight? That was likely the case.

When they reached Theondor on their fifth day of travel, William pulled the horse to a halt, swung off without a word, and grasped her around the waist before she could lodge a protest. The minute his strong hands encircled her waist, the cold December chill that had burrowed into her bones was chased away by the warmth he radiated. A longing for his arms wrapped around her in tenderness uncurled within her. She clenched her teeth against the foolish, hopeless yearning, and suddenly another feeling gripped her.

Loss. Death.

But whose? And why? Unaware of what she was sensing and the spinning in her head, William set her on the ground and started to pull away. She grasped his forearms, unsteady and hoping more intuitions that would aid William and Bram would come.

She could hear William calling her name, but he sounded very far away. She clenched her jaw, concentrating. Dark shadows danced around him, deathly shadows. She gasped, her body shaking and worry seeping into every part of her. But that wasn't all she felt. She *loved* him. She did. He didn't deserve her love, and he didn't want it, so she'd keep it to herself, but it was there in her heart and she had to guide him to keep him safe.

Was the feeling implying he should not go to the island? Sickness coiled within her, and she shoved William away. She fell to her knees, three words pounding in her head: *He should go. He should go. He should go.*

Then two more words came: *Take Grant.*

Noise started ringing in her ears, and William crouched before her, blurry and reaching for her. She felt herself falling backward. She screamed, and before she hit the ground, she had another feeling, this time one that told her she had to stay here and stop Brothwell.

Horrified at the sight of Ada in an almost trancelike state and falling, William lunged for her. He caught her by the arms right before her head hit the earth, and he pulled her to him, her body slumping and her head lolling to the side. Black fright gripped him. Was she dead?

He recoiled at the thought and brought a shaking hand under her nose. For a moment, he felt no breath, and the idea that he might have lost her sent panic rioting through him. Then warmth fanned his skin, and he nearly cried out his relief. He just managed to contain it, but the knowledge that he had come to care for Ada despite his best efforts not to, despite his pushing her away, lying to her, and hurting her, twisted icy fear around his heart.

He glanced down at her now-peaceful face, and his chest squeezed. He cared. He cared so much it hurt. He could never show it, and he damn well had to separate himself from her as soon as possible before the caring grew. But not at this moment. Right now she needed him. Trembling, he cradled her unmoving body against his, allowing himself to savor it for a breath—the soft, womanly feel of her against him, her silky hair fanning over his arm.

Grant crouched down by William's side. "Is she—"

"Nay," William interrupted, his voice harsher than he'd intended. His concern for Ada had not subsided, and with her in such a weakened state, his need to protect her and touch her only intensified.

"I'm sorry," he said to Grant as Marjorie kneeled at his other side and gave him a knowing look. Could she see how much he cared for Ada? He turned his head from her scrutiny to find Grant staring at his arm.

"MacLean, ye're bleeding."

William glanced at his arm where Ada had grasped him. Her nails had left eight bloody half-moon cuts in his arm. What had she felt? Had she gotten another vision of forthcoming danger? He hated her damned gift. "Ada?" He brushed her hair back from her forehead to stroke it gently. "Ada?" She stirred but did not open her eyes. "Her gift is more like a curse," he muttered. "I wish she did nae have it at all."

Behind him, barking resounded, and then Hella and Freya bounded toward them. The relief William felt to see the two hounds made him frown. He resolved to push the hounds away as he had Ada.

William caught Grant's eye just as Grant said, "Those hounds are uncommonly fast. I'd nae think how quickly they travel possible had I nae seen it."

"Nor I," William agreed, stroking Ada's forehead again. He trailed his finger over the perfect arch of her brow, and his chest jerked.

"What do ye think she sensed?" Marjorie said, her voice tight. "Something about Bram?"

"I dunnae," William said, "but the sun is setting, and the only hope of getting across the water and to Bram will be in the dark."

"So we'll go," Grant said. "Marjorie will stay with Ada."

"Nay," William said. The idea of leaving Ada unprotected clenched his stomach into hard knots. "We'll take them with us."

"Dunnae be daft, William," Grant said. "She'll be slow and groggy likely, and her and Marjorie's presence may cause us to lose our chance to save Bram. And the lass said herself that Brothwell was coming. If he reaches us before we can get away…"

Grant did not need to finish his sentence. They'd be outnumbered. They'd likely never escape, and they'd die here. He didn't fear death, but the thought of Ada falling into Brothwell's clutches again filled him with murderous rage. She was his.

"William," Grant said, "ye are letting yer emotions rule yer decisions. Ye must leave her behind if we are to keep all of us safe."

He looked down at her, her eyes moving rapidly behind her eyelids as if she was dreaming. The words that Esther told him about the gift ran through his head. He had said he did not want Ada's heart, and he had believed it, but looking down at her now and recalling all they had shared so far, he had the notion that he'd lied to himself. He wanted her heart. The wanting was there, but so was the fear that what she might give today, she could just as easily take away tomorrow.

She jerked then, and her eyes flew open. They locked with his for one moment, and then she said, "The moon will soon disappear from the sky, blanketing the land in near-complete darkness. Swim to the hill, scale it, and follow the path to the cell that overlooks the cliff. Bram will be there. Jump from the cell into the waters far below without fear of death, and then swim back to us to escape. Ye both must go now or none of ye will survive." He frowned and opened his mouth to question her, but she spoke again before he could. She clutched his arm. "'Tis nae me who will keep King David on the throne. 'Tis Bram."

Eighteen

William could do little more than stare at her, his shock was so great. "Ye're certain?"

She nodded her head. "Ye must make haste."

He rose, uncertainty gripping him, but made his way close enough to the water's edge that he could study the towers. He looked up at the moon, which was disappearing before his very eyes already. Ada was right. He could hardly believe it. He'd never seen such a thing.

"Is she *ban-druidh*?" Grant asked, coming up beside William.

"Nay," William replied. "She had an instinct, as she told us. 'Tis the gift from the fae."

"But if it's nae working properly—"

"Dunnae fash yerself."

"But she said Thomas was the one who would stop the Steward, and now she says 'tis Bram."

William nodded. Her gift had only been half working, and now... He refused to reveal it to Grant just to ease his worry, but William suspected her gift was functioning properly now that he had realized that he wanted her heart. But he'd not give in to the desire to accept her love and give it in return. Still, he did not think that mattered when it came to her gift. William had seen the complete certainty in Ada's eyes when she'd told them what they must do.

Her words drifted through his mind:

The moon will soon disappear from the sky, blanketing the land in near-complete darkness. Swim to the hill, scale it, and follow the path to the cell that overlooks the cliff. Bram will be there. Jump from the cell into the waters far below without fear of death, and then swim back to them to escape.

It seemed simple. Too simple. But what choice did he have?

"The moon will be gone soon," William said, turning toward Ada. She stood there swathed in moonlight, looking very much like a forest fairy with her hair tumbling down over her shoulders and her pale skin glistening. A deep ache pierced him, but he shoved it away and looked at Grant again. "Go arm Marjorie with a dagger; I'll do the same for Ada." The daggers would be no match against men with swords, but it was better than nothing. The thought offered precious little comfort. "I want to talk to Ada before I depart."

Grant inclined his head, and they turned together and made their way to where Ada and Marjorie stood in the small clearing. Grant motioned for Marjorie to follow him away, and once they were out of earshot, William took his dagger out of its sheath and handed it to Ada.

"Do ye believe ye could stab someone if ye were in danger?" he asked.

Her steely gaze met his, and he blinked at how her eyes shone like silver in the light. "Aye." She took his dagger by the hilt. "Show me how to do it."

He nodded and demonstrated how to aim for a man's throat or his heart—the two places that were likely to cause instant death. When he was done, he stood there engulfed in the silence of his own misery and doubt, his throat aching with the need to say something, to offer an explanation as to why he had hurt her. But that would be akin to asking her to scale the wall he was trying to keep between them. So instead he said, "Will ye kiss me for luck?"

Her lips parted with her obvious shock. "Ye dunnae need luck," she replied, her voice hard.

The realization that she had now withdrawn from him as he had her struck a powerful blow to his chest and made his breath solidify in his throat. It was for the best, he decided. He would return for her when this was over, and then he would take her to her new home to be safe.

"Stay here until I return," he said. She nodded so quickly he was suspicious. "I mean it, Ada. Vow it. Vow ye will be here when I return."

A memory he'd long forgotten of his mother surfaced in his mind's eye: him making her promise she would be there in the morning when he awoke. It was as if he'd sensed she would one day leave.

Blood rushed through him, making a whoosh in his ears. "Ada," he pressed, needing her vow, feeling he could not leave without it.

"I vow it," she finally said.

The relief her words brought made him feel weak. Eventually, he would not yearn for her touch or have the desire to possess her heart, but that day was not today.

Hella and Freya trotted out of the woods and toward them. He expected Hella to come to him, but she positioned herself on one side of Ada as Freya sat on the other. Even the hound had distanced herself from him. That was a good thing, he reminded himself as he turned from her. It was what he wanted, *needed*, to remain cold and strong. So why did he feel so damned weak?

Denying William's request for a kiss and then allowing him to walk away was the hardest thing Ada had ever done, but she sensed it was what she had to do to keep him alive and keep the king on the throne. Additionally, not kissing him was best for her.

"He cares for ye, ye ken," Marjorie said beside her.

Ada snorted at that as she stared out at the dark water, looking for a glimpse of William or Grant but not finding one. That was good. If she could not see them, then it was unlikely the guards on Trethway Island could, either.

"Ada, did ye hear me?"

Ada turned toward Marjorie's voice in the utter darkness. "I heard ye. He dunnae care for me. He needed my gift to work, as did the king, but he dunnae want my love."

"And do ye love him?"

Ada bit her lip, wanting to deny it, but what was the point with only Marjorie here? "Aye. But he dunnae want it." The pain of his denial was an open wound still. "Ye need to hide," Ada added, sensing it in her bones.

"Dunnae ye mean the both of us need to hide?"

Ada reached across the blackness and grabbed for Marjorie, feeling the other woman take her hand. They stood there, hands clasped. "Nay, I mean ye. I have a task I must do."

"Ada, ye vowed ye'd be here when William returned." Marjorie sounded scared.

Ada didn't blame her. She herself was terrified. "Aye, I did. But I lied. The only way the four of ye will escape is if I go to meet Brothwell and convince him William took me and that we must ride hard to the Steward. So I had to lie. Besides, William will be fine without me."

"Are ye certain it must be this way?"

"Aye," Ada replied, fear making her tremble.

Her stepsister frowned. "I'm sorry for everything, Ada. I was jealous for years, and then I was afraid of Brothwell, afraid to defy him and stick up for ye."

Ada squeezed Marjorie's hand. "I ken it. I'm glad ye found Bram, and he ye. Love has changed ye."

"Love does that. It changed Bram, too, and I believe it can change William."

"He would have to be willing to accept love for it to change him," Ada said sadly.

"Bram was cold at first to me," Marjorie admitted, "and he did nae want to let me close, but before Bram was taken away to be imprisoned, I went to see him and he told me that I had seduced him into loving me." Marjorie laughed at that.

"I dunnae think that would work with William, especially since he has decided to nae ever touch me again."

Marjorie sighed. "I imagine William is struggling with many demons. Bram was, and he did nae have it as bad as William has."

Ada frowned. "What do ye mean?"

"Their mother left them. Did ye ken that?"

Ada shook head, then realized Marjorie could not see her. "Nay, I did nae ken it. Were they verra young?" Her heart ached for William.

"Bram was nae, but William was only thirteen summers."

"Do ye ken why she left?" Ada asked, seeing William in her mind as a frightened, sad child. If his own mother had abandoned him, it was no wonder he did not want to allow himself to have love. He did not *trust* love.

"Bram said it was because of all the missions their father

was always on. He thinks she was lonely."

"But to abandon her children?" Ada whispered.

"Aye. 'Tis an awful thing. And their clan believes their father and Bram betrayed the king when they were actually working *for* the king. I'm certain William has endured a great deal as a result. Bram himself said the clan had turned against the two brothers after their father left, and that was even before Bram seemingly betrayed the king."

"Good God," Ada muttered. She understood now why William kept her at a distance. He was scared. He was a ruthless warrior, but he was fearful of love. Of trusting people. He'd been betrayed and abandoned. Her anger disappeared, and searing regret replaced it. She wished she could redo their parting. She would kiss him and tell him she loved him, that she always would, and if he ever decided he wanted her love, she would offer it gladly if he would give his in return. Instead, she'd given a vow to stay here that she had known she could not keep. She was leaving him just as his mother had, but she was doing it to protect him.

She didn't know if that distinction would matter to him. As she quickly ran through a plan of how to escape Brothwell, the ground beneath her feet vibrated with the pounding of horses' hooves galloping toward them.

"Marjorie, run and hide," she ordered. "Dunnae come out, regardless of what happens, and tell William that if I escape Brothwell, I'll head to Iona Nunnery."

"Why the nunnery?" Marjorie asked even as she nodded.

A torch flickered in distance and then another and yet another. The irony that someone as dark as Brothwell was filling the blackness with light ripped a bitter laugh from Ada.

"Ada, why the nunnery?" her stepsister repeated.

"They'll shelter me and protect me from all the men who wish to use me, including the king, the Steward, and William. Promise me ye'll tell William."

"Aye," Marjorie said. "I vow it."

He would come for her, and then he would have to decide if wanted her love and would open his heart to her in return. Otherwise, she would stay at the nunnery and declare herself a servant of God. If William still wanted to be rid of her but wanted to ensure she was safe, this would be the solution he sought. The thought made tears leak from Ada's eyes, but there was no time for tears.

As a flickering torch appeared in the distance, followed by another, and another, she pushed Marjorie away, hissing, "Make haste to hide!" Without hesitating, Ada started toward the flickering flames that seemed to be floating in the blackness as the thundering of the horses grew louder.

She walked at first, becoming accustomed to the total darkness, but then she began to run, feeling more sure-footed and keenly aware that she needed to put as much distance between herself and Marjorie as possible. She ran down the same path they had taken to the edge of the woods, and without her sight, branches scraped her cheeks and snagged her dress as she ran. The closer the flames drew to her, the harder she pushed herself. Soon her side was pinching and she was gasping. A branch smacked against her forehead with a *thwack*, and she cried out in pain and fell forward onto her knees.

As she righted herself, she could hear the braying of horses and smell the many days of sweat on the warriors and their steeds. Before she even gained her feet, the riders were there, galloping toward her, Brothwell leading. The torch in his hand cast his face, half in shadows and half bright, so that his determined expression was clear.

He yanked his horse to a stop in front of her, and her mind raced, knowing she must speak first, convincingly, and quickly. "Brother!" she exclaimed, rushing to him and clasping her hand on his shin. "I'm so glad ye found me! William took me! He wanted me to aid him in getting his brother back, but I've the last laugh."

Brothwell leaned over his horse, the torch flickering and illuminating his face. Much to her relief, he looked uncertain. "Ye did nae flee with him?"

"Brother, nay!" Impulsively, she cupped his cheek with her palm. "We are family." The lie filled her mouth with a bitter taste. "He took me against my will."

Brothwell's eyes narrowed. "I'm going to cut out his heart and shove it down his throat."

Ada forced herself not to recoil from Brothwell and his words. Instead, she shook her head. "Ye have more pressing matters. The Steward's castle is under attack by men William sent there. As for William, I've taken care of him. He thinks he will free his brother and escape the island because I told him so, but I lied."

"Did ye now?" Brothwell said, his tone pleased. "What will happen to him?"

"He'll die there," she said, matter-of-fact. "As will Bram. And Marjorie." Ada expected some sort of response of sorrow about Marjorie or even bitter words of betrayal.

Instead, Brothwell said, "Good. While I wish I were the one to deliver their deaths, protecting my father must come before my own selfish wishes. "Let us make haste, King Maker" he said, rising to pass the torch to the rider next to him before Brothwell extended his hand to her.

Nineteen

The water surrounding Trethway Island was so deathly cold that it was all William could do to concentrate on forcing his body to cooperate and swim the distance from the woods to the hill that Ada had instructed them to scale. He'd known the water would be colder than he could have imagined possible, for Brodee had told him of the numbing temperature when he'd swum these waters. Ice chunks floated around him, and every few strokes, William would hit one with his hand or kick one with his foot, and the ice would slice into his skin. His motions were slow, dangerously so, as if at any moment his body would simply not do what he asked. He breathed as Brodee had told him he'd done, and William conjured up an image of Ada—whom he had to survive for.

Her image floated before him, teasing and tantalizing, as well as encouraging, and he continued to thrust his hands through the water. He could see nothing around him, the night was so black, but the faint swish of Grant swimming beside him assured him Grant was still there.

After what seemed like an eternity, his foot brushed the ground beneath the water as he kicked, and he stood, knowing they were now close to shore. Beside him, Grant stood, as well, and though he could still not see the man, William whispered, "Now we scale the hill."

"Aye," Grant replied, his tone low.

Silent and intent, they moved as one out of the water, and with footsteps slowed by the lingering numbness of the cold, they trudged toward the hillside. William touched a hand to his only weapon, his dagger, and wished he had not needed to leave his sword in the woods. But to swim with it would have slowed him greatly.

"Straight up?" William asked. Ada had not said the direction to climb.

"Aye," Grant replied. "Seems as good a direction as any."

And so together, they began the climb. The hill was steep and the rocks sharp. They moved slowly in the beginning, but as William scaled the cliffside, his body warmed and thoughts of reuniting with his brother sped his progress. Rock cut into his skin as he found purchase, hand over hand, but the pain was nothing compared to what gripped him when he contemplated not rescuing Bram. He had no notion if they were even close to the top until he reached up a hand to grasp the next rock and suddenly felt a flat surface. Relief flooded him as he hauled himself over the ledge, then lay on the ground for a moment, listening. Complete silence greeted him. Wherever the guards on this island were, they were not standing here, expecting someone to appear over the cliffside from the frigid waters below.

He thanked Ada in his mind, and at that moment, Grant said, "I do believe we owe our lives to yer wife."

"Aye," William said low, the mere thought of her making him yearn to be back at her side. He pushed the thought of her to the recesses of his mind. Distraction killed. He came to his feet, as did Grant, and sweeping his gaze through the consuming blackness, he saw a flicker of a torch. His hand immediately went to his dagger, and he withdrew it, expecting trouble. But after a breath, he realized the light was not moving as it would be if someone had been carrying a torch. This one was still, as if in a holder. And upon further inspection, he counted eight such torches, which seemed to form—

"A path!" Grant exclaimed, elbowing William. "Do ye see it?"

William grinned. "I do."

"I do believe I've just fallen in love with yer wife," Grant said.

The words were meant to be teasing, William knew, but they stirred something in him, some emotion that he could not face. Not at this moment.

"Come," he urged. "We need to find Bram and leave this place behind before daylight steals the chance from us. He moved toward the torches, then simply followed them down the twisting path. With each step he took, the surety that he would soon find Bram increased. The light from the torches illuminated the area enough that he could see they were winding along a path that twisted close to the edge of the cliff, and ahead, he saw a lone stone cave that seemed to jut out above the water. In front of the cave, sitting on the ground with his arms and legs crossed and his chin resting on his chest, was a guard. He was snoring loudly.

William motioned to the guard's sword, which lay by his leg, and Grant nodded. As Grant moved toward the sword, William advanced upon the guard. When he stood above the man, he raised his dagger, and just as he brought its hilt near the guard's head, the man jerked awake. But it was too late. William knocked the man on the head, hard enough to put him back to sleep but not so hard that he'd killed him. The guard slumped sideways to the ground, and

William made quick work of relieving the man of the key secured to a rope on his waist. He then used the rope to tie the man's hands to his feet, and just as he was stuffing a piece of fabric torn from the man's plaid into his mouth, the guard woke with a moan.

Together, William and Grant dragged the man well away from the door and to the side of the cave that was cast in darkness. Then in silence, they moved to the entrance and William unlocked the door. It creaked open. Grant stood behind him, now holding a torch, and when they entered the cave, William could see that the back of it was open to the water below. He felt his mouth slip open at how accurate Ada's feeling had been thus far.

In the corner, a man lay on the floor. He stirred, not sitting up but seeming to shift positions, and then he said, "Ye're early for my morning beating." Bram's amused tone made William smile. It was so like his brother to have kept his sense of humor, even in this situation. Before William could respond, Bram spoke once more. "I dunnae yet see daylight. Either ye're confused or stupid, as I've been telling ye."

Swallowing the lump in this throat, William said, "I'm nae stupid, just damned sorry that I did nae have faith in ye and Da."

Bram's head jerked up, and then he was scrambling to his feet, the speed of the movement letting William know his brother had not been so injured that he could no longer move properly. Relief nearly choked William as Bram stood there, gaping at him. For a moment, silence stretched, and William let it, simply staring at Bram. He was thinner than last William had seen him, and one eye was swollen shut. Bram's left hand had a swath of ragged material wrapped around it.

"William? Am I dreaming?"

"Nay," William said, his throat tightening painfully with the emotion he was restraining. He closed the distance between him and his brother and gripped him in a hard hug. "I ken everything about ye and Da," he said as Bram hugged him back. "The king told me everything."

Bram nodded, and they separated. "How did ye—"

"I wed Ada MacQuerrie," William interrupted, knowing they had to flee soon. "Ye ken about her gift."

"Oh aye," Bram replied. "Is it really true, then?"

"Aye, she is the reason we're here. She told us exactly what to do to save ye."

Shock swept Bram's face, followed by acknowledgment, and then he looked toward Grant. "It's good to see ye, Grant."

"Same to ye, Bram," Grant replied, grinning. "But this little reunion has to wait. We need to get ye out of here. Seems ye're the key to keeping the king on the throne, according to Ada."

William half expected Bram to declare that he didn't know what Grant was talking about. Instead, his brother nodded. "I was writing a message to the king about what I discovered when I went with Brothwell to the Steward's home for a meeting, but I never got to finish it. That was the day Brothwell imprisoned me."

"What did ye discover?" William asked, moving away from Bram to the opening in the cave. Wind blew in, sweeping cold air over him. He looked down, but in the darkness, he could not see how far the jump was to the water below.

"I discovered a secret passage," Bram said from behind him. He paused, and he and Grant both came to stand at the cave's opening with William. Grant, knowing as William did that they would be jumping, raised the torch, and the two of them glanced at the steep drop as Bram continued to talk. "The passage leads to the Steward's chamber, and it begins outside of the castle. It is how we can get to the Steward. What are we doing?" Bram finally asked.

William turned to his brother. "We're jumping. 'Tis how we will escape."

"Are ye mad?"

William and Grant exchanged a look. "Nay," William said. "Ada said this was how we would escape. She had a feeling, and so far, all her feelings have been correct. Will ye trust me, Brother?"

Bram's brows dipped together. "Do ye trust her?"

"Completely," William responded, the truth of his words hitting him.

"Then let us jump," Bram agreed.

And with that, Grant set the torch in a holder on the wall and the three of them leaped into the darkness below.

Twenty

"What do ye mean she went to meet Brothwell?" William roared at Marjorie.

The first rays of dawn chose that moment to crack the blackness of the sky, giving William a perfect view of the pitying look Marjorie was casting his way. She and Bram stood side by side holding hands. Marjorie had her other hand on Bram's bicep, as if she were holding him there to ensure he didn't disappear again, and Bram had his arm around Marjorie's waist, as if she too might be taken from him.

William understood the compulsion to cling to each other all too well. He fought it every moment Ada was near, and now Marjorie was telling him that his wife had gone with Brothwell.

"Let her explain, Brother," Bram said, his tone gentle.

William's chest tightened with the reminder that he had his brother back. One person he loved had been returned to him, and another—He stopped himself short of thinking it.

Marjorie released her hold on Bram, but when Bram did nae relinquish his hold on her, she said, "'Tis fine. I'm here." Bram gave a reluctant nod and then let her go.

She came closer to William and Grant, who was standing beside him. She set her hand on William's shoulder. "She said the only way the four of us would escape was is if she met Brothwell, convinced him ye had taken her against her will, and then persuaded him to ride hard to the Steward."

"She lied to me," William choked out. While he was awed by her bravery, he was shocked at her defiance—though he shouldn't have been—and furious that she willingly put herself back in Brothwell's hands. Yes, he knew it was to save the rest of them, but at what cost to her? What horrors would she be forced to endure?

Fury roared through him at the thought of her harmed, of another touching her, of never seeing her again. And then something else coursed through him, an emotion he did not want to feel but could not deny any longer—love.

He was almost struck dumb by the realization that he loved her. He'd thought to keep a wall up, but she'd slipped in through a crack. He'd thought he would be stronger without her, but the idea of never seeing her again—hell, of being separated from her at all—made him feel weak. He'd thought to protect his heart, but she'd already taken it.

Damn it all. He had to get her back. He could not live without her. Before her, he'd not been living, not truly. He'd been cold and withdrawn, and she'd warmed him, brought him back from the icy abyss of abandonment and betrayal his mother and his clan had thrown him into. In the short time he'd known Ada, though, she had proven time and time again that she would give her life for him.

"Marjorie, how much time do ye think has passed since she fled to intercept Brothwell?" At least Brothwell would not harm Ada. Not yet anyway. Brothwell needed her too much. What set his blood cold was that if Brothwell reached the Steward's holding and still had her, she would refuse to aid the Steward in an attempt to protect King David. And she would do that. She was that brave. But then the threat from Brothwell and the Steward would be imminent.

"Nae long," Marjorie said.

"I'll ride with ye," Grant said, clasping him on the shoulder and reading the thoughts he'd not even voiced yet. "We'll catch up to them if they are on the path to the Steward's home. Ada will slow them down, undoubtedly. She'll expect ye to be coming for her."

She would expect it, it was true, but it filled him with self-loathing that she would think he'd come for her only because of her gift. It was working perfectly now, if this day was any indication. Everything she'd told them to do to rescue Bram had been correct, and she had known exactly what she needed to do to aid them. And if he knew her gift was now working properly, did she? It gave him hope if she did, because that meant she had undoubtedly realized he wanted her heart, maybe even before he'd realized it.

"There's something else," Marjorie said, her tone as nervous as the expression she wore.

"What is it?" he demanded.

"Ada said that she was going to try to escape Brothwell, and if she did, to tell ye she would head to Iona Nunnery."

He frowned. Trying to escape Brothwell once she got him far enough away from here made sense if her aim had been simply to allow them time to flee the island, but... "Why Iona Nunnery? If she makes her way to the nunnery, then she's verra close to the MacLean holding. Why nae go there?"

"Well," Marjorie said, her gaze darting to Bram who drew to her side and then back to William, "she made me vow to tell ye that the sisters at the nunnery would shelter her from all men who wished to use her, including the king, the Steward, and yerself."

Ada's message was the hardest blow he'd ever taken in

his life. Men twice her size had struck him with fists and swords. But this hit, knowing she thought she had to protect herself from him, cleaved him to his core. He'd failed her. He'd wanted her for her, but he'd lied to her to protect himself. He was a coward, and now she might suffer the consequences of his actions.

Pushing his emotions down, he focused on Bram. "Ye must ride to the MacLean holding," he said.

"Aye," Bram replied. "I ken it well. The MacLean will be all too glad to help me gather a contingent of men to capture the Steward and, if luck is on our side, his sons. Once they are imprisoned, talk of putting the Steward on the throne should cease."

"Aye," William agreed. "Especially once the other remaining lairds who conspired with him are dealt with. But Bram, the MacLean might be with Thomas Fraser and the king, dealing with the other conspirators, and the MacLean men, our clansmen, they—"

"Believe me to be a traitor," Bram finished. He offered a hard grin. "I'll enlighten them. Dunnae fash yerself. I can still fight any man who wishes to harm me."

William chuckled. "I've nae any doubt ye will prevail. I'll return to the holding and join ye as soon as I can, but first I must—"

"Go after yer wife?" Bram asked, his eyebrows raised.

"William has fallen," Grant teased, to which Bram and Marjorie both laughed.

"'Tis a glorious fall," Bram said, eyeing Marjorie.

The look of love she gave Bram made William's gut twist. Would Ada ever look at him that way, or was it too late to offer his wife his heart?

Much to Ada's relief, power-hungry men were so pompous that they discounted that a mere woman could dupe them. Ada could see the glow of the fire that Brothwell's men had made to sit around for the night. She released the edge of the blanket that served as the door to the shelter Brothwell had ordered constructed for her.

He was being most courteous, and why would he not be? She laughed bitterly. He believed she had been taken against her will, and he wholeheartedly believed he had to ride hard to his father to save him from an eminent siege. The Steward *would* fall. Of that much Ada was certain, but it would not be a bloody battle. He and four of his sons would be taken quietly in the night by Bram, the MacLean laird, the MacLeod laird, and Thomas. She did not know the details, but she didn't need to. As for Brothwell, she felt no future for him, which made her think he did not have one. Then again, she felt no future for herself, either.

The feelings and intuitions had been coming to her gut regularly and swiftly since Brothwell had ridden away with her almost a sennight ago, but today there was nothing. It seemed the closer they rode to the Steward's home, the more her senses dulled. She'd had no foresights at all since Brothwell had announced they would reach the Steward holding by midafternoon the following day; she had only an odd sensation in her stomach. But it was not at all like the sickness that had come over her with her intuitions. This was different. She *felt* different.

Freya and Hella nuzzled her, and she petted them both, glad they had been able to catch up to her each night. Without their company, she likely would have fallen apart thinking of William. Where was he? Was he far behind? She didn't doubt he was pursuing her. What she didn't know was if he would ask for her heart and give her his when he found her. She could accept nothing less from him. She suspected that he did truly want her heart since her intuitiveness had become so much sharper before she'd fled him, but what did it even matter? Wanting her love and actually accepting it and giving it in return were very different things, and if he came to her with barriers still around him, she would rather kill her hope for good and live apart from him at the nunnery. She would not stay at some remote castle, hoping and awaiting his return as though a change would ever come.

Raucous singing filled the night. That was her signal to flee. She knew the direction in which Iona Nunnery stood, thanks to one of Brothwell's chatty men orienting her, but just heading in that direction did not mean she'd actually make it there. Yet her instincts had told her she would, indeed, arrive safely. She hoped the nuns would shelter her as she had thought, and she hoped her asking it of them would not put them in danger. Convents were supposed to be sacred places, where even men at war with each other would not dare to do evil, but would that hold true?

Clicking her tongue at Hella and Freya, who both immediately popped up from where they had been lying on the ground, she pulled back the flap to look outside again. No one was looking her way and no guard had been set to watch her, as Brothwell did not expect her to flee. She stepped out of the shelter but stayed low, just in case someone did glance her way. Then she crept toward the woods, the ground icy under her fingers and the cold wind blowing her hair and chilling her to the bone. Once she made it to the shelter of the woods, she rose, got her bearings, and started her journey west to the nunnery.

Fear and chill kept her moving at a fast pace. She wanted to put as much distance as she could between herself and

Brothwell's party before the sun rose and Brothwell came to wake her. Feeling increasingly nervous, she started to run, dodging low-hanging branches and shoving limbs out of the way as she did so. She raced down a rather winding path and glanced behind her to ensure Hella and Freya were keeping up. Her foot caught on something on the trail, and she flew through the air to land hard on her knees a few feet forward.

"Foolish, foolish," she muttered to herself, pressing her hands into the cold, wet leaves as Hella and Freya whined. Then from somewhere in front of her, a branch snapped, the dogs started to bark, and the hair on the back of her neck prickled.

Beset by fright, she forced herself to look up. Brothwell himself stood there. She choked back a cry as Brothwell offered a dark smile. He crouched down to look at her. "I kenned I could nae trust ye because ye were being so verra biddable. Ye have nae ever been that way in yer life."

She felt a momentary panic as her mind jumped to what would happen to her if she was captured and dragged to the Steward's home. Summoning courage she did not feel, she said, "Hella, Freya, attack!"

The dogs surged forward springing on Brothwell with vicious snips and growls. Her only thought was to get past him, but as she stumbled to her feet, he managed to throw off Freya and then he sprang toward Ada. She stumbled backward, tripping and falling hard on her bottom. Pain shot up her back and made her feel dizzy. But as Brothwell advanced, kicking Hella off him, Ada reached for the dagger William had given her, and yanking it from the sheath, she whipped it up and plunged it straight toward Brothwell's heart. The blade sunk deep into his chest, and Ada released it, watching him stagger side to side, his mouth parting.

When he fell to his knees and then forward, so did she. She retched and retched as Hella and Freya whimpered beside her. After a moment, the sickness subsided and she drew to sitting on her knees. She glanced at Brothwell, who lay unmoving in the grass. Her heart thundered as she crept over to where she could see his face. His eyes were wide and still, drool ran out of his mouth, and a circle of blood was growing larger around the dagger. Her hand shook as she moved it under his nose to feel if he was alive. No breath. She'd killed him. There was no relief, only hot tears coursing down her cheeks and a stark awareness that his men would come looking for him soon, if they were not already.

"Hella, Freya," she called softly and rising to her feet. She stumbled away from Brothwell and in the direction she prayed to God was west. Her mind felt slow and foggy. Her steps sluggish. Whether it was shock, grief, or a combination of the two, she did not know, but she feared she was never going to make it to the nunnery.

She alternated between walking and running all day, with only two stops to get water. By the time night started to fall, she was exhausted and staggering more than anything. Hella and Freya stayed by her, stopping when she did, barking at her when she found herself weaving. She paused on the narrow path that twined around the mountainside she was on, gasping for breath, her side pinching and her head pounding. She had a sinking feeling that she should have reached the nunnery by now. Raising her hand against the last bit of sunlight, she stared in the distance and cried out in dismay. It was not a convent she saw in the distance, but a castle.

Her heart began to thump hard in her chest. She had, indeed, gone the wrong way, and the only castle she knew of near the nunnery was the MacLean holding, which was the last place she wanted to be. Frustrated tears sprang to her eyes, and she jerked around to discover where she had made her mistake. The ground she stood upon suddenly gave way, and she fell with it, tumbling down the mountainside, hitting branches and hard ground as she went. She landed in a heap, hitting her head on a rock. Pain exploded in her temples, and she had the sensation of sliding into warm water.

"Ada?" a familiar voice called.

Her eyelids were far too heavy to open, but she knew that voice.

"Ada? Where's William? What are ye doing here?"

Thomas!

She reached out blindly, hoping that if she touched Thomas, grasped his hand, he could keep her from succumbing to the beckoning sleep. Fingers grazed hers, but the warmth was nearly all the way over her now, and she was deadly tired.

"The nunnery," she said, her voice sounding small in her ears. "Take me to Iona Nunnery."

Twenty-One

Hell truly did exist, and William was in it. Five days of hard riding and Ada was nowhere to be found. He'd come across Brothwell, dead, and he'd seen Brothwell's men scouring the woods for him, but Ada was gone. She had not made it to the nunnery, and he wasn't sure where to go from here.

The two silver-eyed, silver-haired nuns who were seeing to his horse and getting him food before he rode out were peculiar at best, mayhap crazed at worst. They giggled to themselves as they shot odd looks at him over their shoulders. He wanted to leave, but they were dawdling bringing his horse back to him.

He cleared his throat. "Did ye say the stable master was fetching my horse?"

"Aye," the nun replied, arching her eyebrows at the other nun.

William frowned, his ever-increasing worry making him irritable. "I'll just fetch the animal myself," he blurted. Every moment he waited here was a moment that Ada could be in danger.

"Nay!" the nuns bellowed in unison. The slighter of the two practically pounced on him. She grabbed him by the arm and yanked him back down onto his chair. His brows dipped together. There was something very odd about these nuns.

"She'll be here any minute," the slighter nun mumbled.

"Ada?" he asked, confused. To his astonishment, the nun nodded. "But ye said ye had nae seen her. Why did ye—"

"She's here!" the heavier set nun exclaimed, clapping excitedly and grasping the other nun. They seemed to practically float to his chair and glare down at him. "Ye must nae muck this up," the heavy set nun chided, to which the other sister nodded.

"We ken ye ken yer heart, but ye must ensure *she* kens ye ken it," the slighter nun said.

Just as he was untangling her words, the thin nun looked to the other and asked, "Hortense, shall we tell him?"

He felt his lips part in shock. *Hortense.* "Hortense?" he said, the meaning of the name making his thoughts spin for a moment. "Hortense and Portense?"

Portense nodded and Hortense said, "Aye."

"She dunnae have her gift any longer." Portense set her hands on her hips and scowled at him. "What think ye of that?"

He stood at the sound of horses in the courtyard of the nunnery. He started to move to the door, but the nuns both said, *"Stillande,"* and he found he could not move his legs.

"Ye're fae," he said, disbelief coursing through him but acceptance of the truth flowing alongside it. It was an odd feeling to know something to be true yet find it almost impossible to believe.

"Aye," they said in unison.

To hear it confirmed that these were the fae who so long ago gave Ada the gift that made her the King Maker rendered him momentarily speechless.

Then Hortense said, "Banished here by our father until we set our mess right with nae anyone to aid us but our dogs, the woman—Esther—whom we compelled, and our misconceived gift to Ada."

"Esther?" William asked, baffled what Ada's companion had to do with aiding the fairies.

"'Tis a long story," Hortense said.

"One that must wait until Ada is present," Portense added.

"Hella and Freya are *yer* hounds," he said slowly, his awe growing. That explained a great deal about the creatures.

"Aye," Hortense said. "Now ye did nae answer my sister's question. What do ye think of Ada nae having her gift any longer?"

"I'm glad," he replied honestly. "All I want is her. If she'll have me…"

The fae smiled at each other, and Hortense patted at her eyes, which filled with tears.

"That remains to be seen," Portense said. The fairy waved her hand, and he could suddenly move.

Without hesitation, he was out the door and surging into the courtyard just in time to see Thomas helping Ada down from her horse. In that moment, William didn't give a damn how she came to be in Thomas's company. Instead, he was focused solely on her. He drank her in as she dismounted. Her hair tumbled in wild disarray over her shoulders, her gown was filthy and torn, and when she turned toward him, she gasped and he saw that she had a split lip and a purple bruise on her left cheek.

He crossed the courtyard in a breath, catching her hand as she raised it to hide her cuts and bruises. William met Thomas's eyes, and Thomas shrugged. "Turns out the importance Ada felt I had was to rescue *her*."

William slid his hand around Ada's waist and held her in close, overwhelming gratitude filling him. Without taking his eyes off hers, he said, "Then surely ye had the most important role of all, as she is *my life*."

Ada's eyes widened, and she inhaled sharply. He must have been choosing the right words, he thought with a smile.

As Thomas strode away from them and across the courtyard to where the nuns were standing, William moved his hand to the back of Ada's neck and cupped her unbruised cheek with his other hand. "I did nae want to love ye, but I see now that there was nae ever a choice. The moment I met ye, ye slipped under the barrier I had built around my heart."

She smiled at that. "Ye did nae think about the cracks at the bottom?"

"I did nae," he answered, lightly brushing his lips to hers. "It was nae ever about lust for me, Ada; it was about warmth. I was afraid to feel warm in here again." He took her hand and placed it on his heart, which he knew she would feel drumming madly. Her fingertips curled against his skin. "I ken what it is to love someone and then have them disappear, or to trust and then have it taken away, but I'd rather risk letting ye in than living my life without ye." He paused to kiss her softly once more. "If ye'll still have my love, I want to give it. Every day. All day. In a thousand ways I've yet to think of, and a few we've already experienced."

"Oh," she said, her voice husky, "ye're attempting to seduce me."

"Aye," he agreed. "Is it working?"

An uneasy look suddenly came over her face, but he

knew instinctually what her worry was. He pressed a very gentle finger to her lips. "I dunnae care if yer gift is gone. Frankly, I'm glad."

She grinned for a moment, but then her brows dipped together. "How did ye—"

He motioned behind him to the fae. "They told me. I believe those two have been waiting for ye for a verra long time."

He watched as his beautiful wife's eyes went even wider. She stepped away from him as if to go to them, but then she glanced over her shoulder. "Stay with me?"

He took her hand and entwined her fingers with his. "Always."

When William's fingers captured Ada's and he looked at her as if she was the most prized treasure in all the world, happiness flooded her. And then—

"Ah!" she exclaimed, her hand going to her stomach.

"What is it?" William asked, his hand moving atop the one on her stomach.

"'Tis the oddest thing," she said with a frown. "It almost feels as if—" She glanced sharply at the fairies, who were grinning. "That's impossible," she whispered.

"Aye, usually," one of the fairies called from across the courtyard.

Ada's heart sped up. "Which fairy is that?" she asked William, but before he could answer, the fairy did.

"I'm Hortense."

"And I'm Portense," the other one said. "I gave the wee bairn a little gift."

At Portense's grin, Ada groaned. "I dunnae want any

gifts at all, wee or large, for my bairn." She tried to sound stern, but she was so happy she knew she had not quite done so.

"Ada?" William turned her to face him, his gaze delving into hers. "Are ye with child?"

"She is!" Portense called, not giving Ada the chance to answer.

"We heard his heartbeat when she arrived," Hortense offered.

His.

Ada laughed and cupped William's cheek even as he reached for hers. "A boy!"

"A boy," he repeated, reverence ringing in his voice. Concern suddenly filled his eyes. "Ada, I'm glad the fae told us, but—"

"Please," she said, turning to them. "What sort of gift have ye given the babe?"

"Just a little nudge, so ye could feel him this once, nae anything more," Portense said with a smile. "But if ye would like us to, we could give the lad a gift to make him—"

"Nay!" Ada and William said together. Joy filled the air around them as the four of them laughed.

William drew Ada into his arms, and she lay her head against his chest, pleased he felt exactly as she did. "As long as we have each other," her husband said, his voice rumbling low and lovely in her ear, "we have the greatest gift of all."

Epilogue

One Year Later

Ada stood beside William in the great hall of Tantallion Castle, which the king had bestowed upon William for his service. The Steward and his sons had been captured and imprisoned, and the rogue lairds' castles had been seized, and all felt well in the world.

She gazed in complete and utter happiness at the gentle and protective way William cradled their son in his arms. For a warrior known far and wide as Wolf, it made her chuckle to see him coo at Rhys as he was doing now.

The hall buzzed while all the people who had come to witness Rhys's blessing day chattered happily. Ada smiled contentedly, as did William, but to their right, Bram and Marjorie appeared tense, and to the left, Thomas and Grant did, as well. Esther, who stood by Thomas, was the only one of their closest friends who had a calm expression upon her face. That was no surprise, seeing as how Ada now knew Hortense and Portense had long ago worked the little bit of magic their father had allowed them to use to compel Esther to leave the nunnery and journey to Ada's home to watch over her after her mother's death.

Ada caught William's eyes upon her, and when he cocked a questioning eyebrow, she nodded, giving her husband permission to reveal their well-guarded secret to their most trusted family and friends. Before he could speak, however, Marjorie stepped close, wringing her hands, and whispered, "Are ye nae worried the fae will come and try to give Rhys a gift?"

Ada shook her head, knowing well that Hortense and Portense were just about here. Maximilian, who she'd discovered the fae had blessed with the breath of life when he was a babe discarded near the woods by the nunnery, would be accompanying them, as well as Hella and Freya, whom Ada had missed terribly.

Bram moved to Marjorie's side, putting him directly in front of William. "Brother, why do ye nae seem concerned?"

"Because," William said, keeping his voice low, "I ken the fae will give Rhys a gift."

"But it will be a good one," Ada finished just as quietly.

"How do ye ken such a thing?" Grant asked, as he too had moved close to them.

"Aye, tell us," Thomas said, moving in beside Grant once more.

Ada smiled and motioned them all forward. "Because," she said, "after Rhys was born, my intuitions returned. But," she hastened to add, lest they misunderstand, "they are only about him. And I have a strong instinct that the fae are going to gift him with something…furry."

In that very moment, the door to the great hall swung open, and Hortense and Portense entered with Hella and Freya trotting beside them. Maximilian walked behind them, leading along three snow-white puppies with silver eyes.

Excited to see William's reaction at the secret she'd kept from him, she turned and laughed at his confused look. "Three pups?" he asked, his voice cracking. "I thought ye said one."

Ada grinned. "I lied. I wanted to surprise ye."

"Why three?" He still appeared baffled.

She grasped his hand and brought it to her stomach. "One for Rhys, and one for each babe in my belly."

"By God!" he exclaimed. "I have nae ever been happier in all my life."

And with that, he pulled her into his arms, wrapping her in the love she had always dreamed of.

I hope you enjoyed ***The Heart of A Highlander***. If you feel inclined to leave a review, it would be much appreciated. Reviews are the single best way other readers can discover my books!

If you loved my **HIGHLANDER VOWS: ENTANGLED HEARTS** series then I think you will love my new Historical Romance series, **RENEGADE SCOTS**! The first book in the series, **OUTLAW KING**, is now available. Enjoy a glimpse into the story below.

Prologue

1296
Northern Scotland

Revolt had its own scent. It was one of burning wood and flesh, fetid wounds and rancid sweat, and it lay heavy in the air. Robert the Bruce, Earl of Carrick, smelled it with every breath he took.

"Rebellion surrounds us," Laird Niall Campbell said, pride ringing in his voice.

Bright-orange flames leaped into the sky from the destroyed guard towers that flanked the raised drawbridge to Andrew Moray's castle, which Robert had been commanded to invade. *Commanded.* The word reverberated in his head, making his temples throb. He glanced to his friend who sat mounted beside him. Perspiration trickled down Robert's back beneath his battle armor, and the moans of captured men reached his ears. Gut-hollowing guilt choked him. "We're on the wrong side of the fight," he said low, acknowledging out loud what they both knew.

Niall hitched a bushy red eyebrow as hope alighted in his eyes. "Dunnae tease me, Robbie," he whispered, ever careful, though they were far enough away from Richard Og de Burgh that the King of England's man would not be able to hear them. "Dunnae say such a thing unless ye are ready to disregard yer father's dictate."

"I'm ready," Robert replied, meaning it. The desire to follow his heart and defy his father, who demanded blind obedience to a plan that no longer had worth, had been building for months. Now, in this moment, it felt as if it would cleave him in two, it beat so strongly within him.

The time was not yet ripe to act, his father kept claiming. It was, and it had to be, now. Today. He could not take up arms against his own countrymen. He could no longer submit to his father's foolish order to remain aligned with King Edward in hope of gaining the Scottish throne, which had been stolen from their family by the usurper John Balliol.

"I'm a Scot, for Christ's sake," he muttered.

"Have nae I been reminding ye of that verra fact for nigh a year?" Niall's hand lay on the hilt of his sword revealing the danger of what they were about to do.

"Ye have, my friend, ye have," Robert said, his mind swiftly turning. His father should now rightfully be King of Scots, but instead Robert sat here ordered by the ever reaching King of England to destroy a stronghold in the land he loved, while his father seemed perfectly content to stay in England amid the comfort of the Bruces' plush English holdings rather than venture back to the wilds of Scotland to rise against King Edward and risk losing everything. Robert could no longer deny the truth—his father lacked the iron will to do what was right.

War meant blood, strife, and possibly death, but subjugation to an English king was a different sort of death, one of the spirit. He could not live that way. "We'll no longer be safe if we rise against Edward this day," he said, accepting it, but wanting to give Niall, who was married and had a daughter, one last chance to change his mind and keep his submission to Edward intact.

Niall snorted. "I thrive on danger."

God knew that was true enough. Niall had always been right there with Robert at the front of every battle, even on the day the Scot's daughter had been born. Still...

"We will be hunted," Robert added.

"Let them try to catch us," Niall said with a smirk. "The devil English king will nae stop until he sits on the throne of Scotland. He will kill all who continue to rebel, and that includes our people. I'd rather be hunted than aligned with King Edward."

"We will be outlaws, enemies of Edward."

"Shut up, Robbie," Niall growled using the nickname only those close to him dared use. "Quit trying to dissuade me. Ye need me."

"I do, but yer wife and yer daughter—"

"My wife will dance a jig when she hears we've taken up arms with our countrymen. Dunnae fash yerself. Tell me what ye want me to do."

Robert slid his teeth back and forth, contemplating that very question. He needed to be canny and proceed in the best way to protect his men. The wind blew from the west, sending billows of white smoke and heat toward them and de Burgh—the king's closest friend and advisor—who was mounted on his steed, some thirty paces ahead of them. De Burgh looked away, but Robert faced the wind. He, too, would suffer every hardship he demanded his men to endure, and most of the men who had ridden here on his command were in the path of the smoke. It burned his throat, nose, and eyes, making breathing nearly impossible.

Death by fire would be an awful way to die.

Robert swiped a gloved hand across his watering eyes and focused on the falconry building that stood vulnerable behind them. It was on the wrong side of the moat—the land unprotected by the drawbridge. Counting, his gaze moved over the captured Scots lined up in front of the outbuilding by de Burgh's men. Twenty of the Scot rebel Andrew Moray's men would die this day on de Burgh's command, unless the Moray warriors lowered their drawbridge and sent their lord, a leader of the Scottish uprising against Edward, out. Robert could not allow their deaths or Moray's.

"Andrew Moray!" De Burgh bellowed toward the castle, which was separated from them by the moat alone. The powerful Irish noble's accent sounded especially thick with anger. "Lower your drawbridge and surrender, or we'll burn your men alive."

Robert's hands tightened reflexively on his reins as the captured men moaned their protest, only to be silenced by the swords upon their chests, no doubt pricking flesh in warning. There was no more time to ponder. He had to act. These men would not lower the drawbridge.

De Burgh was a fool to think he could ride here from England and command these Scots. They hated Edward for his attempt to put himself on a throne he had no right to occupy. "Ride to the head of my men," he said to Niall, "and wait for my signal. If I can avoid bloodshed I will."

"Och," Niall said, "blood will be shed this day, but it will nae be Scot's blood."

"We can nae guarantee that, Niall," Robert replied.

Niall nodded. "I ken," he said, his shoulders sagging a bit. "Try to prevent a battle then," he relented, "but I feel in my bones it's imminent."

Robert felt it too, but he had a responsibility to do all he could to protect his vassals. "Go to the men," he urged.

With a nod, Niall turned his horse from Robert and headed down the hill toward Robert's vassals. Three hundred and fifty of his men who were loyal to him stood mixed with three hundred and fifty of the king's men. Robert clicked his heels against his steed's side and closed the distance between himself and de Burgh who flicked his gaze at Robert and then yelled toward the castle, "You do not have long to decide!"

"De Burgh," Robert growled, "ye can nae burn alive innocent men. They follow Moray's orders."

De Burgh jerked his head toward Robert. "Innocent?" he snarled. "These Scots rebel against Edward, their liege lord. They deserve their fate."

"Edward is nae their liege lord," Robert said through clenched teeth. "John Balliol was their king." The words sliding from his tongue were bitter but true.

"They should be glad to see such a weak king as Balliol driven from the throne," de Burgh retorted.

"Edward's plan all along, I'm certain," Robert snapped.

De Burgh flashed a smile. "Your people are the ones who appointed Edward to choose the next king of Scotland, all those years ago, if you recall. And he saw Balliol as the man with the best claim to the throne."

"He saw Balliol's weakness, and my grandfather's strength, and that's why Edward chose Balliol," Robert growled.

"You sound as if you wish to rebel," de Burgh said, smirking. "Where is your father, then?" De Burgh made a show of twisting around in his horse as if searching for Robert's father before facing Robert once more. His lip curled back in a taunting smile. "Ah yes, your father does not have the fortitude to rule Scotland. If he did, he would have risen in rebellion with the people who would fight against Edward in Balliol's name. Fall in line with me, Bruce," de Burgh threatened. "You have no other choice."

"There's always a choice," he spit out, finding the hilt of his sword and flicking his gaze toward Niall and Robert's vassals some one hundred yards behind them. Robert looked to de Burgh once more and motioned toward the captured men. "Release them."

"You insolent, foolish pup!" de Burgh growled, spittle flying from his mouth. "Stand down! Moray!" de Burgh roared. "I give you to the count of ten before I order my guards to fill the outbuilding with your men, and we can all watch them burn."

A window at the front of the castle banged open, and a woman—Lady Moray, Robert realized—appeared. "My husband is nae here, so we kinnae send him out."

De Burgh snorted. "She expects us to believe Moray did not come here to gather more men?"

"Perhaps he did nae," Robert said, seeing a chance to prevent bloodshed. "Moray rebels by the renegade William Wallace's side, and Wallace's men keep to the woods. Perhaps Moray went there first."

"I don't believe it," de Burgh snapped. To Lady Moray he shouted, "Lower your bridge. I will see for myself if you speak the truth."

"Nay, ye Irish scum! Ye simper and cater to the English king!" Lady Moray bellowed.

Robert's fingers curled tighter around the cool iron of his sword. There would be war today, after all. Lady Moray had just shot an arrow of barbed words at a man who wore his pride like a cloak.

De Burgh's face turned purple. "Burn them!" he cried, his voice trembling with rage. The two guards standing near the door rushed to open it, and as they did, de Burgh flicked his hand to a slight guard who held the torch. "Set the fire when the door is closed."

Shouts erupted from the captured warriors, and Robert's blood rushed through his veins and roared in his ears. His life was about to change forever. But his honor would remain intact. He would rise in rebellion, not for Balliol to be returned to the throne as king, but for the people of Scotland to keep their freedom. He could worry of nothing else now.

The terrified shouts of Moray's men as they were locked in the falconry pierced the roar of blood in his ears. "Tell yer men to halt," Robert yelled to de Burgh. "Do so now and take yer leave from Moray's land, or I'll kill ye." His heart beat like a drum.

De Burgh bared his teeth. "You have misplaced your loyalty, Bruce."

Robert flicked his gaze past de Burgh, over the rocky ground that separated the two of them from the warriors in the distance, to Niall at the front of Robert's vassals. He raised his right hand and swiveled it round, giving the signal to rebel.

Niall smiled, a flash of white against his sun-bronzed skin. He raised his own hand and returned the signal. They would live or die this day, but they would do it with honor.

Tension vibrated through every part of Robert's body as he yelled, "To arms for Scotland!"

All at once, the hissing, scraping, sliding, and singing of seven hundred blades filled the air, and the clashing of steel sounded in the distance. A woman's scream ripped through the noise, shocking Robert by how close it was. De Burgh swung his sword at Robert, but Robert parlayed the blow and unseated de Burgh with one move. With no time to waste, he turned his horse toward the outbuilding, and he gaped at the scene before him. The squire who held the torch was running from de Burgh's guards and toward

Robert. The young man suddenly swerved toward the moat and threw the torch toward it. The bright flame disappeared into the water, and Robert raced to save the man who would likely be killed for his actions.

Robert met the guards halfway to the squire, who was now running back toward him. He parried a blow from the left, then the right, and caught a glimpse of Niall riding fast toward him.

"Release the trapped men!" he yelled to the Campbell, but in a breath, de Burgh's warriors descended on his friend, now engaged in a battle for his life.

Behind Robert, the loud grating of the drawbridge being lowered stilled all motion for a moment. God's teeth! Surely, Lady Moray was not lowering it in surrender. Within a breath, the thundering of hundreds of horses' hooves against the wooden bridge set a buzz in the air that seemed to vibrate into Robert's very bones.

When he glanced around for the squire, he saw nothing but English knights heading toward him. He raised his sword in defense of an oncoming hit, knocked the blade out of the knight's hand, and nudged his mount out of the way of another Englishman. It had turned him directly toward the bridge where Lady Moray herself came riding out, her red hair billowing behind her as she led her husband's warriors in a charge. They appeared to number almost two hundred, not near enough that they could have withstood an attack from the combined forces of the Bruce men and the English garrison, but they had more than enough to overcome the English if the lady intended to join forces with Robert. But did she?

As she rode, she shouted, "Free our men. Free our men! Someone free our men!"

Robert swept his gaze back to the outbuilding, and the

breath was snatched from his chest. The young squire had somehow managed to get to the outbuilding. Niall was there, as well, along with six more of Robert's men. They held the English guards back, but one broke free and raised his sword to strike down the squire as he stepped toward the door and seemed to be opening it. Robert ripped his dagger from its sheath and flung it with all his might toward the knight. The dagger pierced the man's hand as he was bringing his sword down and he dropped his weapon. The squire, who'd turned toward his attacker, eyes wide with fear, twisted back around to the door and slung it open. Moray's men poured out, weaponless.

Robert unhooked his shield from his saddle, and then dismounted amid the chaos, his sword in one hand and his shield in the other. He raced toward the stumbling Moray men and the squire, parrying blows as he went. When he reached the boy, a call to fire at the lad and the Moray men went out from de Burgh. Cursing, Robert looked to his right to find that a line of knights had covered the distance from the scrimmage below to the castle, and they were lined up to shoot. Robert shoved the boy behind him, as a volley of arrows flew through the air. They clanked against his shield.

"Again!" de Burgh shouted, clearly not caring if he struck down his own men.

Robert moved to shield the boy once more, but the squire stepped out from behind Robert and ripped off his helmet. Long blond hair tumbled out over his—no, *her*—shoulders. Robert could do no more than stare in shock at de Burgh's daughter, Elizabeth de Burgh. Her clear blue gaze met his for a brief moment.

"Cease fire! Cease fire!" came de Burgh's frantic call.

The chit's eyes, bluer than any Robert had ever beheld,

widened with what appeared to be shock. Had she thought her father may not save her?

She turned to Robert. "Thank you for your aid, my lord." The words tumbled from her mouth in a rush, and then to Robert's surprise, she dashed, as graceful as a deer fleeing a predator, past him and toward her father.

Robert stood dumbfounded for a moment at the young chit he'd seen at court but had never met. One of his men lunged toward her, and Robert shouted, "Leave her!"

She raced through the melee, surprisingly agile and quick, and she managed to reach her father unscathed. At once, she was snatched up by the hand she stretched toward her father and slung on the back of the destrier he had mounted once again.

Lady Moray and her husband's warriors came into the fray of the battle that was now moving ever closer. English arrows flew toward them. She raised a hand as she raced forward, and Robert looked to the rampart of the castle, relieved to see four dozen or so bowmen. Within a breath, more arrows soared through the air, but this time toward the knights lined up to shoot at her. As she reached Robert, he said, "My lady, I would stand in defense of yer home if ye will allow me to."

She arched her eyebrows over glittering gray eyes. "It's about time a Bruce came to his senses," she said with a nod. "I'll fight alongside ye, for this day ye have saved many Moray lives."

Robert glanced around at the already fallen men from both sides and made a decision. "De Burgh!" he bellowed, before any more casualties came to pass. "The Moray men fight with me. Stand down and leave, or be prepared to die."

De Burgh twisted his mount toward Robert while calling an order to his men to hold, and Robert did the same to his and Lady Moray's men. De Burgh was an astute man. He had to see he was outnumbered and that the best option would be to flee as Robert had graciously offered to allow.

"I name you traitor, Bruce, and I'll inform King Edward of your treachery."

"I can nae be a traitor to a man I do nae call king!" Robert reminded de Burgh. A roar of approval arose from his men and the Moray men alike.

A command to his men to depart was the answer from de Burgh, and the English garrison quickly complied, taking their mounts and turning to ride out. As Robert watched them leave, Elizabeth de Burgh twisted in the saddle, her unwavering gaze meeting his.

Beside him, Lady Moray spoke. "That girl forever has my debt. I pray the punishment for her deeds this day are not too grave.

Robert nodded. Elizabeth de Burgh had mettle, that much was certain. It would remain to be seen if it was not beaten out of her after today.

"What will ye do now?" Lady Moray asked.

Robert thought briefly of his father ensconced in Durham at one of their English manors. He would need to send a messenger to give his father fair warning of what had occurred this day. What he did with that information was on his head.

"My lord?" Lady Moray said.

He caught the lady's inquisitive gaze. "I'll send word to my father of my actions—"

"*Honorable actions,*" she said, reaching out and squeezing his forearm.

He inclined his head in gratitude, certain his father would not feel the same. Swallowing a sudden swell of emotion for the rift he had placed between himself and his father this day, he said, "then I'll ride to Hugh Eglinton's Castle. I've received word that the nobility leading the rebellion have been given safe haven there to meet and plan, and amongst the party is also William Wallace."

Lady Moray's eyebrows arched. She bit her lip for a moment then spoke. "Ye ken many of those men fight in the name of Balliol. They fight for his return to the throne."

"Aye," Robert replied. "But Balliol abdicated and I have heard that the Comyns—" saying the name of his family's bitter enemies who years before had put the force of their great power behind their cousin Balliol to have him named as the man with the best claim to the throne over Robert's grandfather, always made Robert's throat tighten. "—are imprisoned by Edward. I go to fight for Scotland, as I did this day."

She nodded. "I pray for ye that it will be enough to see ye well."

"I'll gladly take yer prayers, he replied, sensing deep within that he would need them.

"I'll send a messenger ahead of ye with word of yer deeds for me to my husband who is at Eglinton Castle," she revealed with a secretive smile. "That way, ye are more likely to keep yer head when ye approach the Scots. Many think ye a traitor."

"I know it well," Robert said, "but I will face it and prove them wrong. Do nae risk yer man."

"I owe ye," she whispered fiercely. "Ye saved my men. I will pay my debt by aiding ye in hopefully saving yer life when ye approach Eglinton. Grant!" Lady Moray bellowed and within a breath a young Scottish warrior appeared. Lady Moray smiled at the young man mounted beside her. "Grant rides like the wind. He should reach the castle before yer large gathering of vassals." Robert inclined his head at her words. To Grant, she said, "Ride to yer laird. Take word of Bruce's actions here today, and tell my husband, Bruce is our friend."

"I will, my lady," the warrior said, before turning his horse and galloping away. They watched him in silence for a moment before Lady Moray spoke again. "Dunnae tarry, Bruce. Scotland needs yer fighting strength. Ride hard."

"I vow it!" he swore, turned from Lady Moray, and gave the signal for his men to follow suit. Niall brought his horse beside Robert's and together they led the men away from Moray's castle. As they did, Robert felt Niall's steady gaze upon him. "What is it?" Robert finally asked.

"Please tell me this means we dunnae ever have to go back to the English court and pretend to admire the English king nor like English food."

Robert chuckled, some of the tension unknotting from his shoulders. "God willing. Niall, I will ride to Eglinton with my men to join the rebellion are ye certain ye wish to ride with me? What of yer clan, yer wife, yer daughter?"

"My clan is secure under my brother's care in my absence. As for my wife and daughter, it is thanks to ye that my daughter is alive. Dunnae think I've ever forgotten, nor has Calissa, how ye saved our Brianna when those English knights captured her. Brianna is safe at home with Calissa, and I will stay with ye and fight for our land and to free our people."

"If ye ride with me, ye may ride to yer death," Robert said, his tone grave.

"I've ridden next to ye since we were young and trained together at the Earl of Mar's castle, Robbie. If I'm to ride to my death, there is nae anyone I'd rather be beside, but I think we ride to freedom. Let us see it together, aye?"

"Aye," Robert agreed. There would be no changing Niall's mind, and Robert both appreciated his friend's loyalty and feared for him. But Niall's decision was set, and there were no arguments left to be made, so Robert urged his steed into a gallop to which his men matched the pace.

They rode relentlessly through the remains of the day, over hard terrain, under the baking sun, and into the early evening hours. When he finally spotted Eglinton Castle in the distance, he ordered the party to halt and turned to Niall. "I'll venture up alone," he announced, determined to protect Niall should the other Scottish nobility greet them with swords and wish to fight, despite Lady Moray's sending word. Many saw them as traitors, thanks to his father's orders to continue obeying Edward even when the Scottish nobility started to rebel against his rule, and Robert was not convinced Lady Moray's words would have much effect on those who distrusted him.

"The devil ye will," Niall replied, his tone hard. "I'm nae going to linger back here with the men and let ye get all the glory. I'll go with ye, thank ye. All those who dared to call us traitors will ken the part I played in striking against de Burgh and, therefore, the English king."

Robert opened his mouth to argue and then promptly shut it. It would do no good. "Ye're as stubborn as a goat," he grumbled instead. "And I do nae have time to mince words with ye. Come along."

Niall chuckled as they moved their horses down the path that wound up to the castle gates. As they rode, Niall said, "It's heartening to see that ye have finally learned I'm the stronger of the two of us."

"If ye think I'd ever believe that," Robert teased, "ye must have hit yer head."

"Name yerself," a guard bellowed, interrupting their

banter as they approached the gate.

"Robert the Bruce."

"Laird Niall Campbell," Niall added.

"The turncoat arrives," the guard hissed.

It was as Robert had expected. He whipped his sword up to the man's throat. "I'm nae a turncoat. My family did nae support Balliol, but that does nae mean I will nae fight for Scotland against Edward."

"Come along, then," the guard relented in a begrudging tone. "The others will decide if ye should keep yer head."

"Everyone always wants my head," Robert said lightheartedly, "yet it still sits upon my shoulders."

Niall chuckled, and the guard glared at the two of them. He guided them up the stone steps, past more guards, and into the torchlit castle. Silence blanketed much of the estate at such a late hour, but muffled voices drifted from down a dark corridor. A flicker of light flamed at the end. The guard stopped and motioned toward it. "The leaders of the rebellion are in the great hall discussing strategy."

Robert nodded, and he and Niall fell into step behind the guard once more. As they made their way down the corridor, the voices coming from the great hall grew louder and more distinct.

"I'm nae going to risk my life to put Bruce on the throne!" someone bellowed.

Robert flinched, knowing they were referring to his father.

The guard who was with them snickered, and Robert glared the man into silence.

"Bruce is the rightful claimant," came another voice.

"Bah! Bruce swore fealty to Edward as overlord of Scotland!"

"Ye ken he did that to avoid swearing allegiance to

Balliol!" someone else shouted.

"Where is he, then?" the other man thundered. "Balliol has abdicated, and Bruce, the elder, does nae return to Scotland to help us stop Edward. What does he do instead? He sits in his lavish English estate! He has no backbone to rebel! Let us look to John Comyn to lead us in Balliol's absence. He has managed to escape the imprisonment that befell many in his family."

Their words were like harsh blows to Robert's chest. John "the Red" Comyn came from one of the most powerful families in Scotland—Robert's being the other—and that was the heart of the conflict between his family and the Comyns. The Comyns wanted all the power, including the throne, but not for the good of Scotland—for greed. Comyn cared for the rebellion only insomuch as he wished to protect his vast estates and current power. He did not truly care for the people and their freedom.

Robert gritted his teeth. He would have to fight beside a man who wanted to destroy him in order to save the land he loved. He shoved the guard out of the way, but a hand came to his arm. He turned to find Niall staring at him. "I'll nae bend the knee to a Comyn," Niall said. "Ye ken as well as I do that they will do all they can to gain the throne if there is nae any hope to return Balliol to it."

Robert nodded. "We will fight for Scotland." He didn't say that he hoped his father would join them, though the hope lingered.

Suddenly, the door was flung open, and a giant of a man appeared at the threshold. He had to duck to exit the great hall. He strode toward Robert and Niall, his boots thudding against the floor. He stopped in front of them and smiled, a genuine expression that reached his clear blue eyes and made them crinkle at the edges. "I thought I heard a noise out here," he said in a deep, friendly voice.

"Ye heard us despite all the commotion within?" Robert asked, exchanging a quick glance with Niall.

"Aye." The Scot nodded as he scratched at his russet beard. "I've had to learn to listen carefully, especially when surrounded by chaos. 'Tis how I still survive though the English hunt me. I'm William Wallace of Elderslie."

"We've heard of ye," Niall replied. "I'm sorry to hear about yer wife."

Grief swept over Wallace's face for the space of a breath before murderous rage replaced it. "I thank ye. The English are suffering for the murder of my wife and will continue to do so. And ye are?" His curious gaze took in both Robert and Niall.

"Niall Campbell."

"Carrick," Robert said, giving only his title, as was customary.

"Ah, Bruce," Wallace said, ignoring the given title. "Word of yer deeds have been brought to us by a messenger from Lady Moray."

Robert nodded Wallace grinned. "Seems ye made a friend in the lady and she thought to save yer head should anyone want to take it off." He gazed intently at Robert. "Why have ye come here to us?"

"To help retain Scotland's freedom, just as ye, Wallace." Wallace looked unconvinced, so Robert added, "I've heard some things about ye as well."

"Aye? What do they say?" he asked, a twinkle in his eyes.

"That ye fight like a brute beast."

Wallace chuckled. "How would ye have me fight?"

"To win," Robert replied easily enough.

Wallace set a large hand on Robert's shoulder. "I do

believe ye are the first noble I've met that I have actually liked," Wallace said, winking at Robert. "Let us see if my opinion is enough to keep yer head on yer shoulders."

Robert nodded and fell into step with Niall by his side behind Wallace. Wallace entered the room of disagreeing Scottish nobles and rebels, and when Robert and Niall followed all arguing ceased, chairs scraped, and the singing of swords being unsheathed filled the air.

England

Elizabeth pressed her hands against the cold glass of her bedchamber window, which overlooked the beautiful gardens at the king's court. Her breath caught when her father and the king turned to look up at her as one. She scurried back from the window and bumped into the table behind her. The vase teetered, and she lunged for it, catching it before it hit the floor. But her foot slid out in front of her, and she went down with a hard *thud*, the breath whooshing out of her and the water in the vase spilling down the front of her gown.

She sat there with her bottom pulsing in pain, and her mind awhirl with horrid possibilities about what punishment the king was demanding her father dole out after what she'd done at the Moray's castle. Banishment from her parents, her brothers, and sisters to some remote place? A nunnery for life? She shuddered. She may only be twelve summers, as her mother and older sister always loved to remind her, but she did know some things, contrary to what they seemed to believe. She understood fully that she had far too much zest for life to spend hers in a nunnery or someday be a docile wife, for that matter. She inhaled a long breath and tried to slow her racing heart. Her father loved her. He would reason with the king. He would protect her.

Wouldn't he?

Worry niggled at her as she set down the vase beside her and drew her legs to her chest, shivering with a chill of which she could not seem to rid herself. The memory of her father giving the order to burn men alive filled her mind. There had to be some explanation. There simply had to be. Because if there was not, then her father was not the man she believed him to be. And if he was not good and honorable, then how could she trust he'd protect her?

Still quivering, she set her palms to the cold, wet floor and scooted over enough to see in the slash of sunlight coming through the window. She could recall her father's face just before he had locked her in this bedchamber, and the hairs on the back of her neck prickled. Never had she seen such rage from him. He'd been nearly purple and unable to speak, and it said a great deal that he had not come to see her even once in the past sennight, nor had he allowed her out of her bedchamber. She had thought he would have by now. In fact, she had been sure he would visit so he could tell her he was vexed, very vexed, but that he loved her and had been compelled somehow to give the horrific order to burn the men.

She twined her hair around her finger, her agitation increasing. She was not sure how much longer she could endure being locked in here alone. The only person she had seen since returning home was the chambermaid who brought Elizabeth a tray of food three times a day and emptied her pot. She let out a ragged sigh. Perhaps she should be grateful she was being fed. She began to rock back and forth, going through the events which had led her to disguise herself as a squire and ride out with her father, his men, and Lord Carrick, Robert the Bruce.

It had been two things truly. She'd been irritated that her father had dismissed her request to ride with him that day so completely, loudly, and publicly. She'd not known the "mission," but she had known she wanted to be part of it, and she could not see why she should not. Father had always allowed her to do things other girls did not. She rode as a man did, she spoke her mind, and she had even accompanied her father and his men on hunts.

The other compelling factor had been Lord Carrick himself. She had not met him, though the young man had been at court for some time. He was always surrounded by other lords and lavishly dressed women batting their eyelashes at him, but it was the way his dark gaze looked through the ladies and the simpering lords as if they were not there—or perhaps as if he wished to be anywhere but there himself—that intrigued her so. Once she had overheard her father tell the king that Bruce concerned him. He feared the young lord harbored secret compassion for the wretched Scots' cause. Those words had burrowed into her heart, for she secretly thought that it was wrong of her godfather to try to make himself king of a land to which he had not been born, to a people who did not want him as their king. She did not dare utter such a thing out loud, of course; even she knew it was foolish to *always* speak one's mind.

A soft tap came at the door followed by, "Elizabeth?" in a low, worried murmur.

Elizabeth jumped to her feet at her cousin's voice, nearly slipping in her haste. "Lillianna!" she cried out, pressing her palms to the thick, dark wood of the door. Never had she been so happy to hear her dearest friend's voice.

Lillianna was more of a sister to Elizabeth than her three true sisters were. Lillianna was the only female Elizabeth knew who shared her leanings toward things that were considered restricted to women—riding as a man, archery, swimming, and learning more than how to select food for supper and embroidery. Her cousin also was an excellent eavesdropper, a talent she'd taught Elizabeth when Lillianna had come to live with them two years ago after the death of her mother.

"I'm so glad to hear your voice!" Elizabeth said. "What news do you bring? Is it terrible? Am I to be banished? What did you learn?"

"Not very much, I'm afraid," Lillianna moaned. "Whatever has been decided about your fate has thus far been discussed behind doors too thick for eavesdropping. I'm not even supposed to be here. Your mother and father expressly forbade me from coming to see you, and Aveline has been trailing me, keeping watch."

Elizabeth rolled her eyes at her sister older Aveline being her usual perfectly awful self. "How did you manage to escape her?"

Lillianna snickered. "I told her Guy de Beauchamp wished to see her in the solar."

"Oh, Lillianna!" Elizabeth laughed, feeling so grateful for her cousin and only true friend. "Aveline will be livid when she learns you tricked her. She has a tendre for Lord de Beauchamp. Though I cannot see why. There is something about him that unsettles me."

"Perhaps it's the way he is always staring at you as if you are a great treasure he wishes to add to his collection when you become of age," Lillianna said sarcastically.

"I will never marry a man such as Guy de Beauchamp," Elizabeth vowed. "I don't care if he is one of the wealthiest lords in the land. Aveline can have him!"

"As if you will have a choice of who you marry." Sadness blanketed Lillianna's voice.

Elizabeth wished she could hug her cousin. Lillianna was likely thinking of her mother, who'd been forced to marry her father. Uncle Brice had beaten Lillianna's mother for being unfaithful, and she had died from the beating. But being a powerful lord, he had gone unpunished for the death of a simple Scottish lass.

Elizabeth inhaled deeply, refusing to worry about problems that were years off. "We shall both use our very clever minds to come up with a plot to marry men of our own choosing. We will aid each other!"

"You are so naive and hopeful, Elizabeth. 'Tis one of the reasons I adore you so. I cannot linger, though I wish I could. I came to warn you that your mother is coming to see you today."

Elizabeth tensed. Her mother never had a kind word for her, only criticism, and Elizabeth could only imagine what she would say about ignoring her father's orders. Likely, she was livid. Not out of care for Elizabeth, of course, but out of fury over being embarrassed at court by Elizabeth's actions. "You better depart, then. I'd not want Mother to take out her vexation with me on you." And her mother would; Lillianna knew this. Mother cared for Lillianna even less than she did Elizabeth, which was barely at all. Elizabeth felt sure her cousin had only been permitted to come live with them because it had made Mother look charitable and warm-hearted.

"I'll return tonight if I'm able," Lillianna said.

"Only if it's safe. I don't want you bringing trouble to yourself on my account."

"I'll be careful," Lillianna promised, then the tap of her

footsteps fell on the floor.

Elizabeth stood there listening until the sound of Lillianna's departure faded. Silence descended momentarily but was broken once more by the tap of shoes upon the floor. She sucked in a sharp breath, fearing it was her mother. She hoped Lillianna had not been seen.

A distinct jangling of keys and the clink of a lock made Elizabeth's heart race. The door opened, and her mother, looking perfectly coifed and richly garbed, stepped into the room. Blue eyes that she'd been told a thousand times were the same color as hers narrowed on Elizabeth. "You cannot depart this room looking like that."

Her mother's unfriendly tone made her clench her teeth, but the news that she was to depart hit her like a ray of hope. "I'm to be released? I'm forgiven?"

"Forgiven?" Sarcasm laced Mother's words. She stepped in front of Elizabeth, close enough that she got a full whiff of the pungent oil her mother liked to wear. "You are not forgiven. You are lucky to still have your head, you silly, willful girl!"

The slap came fast and hard, leaving a sting that brought tears to Elizabeth's eyes.

"Marietta!" Elizabeth's father boomed from the doorway. "Don't raise your hand to Elizabeth again!" Relief flowed through Elizabeth, but as her father settled his dark, unfriendly gaze on her, it vanished. "She has to be taken through the great hall to depart, and I'll not have anyone seeing her skin marred with red welts that will remind them of her deed."

"She is the talk of the court!" her mother wailed. "Let them see we punished her!"

Elizabeth's stomach knotted at her mother's words.

"Clearly, you have not been in the Great Hall this

morning," her father said to her mother. "Elizabeth's deed is no longer on everyone's lips. Bruce is the talk of the court now," her father said, his voice lethal. "It seems he left the rebel Moray's castle and rode from there to join the other Scottish lords and renegades to rise against Edward."

"Pity," her mother murmured. "I had a hope to marry Aveline to Bruce but that won't do now. He'll lose his estates for certain."

Her father frowned. "I have a marriage in mind for Aveline already, so don't vex yourself. Now, wait outside. I wish to speak with Elizabeth alone."

"Richard," her mother exclaimed, "you promised me I would have charge of her now!"

The news made Elizabeth cringe.

"Woman!" her father roared. "You will, but you will have it *after* I have spoken to her."

Her mother, eyes wide and no doubt sensing she had pushed Father as far as he would be pushed, backed out of the room, shutting the door as she left.

Elizabeth pressed her back against the wall, wishing she could disappear into it.

Her father's eyes seemed to harden as he looked at her. "You have made a fool of me."

Elizabeth clenched her hands. "Father, no. I—"

"Silence!" The word whipped across the space and hit her just as hard as her mother had.

She flinched away from him and fisted the slick material of her gown in her hands.

Her father's gaze raked over her. "I always had a particular tendre for you, so I allowed indulgencies I did not with your brothers and sisters, ones I should not have allowed."

Color rose in his cheeks as he spoke, and Elizabeth stared at the rosy bloom that spread down his neck. Father saying that he'd *had* a particular tendre for her echoed in her mind. Had she destroyed his love for her, then? Her belly felt suddenly hollow.

He swiped a hand across his red beard, tugging at the ends. "Your mother warned me that I was ruining you, making you into the opposite of what a lady should be—willful, too curious, wild—but I told her to mind her place." He shook his head. "I let you linger when I should have sent you away, and because of my weakness, you believe you can do as you please!" He banged a fist into his open palm. "You—" He pointed a finger at her. "You seem to think you have a place at the table of men!" His hand gripped her chin so swiftly she gasped. "I tell you now, you do not. You are a girl and will grow to be a lady, obedient and lovely, and you will learn that your purpose is to serve my house as I command for the furthering of the family. Do you understand me?"

She fought against the tremor in her body. She understood. Her importance to him lay only with what wealth or connections she could bring to the family one day, just as Aveline had always claimed. Elizabeth had not believed it until now. What a fool she'd been! She had no freedom, only the rights her father gave to her. Did he feel no true affection for her? Was there no explanation for the order he had given that day? Her mind spun, making her stomach roil.

Her father squeezed her chin. "Do. You. Understand?"

She stared at the pulsing vein near his right eye. She knew she ought to respond immediately, yet such worry coursed through her, she could not make herself speak, even knowing her silence would have grave repercussions.

"Elizabeth," he hissed, his color rising again. "Your head is currently on your shoulders because I convinced the king that you could be useful to him eventually. Should I tell him otherwise?"

The king? Her father had convinced Edward that she would be useful to him? But how? Gooseflesh swept down her arms as her father's fingers curled even deeper into her skin. "No," she managed to choke out.

"Good." He released her chin, and she rocked back from him, desperately wanting to rub her aching skin. Instead, she forced herself to fold her hands together and prayed she appeared calm.

Silence stretched between them, and he watched her steadily before he smiled. "You are stubborn and prideful, and you don't know your place. But you will learn it. By God you will." He grabbed her suddenly by the arm, half dragged her across the room, flung open the door, and shoved her toward her mother. "Take her home to Ireland, and make her into a lady who will benefit this family."

The anger and hurt deep inside Elizabeth burst within her and overcame her fear. "You would have burned men alive to keep the king's esteem," she accused with a desperate hope that he would deny it.

"Yes," he replied, his wintery voice and open acceptance of the awful truth making her feel as if her legs would buckle. She placed a steadying hand on the wall as the floor beneath her seemed to sway. "Do you think I became this rich and powerful without currying favors?" he demanded.

"Favors?" She heard herself gasp, yet her voice seemed very far away. Her ears rang horribly. "It is not simply a favor to burn men alive."

"I cannot allow anyone to defy me. *Ever.* That is how I stay powerful. You'd do well not to forget it, Daughter."

She would not forget. As much as it pained her, she would hold close the memory that her father had traded his honor for the king's continued support and the wealth it would bring. Never would she marry a man who would do such a thing.

You can order *OUTLAW KING* now!

Series by Julie Johnstone

Scottish Medieval Romance Books:

Highlander Vows: Entangled Hearts Series
When a Laird Loves a Lady, Book 1
Wicked Highland Wishes, Book 2
Christmas in the Scot's Arms, Book 3
When a Highlander Loses His Heart, Book 4
How a Scot Surrenders to a Lady, Book 5
When a Warrior Woos a Lass, Book 6
When a Scot Gives His Heart, Book 7
When a Highlander Weds a Hellion, Book 8
How to Heal a Highland Heart, Book 9
The Heart of a Highlander, Book 10
Highlander Vows: Entangled Hearts Boxset, Books 1-4

Renegade Scots Series
Outlaw King, Book 1
Highland Defender, Book 2
Highland Avenger, Book 3

Regency Romance Books:

A Whisper of Scandal Series
Bargaining with a Rake, Book 1
Conspiring with a Rogue, Book 2
Dancing with a Devil, Book 3
After Forever, Book 4
The Dangerous Duke of Dinnisfree, Book 5

A Once Upon A Rogue Series
My Fair Duchess, Book 1
My Seductive Innocent, Book 2
My Enchanting Hoyden, Book 3
My Daring Duchess, Book 4

Lords of Deception Series
What a Rogue Wants, Book 1

Danby Regency Christmas Novellas
The Redemption of a Dissolute Earl, Book 1
Season For Surrender, Book 2
It's in the Duke's Kiss, Book 3

Regency Anthologies
A Summons from the Duke of Danby (Regency Christmas Summons, Book 2)
Thwarting the Duke (When the Duke Comes to Town, Book 2)

Regency Romance Box Sets
A Whisper of Scandal Trilogy (Books 1-3)
Dukes, Duchesses & Dashing Noblemen (A Once Upon a Rogue Regency Novels, Books 1-3)

Paranormal Books:

The Siren Saga
Echoes in the Silence, Book 1

About the Author

As a little girl I loved to create fantasy worlds and then give all my friends roles to play. Of course, I was always the heroine! Books have always been an escape for me and brought me so much pleasure, but it didn't occur to me that I could possibly be a writer for a living until I was in a career that was not my passion. One day, I decided I wanted to craft stories like the ones I loved, and with a great leap of faith I quit my day job and decided to try to make my dream come true. I discovered my passion, and I have never looked back. I feel incredibly blessed and fortunate that I have been able to make a career out of sharing the stories that are in my head! I write Scottish Medieval Romance, Regency Romance, and I have even written a Paranormal Romance book. And because I have the best readers in the world, I have hit the USA Today bestseller list several times.

If you love me, I hope you do, you can follow me on Bookbub, and they will send you notices whenever I have a sale or a new release. You can follow me here: bookbub.com/authors/julie-johnstone

You can also join my newsletter to get great prizes and inside scoops!
Join here: https://goo.gl/qnkXFF

Made in the USA
Middletown, DE
30 December 2019